HUNTED

Hunted

The Aztec Saga

J.S. DAVIDSON

Stoneman Creative

Hunted
First published 2014
Second edition 2021

National Library of Australia Cataloguing-in-Publication entry

Creator: Davidson, J. S. (Jan-Sheree), author. Stoneman Creative
Publisher
Title: Hunted / written by J.S. Davidson; edited by Sandra Simmonds.

ISBN: 978-0-6486821-3-4 (paperback)

Series: Davidson, J. S. (Jan-Sheree Stella). Aztec saga ; 1.
Subjects: Fantasy fiction.
Melbourne (Vic.)--Fiction.
Other Creators/Contributors:
Simmonds, Sandra., editor.
Stoneman Creative publisher
www.jsdavidson-books.com

~ 1 ~

CHAPTER ONE

I awake on the cold concrete floor. I push myself up, carefully nursing my bruised body. There are no windows, so I cannot tell if it is day or night. I have no way of telling how long I have been here. The room is dimly lit with a single, bare light globe. The only furniture is a table and a chair; both bolted to the floor. Three metallic boxes, engraved with symbols, sit on the table, meticulously placed. They each have a tiny padlock holding their lids shut.

The metal door of my prison remains locked. It has a small slide opening at the base—a feeding door. I am yet to be fed, and it is taking its toll. My head is light, and I occasionally experience vertigo.

The walls of my prison are solid concrete. I know my captors well enough to realise that every piece of this room has been designed precisely. When I was first imprisoned here, I searched every part of the room for an escape; there is none.

I stand gingerly and catch my reflection in the shining metal in the middle section of the door. My long, dark red hair is no longer wavy and hanging gently by my face. Instead, in many parts, it has been ripped out, and what remains is a matted mess.

My skin, which was once almost bright white and soft, is now dark with filth and coarse to touch. My fingernails are broken and filled with dirt and dried blood. Some of that blood is mine, most is not. The dark clothes I wear are torn; they hang in shreds from my now skinny body. I hardly recognise the person staring back at me.

The feeding door slides open, and I watch as a metal tray slides through and stops in the centre of the room. It holds a single envelope. It is almost comical; after all I've been through and all I have seen, the sight of an envelope could instil such fear in my gut. I bend to pick it up; the smoothness of the paper feels foreign against my rough hands.

I open the envelope to reveal a note within, written on soft, delicate paper:

You will remain unshackled.

Leave if you wish.

That's it—that's all the note says. I turn the envelope up, and two keys fall out. One is a standard key; one you'd expect to find in any regular hardware store. It has a small piece of paper attached to it with the word 'door' written on it. The other is a key of beauty. It too has a piece of paper attached to it, but with the word 'boxes'. I stand in the centre of the room just staring at the keys. Why would they go to such lengths to allow me to leave so easily?

The feeding door slides open again, and this time, a tray with a notepad, one pencil, a bowl of soup and a piece of bread, slides across the floor. The smell of food makes my stomach ache. I want to deny them the satisfaction of eating, but the temptation is overwhelming. I fall to my knees and begin to devour the food, almost choking on the dry bread in my haste to swallow it.

I place the bowl back on the tray and pick up the notepad to inspect it. On the first page is a message:

Fill the notepad with your memories,
Or
Leave.
Should you leave, I will fill more boxes.

Of course, I wanted to flee this place, but I knew it was a trap; I just wasn't sure what kind of trap. I look up to the boxes. What could such small trinket boxes hold that would ensure I stay in this cell and tell them everything?

I stand and walk to them. There is nothing to distinguish one from the other, so I randomly select a box—the middle one—and unlock it. The padlock falls to the ground with 'ting' sound. I hold one hand around the base of the box, as I slowly lift its lid and peer inside. My heart palpitates, and my breath is stolen from me when I see what is inside. A finger with a twisted scar lies on the red velvet casing within the box. I recognise its previous owner immediately.

Beneath the finger, is a small piece of folded paper. I grasp the very edge of the paper and pull it out carefully, trying not to disturb the dead flesh, as though its previous owner would be harmed by me altering its position. Carefully, I unfold the slightly bloodstained note. The words etched across read:

"Not all shackles are made of iron."

I stumble backwards. "No! No! I won't do it," I scream to the empty room. I know what devastation will come about if I fill that notepad. I look at the boxes sitting on the table. I know they are not empty. I clasp my hands to my head and close my eyes. I won't look inside them.

The slide flies open again, and this time, a small box scratches across the floor and stops at my feet. As I pick it up, I notice it is different to the boxes on the table; this one is warm, and without a lock. I push the lid back. An eye stares back at me. It has been ripped out with such haste that the optic nerve still twitches.

I slam the lid closed and fall back against the wall, panting for breath. How could this have happened? They had captured *me*, only me. My stomach knots and the room seems to spin around me. How could it be that they captured another? My stomach moves from knotting to convulsing as its contents spill through my mouth into a foul bucket, which has been left in my cell for other purposes. A person I love is being held in another cell, maimed and tortured. My love for that person is the shackle that binds me. How could I have been so stupid and naive to think that by sacrificing myself I would end this, when my captors know my weaknesses and are prepared to exploit them so ruthlessly.

When I decided to let them capture me, I knew they would torture me until they got what they wanted from me. I had prepared myself for that—but not this. They know that I could never leave my loved one much less allow them to be tortured and killed. I just wanted to run from here and end this nightmare, but not if it meant the death of the one I loved.

There is no choice. I pick up the notepad and pencil and sit at the table. I don't know how they expect me to condense my recollections into this one notepad using just this pencil, but I am certain that once I've filled this book, another will slide through the feeding door.

A memory has the power to move us forward, to do great things, or—to destroy us...

~ 2 ~

CHAPTER TWO

My home was hidden amongst the tallest of pine trees, nestled in a valley between two mountains in central New South Wales, Australia. It was a modest cottage built of cedar logs and warmed with a wood fire. During the winter months, it would produce rolling puffs of smoke. The smell of smoke would linger amongst the dew-covered pines and would tickle my nose as I walked amongst them in the mornings.

I didn't live there alone. I shared it with my two favourite people in the world—my husband Michael and our baby girl, Sasha. I called her my baby girl, but she was far from it, having turned four years old and frequently reminding me of how 'grown up' she was.

Our home was completely self-sufficient, just as we were. Michael was a keen hunter and angler. He would bring home fish from the river that flowed steadily past the front of our home, or game he would hunt from the forest. All the while, Sasha and I would tend to our little veggie patch.

Sasha loved when the springtime would come around. All the strawberries would ripen, and she would take such delight in fossicking through the green foliage to find the juiciest ones.

Each time she would find one, she would pinch it out and hold it up to me. Her little face would be alive and filled with adventure, her rosy cheeks against her white skin looking just like the strawberries she adored.

Michael was without a doubt the most handsome man I had ever seen. His hair was dark and his eyes were deep blue, with intriguing flecks of green. When I looked into his eyes, I could see the world staring back.

Our life was simple. We didn't own lavish cars or wear designer clothes; we didn't need to because we found our value in the love and happiness we shared. One summer evening, however, that happiness was shattered ...

The night was hot and sticky. Michael and I lay on our porch swing, my head on his chest. His arm lay relaxed over my shoulder, and his fingers intertwined with mine. We listened to the melodious sounds of the river, as the wind rocked us gently.

"Alexandra?" he asked as he traced his fingers along my arm.

"Hmm?" My eyes were closing as sleep began to take me.

"I think Sasha needs a brother or a sister," he whispered in my ear.

I tilted my head back and let his lips dance with mine, his rough stubbly face grazing my cheek.

"Yes, she does," I whispered through my kissing lips.

I twisted myself on top him. His hands sat on my hips and slowly slid up the sides of my waist against my skin. His hands were as rough as his face, but my body tingled to his touch.

"How did I get so damned lucky? You're amazing." He tucked my long, wavy red hair behind my ear. His eyes burned deeply into mine so that it felt as though he was staring straight into my soul.

"I love you." The words came effortlessly from me.

"I love you, too." I had heard him say those words to me so many times, and they still made my heart flutter.

A long, groaning noise sounded from behind our home.

"Honey, did you hear that?" I sat up craning my neck to listen more clearly for the strange sound.

"It's nothing, baby." He sat up and kissed my neck. "Now, where were we? Oh, you were in the middle of seducing me," he breathed in my ear. His breath was hot and smooth and made my toes curl.

He laid back on the swing, folding his arms behind his head. I pulled a play, sultry face and began to unbutton my shirt from the top.

I stopped suddenly. "Michael, I heard it again." This time, I knew it was not my imagination. "Would it be the ...?" I didn't get to finish my question.

I no longer lay on the swing with Michael. I was lying on the hard ground. Pieces of rubble protruded into my back. Black smoke filled the air, forcing its way into my lungs and depriving me of oxygen. I tried to gasp for air, but all I was able to inhale was the rancid black smoke.

"She's alive. I need a medic here! Now!" a man yelled as he landed next to me. He was wearing a yellow suit with a clear facemask. "You're going to be okay," he said slowly and clearly. He pressed a mask over my nose and mouth. "Big, deep breaths."

I did as he instructed, sucking in the clean air. Instead of black smoke filling my lungs, pure oxygen flowed into me.

My vision blurred in and out of focus, as I struggled to remain conscious.

Where was Michael?

"Sasha?" I began to panic. I tried to sit up—I needed to find my baby.

"Lay back, Miss." The man pushed down on my shoulders making it impossible for me to sit.

"What? No! I need to find my daughter. Please, where is she?" There was something wrong with my voice. I was speaking, but it was barely audible.

"You need to calm down, Miss. There was an explosion. You have sustained trauma to your head and chest."

His face distorted before me, as once again I felt consciousness slipping from me. I grabbed the ground with my fingertips, certain I was going to fall off the Earth.

A voice came over the radio that hanging from the fireman's vest. "How many trolleys do we need?"

The fireman picked the radio up and said, "Only one—the rest are for the Coroner."

~ 3 ~

CHAPTER THREE

The room blurred, and my eyes burned as my eyelids slowly began to open. My eyes felt heavy and only semi-responsive to my commands, as was the rest of my body.

My mind was dull and distant. I couldn't remember where I was, and trying to sort through my memories was like looking through an opaque window; the more I tried to focus, the more distorted they became.

As I peered through my lashes, I could see the vague outlines of two women moving around the room. They were speaking to each other, but their words entered my ears as though being spoken under water. I could also hear an insistent beeping.

I felt as though I had been awake for a hundred years, so I allowed my eyelids to close gently. I lay still, hoping to feel Michael's hand touch mine. I waited for a moment, but there was nothing. I was waiting for his hand to stroke my forehead while his gentle voice explained the recent events. But there was no voice, and there was no hand.

"Where am I?" I asked, but my voice was so faint I could barely hear it. The figures appeared unaware of my presence as they spoke.

"What's her story?" one woman asked the other. "It's my first week in this hospital, so I don't know the back stories of any of the patients."

"This is Alexandra," the second woman responded. "She came to us about two years ago with severe head trauma. You might have seen it on the news—tragic story. The building she was in exploded! Honestly, I don't know how she survived. There was hardly anything left of the others."

"Oh my God! That's awful. What happened?"

"Turned out the landlord was negligent—something to do with gas cylinders. Anyway, she arrived non-responsive, so was put on life support. We all thought she would pass once the plug was pulled..."

"And she didn't? What a miracle! Oh, I bet her family was so relieved!"

The second woman paused for a moment. "Alexandra does not have one living relative that we know of. Believe it or not, it was Tess who decided when to pull the plug."

"Tess? Are you serious? I bet she didn't even flinch! She's one cold woman."

"There were lawyers in and out of here for a few days and something about a court order. But it was Tess who turned off the support once the legalities were sorted. No one can figure it out, but Alexandra just kept on breathing!"

"But she hasn't been intubated?" she asked surprised.

"Didn't have to be. I don't know how or why, but she's managed to breathe on her own. It's almost like she's asleep rather than in a coma. Still, I kind of hope she doesn't wake up. Could you imagine it?"

The first woman sighed sympathetically. "Oh, I know. To her, it will seem like yesterday when she was with everyone she loved. She would have no idea two years have slipped by."

They continued to converse as they exited my room, but I wasn't listening. The opaque window that sheltered me from my memories had blown open—I remembered everything. My stomach convulsed as I thought of my baby girl in the house, and my beautiful husband who I would never see again. No, it must have been a mistake. If I survived, they would have too.

I had to get out of this bed—I had to find them! I bent my arm into the bed to sit myself up, but as I did, something pinched in the crease of my elbow. I rolled my head on the overly soft pillow and tried to focus my eyes on my arm; a drip protruded from my vein. The drip was the cause of the ever-insistent beeping. Every beep ricocheted inside my head.

I reached my heavy hand across my body and tore the cannula from my arm. Blood dripped steadily over the pristine white sheets. I grunted as I tried to push myself up, but I could not take my weight. I tried again, but couldn't coordinate any movement.

"What the hell?" a woman exclaimed as she ran to my aid.

"I can't stand. Why can't I stand?" I pleaded as panic shot through me. "Am I paralysed?"

"Stand! You shouldn't be able to open your eyes!" The woman snapped as she pushed firmly on my shoulders to position me back into the bed. "You've ripped your drip out. I'm going to have to re-site it in your hand!" she hissed. "What were you thinking? Waking up in a hospital and your first thought is to rip out your tubing?" She held my arm firmly in her hands, inspecting my veins.

"Hospital? What hospital? Why am I here? What's happening? Why can't I stand?" I demanded. "I need to find them! Let me go." I tried to push at her, but my arms failed me again.

"Stop fighting with me and listen!" she ordered as she pushed me back to the pillow. "You've just woken from a coma; a coma no one expected you to wake from, ever! You can't stand because you've lost all your muscle tone. Two years you've been lying in bed! The only time you moved was when we rotated you every two hours."

"Two years? No, it can't have!" My chest tightened at the thought.

"It *has* been two years." Her tone softened. "I am certain of it because I've been your tending nurse for almost all that time."

"The people I lived with ... where are they? Those women said they died; they can't have! Where are they?" I pleaded with her. "They must have me confused with someone else."

The woman leant across to the side table and pulled the drawer out to retrieve a bandage, then began wrapping my arm. "There's no mistake."

Tears started to build up behind my eyes, the hot liquid burning as it seeped down my cheeks. "You're wrong!" I cried. "If I'm alive, so are they! Why won't you tell me where they are?"

She sighed. "Listen to me. You've been in this hospital for two years. You were the only survivor; I assure you."

I laid back on my pillow not bothering to wipe the tears as they flowed down my cheeks. I knew she was right. I knew they'd died from the moment the fireman found me, but I wasn't ready to admit it to myself yet.

She sat on the edge of my bed and tucked the last piece of my bandage within itself. "Look. My name is Tess, and I have been nursing you the two years you have been here. Now, I'm sorry you have found out this way, and I'm sorry you're alone now, I really am, but right now we have to deal with you. Generally, when people wake they might be able to move their eyes or squeeze a hand, but here you are holding a conversation with me ..."

"Well, hello." An unfamiliar voice spoke.

I lifted my head to see a short, stocky man with brown hair walking casually into my room. He was wearing a white coat that was covering a neat shirt and dark pants. A badge was pinned to his lapel saying: 'Dr. Hemmings'.

"Brian, I've never seen anything like it." Tess flourished towards him. "I was in here not three hours ago, and she was completely comatose. Just now, I found her trying to get out of bed, fully conscious and with gross motor skills I'd expect to see only after months of rehabilitation."

"Yes, quite astonishing. You've certainly surprised us, Alexandra. How do you feel?" he asked me as he adjusted his thick glasses.

I glared at him. "How would you be feeling?"

He rocked on his feet and threw a look to Tess. "So you're aware of what has happened?"

"That I'm alone? Everyone I ever loved is gone? That they died horribly in an explosion? Yeah, I'm aware." The words slid across my tongue like poisoned razors.

I could see a perfect image of Sasha and Michael in my mind; they were smiling and happy. I would never see them smile again. I closed my eyes to preserve that perfect memory, but I could already feel it slipping away.

"I am sorry for your loss. I cannot begin to imagine what you are going through; however, do you understand what an anomaly you are? Coma patients do not just wake up as you have, and they certainly do not have the function of their motor skills. If I didn't know your history, I'd never believe you to have been comatose for two years."

He spoke as though my sudden awakening should have impressed me. I was not impressed; I was angry. Why did I have to live a life alone? Why did my family have to die in the explosion?

"I have just woken up to find that the two people I love most are dead. You'll forgive me when I say I don't give a *crap* how much of an anomaly I am," I snarled.

He nodded once and lifted one eyebrow. "Yes, well, I need to check over you. May I?"

"Do whatever you want," I hissed.

He wrapped his fingers around my wrist and watched the seconds tick by on his watch. His fingers were smooth and cool—I didn't like them. After a minute, he released my wrist, opened his folder and scribbled something in my file. He then pulled out a small torch from the chest pocket of his white jacket, peeled my eyelid open with his thumb, and shone the light into each of my eyes.

"Both pupils are equal and reactive." He slid the torch back in his pocket. "I'm going to order a brain scan ... make sure everything is ticking the way it should. In the meantime, you must tell the nurses if you experience any headaches, dizziness, nausea, or anything that seems out of the ordinary." He turned to Tess. "A word outside ..."

I was only half listening to him as an overwhelming sense of hopelessness washed over me. Not only was I alone, but I had no purpose, no reason to wake in the mornings. No one needed me anymore.

Dr. Hemmings turned and began to walk from the room, but stopped short of the door, pausing as he turned to speak to me. "This may not be what you want to hear, but it's something you need to hear. You are alive for a reason, Alexandra. For whatever reason that may be, *you* have been given a second chance. Instead of focusing on your loss, focus on *why* you were given your second chance." He pulled a small smile and walked through the door with Tess in close pursuit.

I closed my eyes. He was right, but I didn't want to hear it.

I'm not sure if time passed slowly or not that afternoon. I don't think I slept, although I might have. My mind was playing memories like a cinema would a movie, and I let them run freely.

The cruellest thing in this world is to regret, and I was filled with regret; the nights I just yelled goodnight to Sasha because I was too busy with something else to tuck her in, or only half listening to the little stories she would go on about because they were the same stories as yesterday. Instead of playing outside with her, I was inside cleaning the house. Really, how important is a clean house? Christ! The house doesn't even exist anymore, much less have anyone to impress. I was angry with myself for letting such insignificant things control my life. Now, I was completely alone, and I ached for my daughter and my husband.

"Still awake, I see," said Tess as she entered the room pulling a small dinner cart behind her. She was small and slender, with her blonde hair pulled up into a tight ponytail emphasising her high-pointed cheekbones and her blue eyes. She was wearing navy blue, loose-fitting pants with a loose shirt to match.

"No one was expecting you to be awake, so I'm afraid you only get what was left in the kitchen," she said promptly with a stern voice. "You have chicken broth."

I didn't care; I wasn't hungry. I felt empty, but it was the kind of empty food would never fill.

Ignoring my cool demeanour, she arranged the food precisely on the trolley and rolled it over my bed. "Now, Alexandra, I want you sip your soup—*slowly*. If you think your stomach is handling it well enough, you can try some bread in a few days. She paused as she watched me begin to spoon the soup. "You know, in all my years, I've never seen anything like what has happened here with you today," Tess said.

"What do you mean?" My voice had become hoarse, and it was beginning to hurt to speak.

"You ... just opening your eyes and moving around like that." She flew her hands in the air and pushed them back onto her hips just as quickly. "And now this! You're sitting when you shouldn't even be able to nod your head! Some people may call it a miracle," she scoffed, clearly not a faith believer.

"I wouldn't call it a miracle. I wish ... I wish I had gone with my family."

Tess spoke quietly, "Look, I know you are grieving, and this is a shock. I know better than anyone does, the *importance* of grieving, but don't let that grieving become self-pity. It doesn't matter if you crawl up into a ball and stay that way for a year, or if you accept the fact that you're alive and get on with your life; either way, they're never coming back."

I looked at her furiously. I could almost feel my blood boil. "I'm *not* ..." But, instead of yelling at her, I began to scream as a searing pain tore through my temples and behind my eyes. It felt as though a scolding knife was slicing my head in two. I clapped my hands over my eyes and forehead; the pain was unbearable.

"Alexandra? Alexandra?" Tess was demanding my response. I could hear the alarm in her voice.

The knifing pain stabbed in again, but deeper this time. With it, came images: a glowing lantern hanging from a dark timber verandah, and a pair of eyes. The eyes were like none I had ever seen. They were the darkest blue—almost black—and they were watching me. The eyes could *see* me. They were filing through my memories. I could feel them forcing themselves through my mind, pulling memories at random. I tried to pull away, but I couldn't; I was frozen. The eyes burned deeper and deeper into my memories, taking each of them past my consciousness as they did.

"Get away from me!" I screeched and punched the air violently.

I felt the cold, hard hospital floor beneath my body.

"Delilah! Stop staring like a mullet and get Dr. Hemmings!" Tess yelled.

I felt her hands on the back of my shoulders as she pulled me from the floor, helping me to stand.

"Alexandra? Can you see me?" she snapped, her bony hands on either side of my face as her wide eyes assessed me.

"Yes," I said breathlessly.

Dr. Hemmings hurried through the sliding door into my room. "What's going on? What's happened?" he demanded of Tess.

Tess inhaled deeply. "She was fine. Then she started wailing around, screaming the damn building down and throwing punches." She pointed to the side of her face. She wore a bruise, which was swelling quickly. "She threw herself from the bed."

"I'm sorry Tess. I didn't mean to hit you. I was hitting the eyes away," I said quickly.

"Eyes?" Dr. Hemmings frowned.

"Yes, eyes. I saw a lantern and eyes. The eyes wanted to take me. They were reading my thoughts," I stammered in panic, my breathing forced and erratic.

"Shh, shh, shh. Calm down." Dr. Hemmings spoke clearly.

I could feel my body heat rise as fear swamped me. "It was real! I could feel them stealing my memories. They wanted to take me," I screamed frantically.

"Okay. I believe you," Dr. Hemmings said as he gave a nod to someone over my shoulder.

"You need to help me." I felt a small jab in my arm. I ignored it. "We neeeed toooo fii, tooo fii ..." My voice slurred, and my body was heavy.

"This will help you to rest." Dr. Hemmings said. It was the last thing I heard.

~ 4 ~

CHAPTER FOUR

My eyes blinked open, but then quickly closed as the lights in the room burned into them. My body ached as though my blood was being forced unwillingly through my veins.

"Welcome back." Dr. Hemmings spoke casually, as he stood at the foot of my bed.

"What happened?" My head was still groggy and my voice still slightly slurred.

"You hallucinated. Don't panic," he soothed. "It is not uncommon in people with head injuries. To be perfectly honest, I am astounded at the level of brain function you have after the injuries you sustained. So on the whole, having a few hallucinations is not a bad outcome." He pulled a forced smile and lifted his eyebrows.

"No, no—it wasn't a hallucination. I know what I saw. I know it sounds crazy! But it can't be ..."

He cleared his throat and pushed his glasses further up his nose. "I am positive. The brain is clever; for example, if you experience extreme emotional trauma it will block out the event until it believes you are capable of processing it. Sometimes it alters our perception; for example, I am sure you've seen people with conditions such as anorexia? They see themselves as grotesquely overweight, whereas, of course, it is the complete reverse. And sometimes we see or feel things that aren't really there. Hallucinations can be brought on by many contributing factors. One of the most common is right before you fall to sleep. You may hear music, or your name being called. This happens because your brain is beginning to relax. In your case, however, it is due to brain trauma. Quite often, hallucinations don't present for many years after the trauma, but in your case, they have begun. So, what happens now you are wondering? We will monitor you. Hopefully, they go away on their own accord. If they don't, I will administer something to keep them at bay."

I rubbed my forehead with my fingertips. "I know what you're saying, and I know I sound ridiculous, but it just felt so real. I could *feel* the eyes searching through me." I couldn't understand how something that felt so real could be just imaginary.

"Do you know what the third floor of this hospital is designated for?"

"No."

"It is a psychiatric ward. Every person there believes what is happening to him, or her, and what he or she is experiencing is, without question, 'real.' There is one man who will only walk in the direction of the Earth's orbit and spends most of his days trying to convince others that to do otherwise will ultimately mean the Earth's destruction. Another chap will never look you directly in the eye because he is certain a spirit is hunting him. He believes this spirit jumps from host to host and is waiting for the opportune moment to 'suck his soul from him', and he believes this is achieved by eye contact."

"I understand that's insane. That's impossible. No one could throw the orbit out, and souls aren't palpable, much less a spirit who sucks it from your eyes." I was starting to feel frustrated.

I didn't care about other patients or what some study found; I wanted him to stop talking and *listen* to me.

"To you, their delusions are absurd. What these men experience on a daily basis would feel no different to your experience of the eyes you say are trying to penetrate your mind."

"You're saying I'm crazy?"

"No, not at all, Alexandra. I am saying that you need to let me do my job. *And* you need to trust me. We are going to monitor you for a while. The hallucinations may go away on their own accord. If they don't, I will be prescribing you medication."

"If they don't go away, will I have to be on the medication forever?"

He nodded. "Usually? Yes."

I dropped my head back onto my pillow. If the loss of my family wasn't enough, I was now facing a lifetime of medication dependency.

"If the medication is required, it will be as simple as taking one tablet before breakfast each morning. Before long, it will become second nature, just as brushing your teeth is a normal part of your routine. As I said, we will monitor you and see how ... if ... the hallucinations progress." He looked at his watch. "I have to see a few other patients this morning, but I'll be back to check on you in two days. As for now, do you have any further questions for me?" he asked as he scribbled in the manila folder.

"No." I lied; I was filled with questions, none of which he could or would begin to answer.

He nodded absentmindedly, as he finished scribbling in his folder.

"Right, well, I'll see you in a couple of days. Oh, I got the scans back—all good!" He smiled and left the room.

I didn't care about the scans. My focus was only on those eyes. The concept of eyes digging through my memories was just as absurd as what the men on level three believed, but it was different for me. It *was* real. I knew it.

Next to my bed was a white side table. On it sat a corded phone and a small black tablet. I reached across and took the tablet. It was old and well used. The screen was no longer smooth to touch and had several scratches down one side.

I unlocked the screen and pressed on the browser. I spent the next several hours searching the internet for anything that may have explained what I had experienced, other than a hallucination. My hopes were quickly dashed as each article, whether written by a 'home help doctor' or a highly regarded psychologist, clearly stated the same thing Dr. Hemmings had explained.

I closed the tablet cover and slid it back across the side table. I was kidding myself. There was no other explanation than what Dr. Hemmings had given me—well, apart from sites that delved into witches, spirits and psychic phenomenon; all superstitious nonsense as far as I was concerned. I wanted *real* answers.

I laid my head back on the soft pillow and stared at the white ceiling. As the minutes ticked by with only my thoughts to stimulate me, I slowly come to realise how absurd I was being. I had been involved in an explosion and sustained serious head injuries. Slowly my rational mind began to take over my imaginative fears. Dr. Hemmings was right.

*****

"How long until I can leave?" I asked Tess.

"Ha! You open your eyes not two weeks ago, and you're already planning your escape. You can leave when I say you can," she answered as she changed the sheets of my bed.

"And when is that?" I asked, trying not to sound rude.

She turned to me with hands pressed firmly on her hips. "Well, to begin with, you've had three additional episodes of hallucinations, each of which you described to be identical to the first and for which you needed to be sedated. Dr. Hemmings has prescribed some medication for you, which you *will* start *today*." She pointed a bony finger at me to emphasise the point.

I growled under my breath. I hated taking drugs of any type. So often, you would hear of people being prescribed an illustrious drug that promised to cure them of all their ailments, only for them to be diagnosed years later with an incurable disease caused by said drugs.

"Growl all you like. You are not leaving this hospital until you take your meds." She folded her arms and pulled a small victorious smile.

"Fine!" I scowled at her through my mirror reflection. I had hoped I wouldn't have to resort to relying on drugs, but I had little option. I needed something to stop the hallucinations.

"Besides, where do you plan on going? I know you don't have any family, and I'm yet to see even one friend walk through that door." She fluffed my pillow as she spoke.

The harsh reminder of being alone struck painfully. I pushed my lips together trying to stop from crying. I didn't want Tess to see me as weak. If I was to get out of this hospital, I needed to be strong, to prove that I could handle myself without needing someone to hold my hand.

She dropped her hands to her sides and let out a sigh. "Look, prove to me that you can eat full meals—and when I say 'full' I *mean* full! I also want you to be up and dressed every morning before I come in. You take *all* your medication without a fuss." She pointed her finger at me again. "And, I need to know that when you leave, you have someone to keep an eye on you. If you do all this, then maybe—*maybe*—you might be out in a month. So long as the medication stops all the hallucinations and your muscles are fully functioning ..."

"A month?" I almost yelled at her. A month was ridiculous. I couldn't stay trapped in here for a month.

"You want to make it two months?" She narrowed her eyes at me.

"A month it is," I agreed reluctantly.

"Oh, and before I forget, I should give you your possessions; or should I say possession." She held up a necklace. The chain was dark red, and the charm hanging from it was a tiny cross-bow, carved from timber. Although I was sure I had never seen it before, it had a sense of familiarity about it. It somehow gave me a feeling of comfort; like standing by a warm fire in your home after being lost in the snow, or seeing an old friend after a long time apart. I just continued to stare at it until Tess became impatient.

"Alexandra! Wake up," she said, waving her hand in front of my face.

I blinked several times. "That's not mine."

"Well, it was in your patient file, so it's yours now." Before I could resist further, she slipped the necklace around my neck. Shivers ran through my body as soon as it touched my skin.

"You really don't remember this?"

"No. It's definitely not mine. I never wore any jewellery, not even a wedding ring. I never liked jewellery. I don't know why—I just didn't." I leant forward to look at the charm that sat centred on my chest. It was quite possibly the most beautiful charm I had ever seen.

*****

The month passed surprisingly fast. Tess spent more time in my room than necessary, but I didn't mind. I actually grew to enjoy her company. She was extremely blunt and direct with everything she said and with every order she gave to either her staff or me. I liked that about her. I liked that if I asked a question, I got a straightforward, truthful answer. I also liked that she never mentioned my family or the funeral.

She hadn't offered to research any relevant medical certificates indicating where my family may have been buried, and I didn't ask. I know many people make peace by taking flowers and toys to their children's graves, but I had never been able to see any sense in it. The moment they draw their last breath is when you lose them. What lies beneath the ground is not your loved one; it's nothing more than rotting flesh and bones. Well, that's what I kept telling myself. The truth was that I was scared to see their graves because that would make it real, and that was something I wasn't prepared for yet.

Everyone grieves in his or her own way. I wanted to ask her exactly what had caused the explosion, and if there was anything left of my home. But every time I tried to ask her, the thought of my family burning would plague my mind, so I remained silent.

During the extended time she spent in my room, she revealed little of herself; however, I was surprised one day when she told me that she had recently found her husband of almost thirty years in her bed with their neighbour. Her teenage daughter had been very close friends with their neighbour and because of her husband's 'despicable actions', her daughter refused to go to school and would hardly leave her room.

Tess described to me how it was the most humiliating experience of her life. Not only was it sick and perverted on his behalf, everybody assumed she knew it was going on because apparently, it had been a repeat occurrence for many months.

It made me realise that although the pain of losing a family was excruciating, there are tragedies other than death. Her family was alive but had completely fallen apart—she was just as alone as I was.

She told me that if not for her job and her daughter's welfare, she would have packed her bags that day, caught a bus to anywhere and never looked back.

*****

"Today's the day." A nurse spoke loudly as she slid the door open.

I turned to face her. Today, like most days, I had been sitting on the tallboy staring out the window at the clouds above, watching them move slowly across the forever-blue skies. They gently bumped into each other and then drifted apart again, changing their form as they moved.

It was a cruel pleasure to sit and watch them. Many times, I believed I could feel Sasha's little fingers hold my hand as I stared at the clouds, and for split seconds, I would forget my reality no longer had her in it. For the tiniest of moments, I would forget that I was alone, and I would look to the door in anticipation of Michael and Sasha bursting through it. Then reality would crash down upon me. Every time it did, I felt as though I was losing them all over again. I was angry with myself for surviving. I should have died with them—eternally at peace.

The nurse was holding a blue backpack and a folded piece of paper. "Today is your last day." She waved the piece of paper in the air excitedly. "Your discharge papers," she sang happily, "although we will be sad to see you leave."

"Really? Has it been a month already?" I asked, genuinely surprised that today marked a month.

When I had first awoken in the hospital bed, all I wanted to do was leave, to run away, to hide from the outside world and convince myself it was all a dream. And when Tess had told me I would be doing 'no such thing' and that I would remain a *guest* of hers for possibly months, I resented her. Now I realised I couldn't have left any earlier. Even as I sat on the tallboy and watched the clouds, I was unsure whether I was ready to face the world again, because, for the first time, I would be facing it alone.

"Tess wanted me to tell you that she'd sign this ..." she held up my discharge papers, "if you take this—*without a fuss.*" The nurse smiled kindly, as she lifted the backpack onto the bed. Tess had obviously warned her of my potential stubbornness.

I looked at her quizzically. "What is it?" I slid down from the drawers.

"Well, it's mainly from Tess, but the rest of us chipped in a few things too." She beamed as she unzipped the bag and pulled out a pair of blue jeans, a white t-shirt and a pair of sneakers.

"Tess said her daughter doesn't want these clothes anymore so she's giving them to you." She carefully put the clothes down on the bed. "There are a few more shirts and another pair of pants in here; might be a few pairs of socks too."

"Oh Tess," I said as I pulled on the jeans. It felt so good to be wearing something other than the paper-thin clothes the hospital offered.

"I think there might be a hair brush in the bottom of the bag." The nurse smiled. "You'll also find a voucher for the *Heavenly Day Spa* from some of us here. We think you more than deserve some pampering after—everything," she said discreetly. She quickly reverted to nurse mode by adding, "Now your meds are in there with a script for refills. Just take them as you have been, but make sure you keep them stored in a cool, dry place."

She was about to say something else when the buzzer around her waist began to beep. "Sorry, I can't stay and talk. Another patient needs me," she said as she walked towards the door. Before she left, she turned back and said, "Oh, and Tess says to meet her outside before you go. Good luck, Alexandra. You'll be great. Just don't dwell on the past." She smiled a warm smile and disappeared through the door.

I walked to the mirror in the bathroom and pulled my hair into a high ponytail, eyeing my new necklace. It hung beautifully around my neck and sat perfectly in the centre of my chest. I was still not sure that it belonged to me, though, as I had no recollection of ever wearing such an item. Maybe a family member requested it to be placed on a relative and one of the nurses mistook me for them. Either way, it was mine now.

The shirt I had been given was about a size too big, but I wasn't complaining. I threw the backpack over one of my shoulders and headed towards the doorway of my room. I turned back, ensuring I hadn't left anything behind. It was such a strange feeling to realise I had absolutely nothing that I could have left behind. Except for the necklace, all that I owned now was what Tess had given me. It made me appreciate the gesture even more.

I walked towards the sliding door that separated me from the outside world. I stood still and stared at the doors, feeling both trepidation and anticipation for my uncertain future. From the moment I awoke in the hospital, I envisaged the day I would leave here; leave the pain behind me and find my place in the world again. Now that day had arrived, I was afraid. Beyond those doors lay a world unknown to me. Was it to be cold and lonely, or might I be able to find happiness in a world without Michael and Sasha?

As I inched closer, the doors slid open. I stepped through to the outside and immediately felt the sun on my face. It was warm and gentle on my skin, much kinder than I remembered it could be. I spotted Tess leaning next to a bricked garden bed by the car park. As I walked to her, I could tell she had been crying; her eyes were red and puffy. I had never seen her show any sign of weakness, so seeing her in this state made me feel helpless.

She leant back on the brick wall, drew in a long breath on her cigarette and blew the smoke out in a long stream into the air.

"A nurse who smokes? That's ironic. Those things will kill you, you know?" I said with a half a smile.

"Yeah well, might not be a bad thing." She drew back on the cigarette again. "My husband's a sick perve who likes to screw anyone but me, and my daughter—just this morning—told me she's a lesbian, that I wouldn't understand, and that she's moving to Melbourne. *And* she never wants to see me again; she blames me for his ... tendencies." She shook her head as she put the cigarette back to her lips. Her skinny fingers were shaking as she drew back on it.

I didn't know what to say or how to comfort her. What could I say? I had only known Tess for a short time, but it was long enough to know that beneath the harsh exterior, she was a very kind and caring woman. She must have been deeply hurt by her husband's betrayal and her daughter's rejection. She squashed out the cigarette in the garden behind her. "Here, take this," she said as she handed me a long white envelope.

"Really, you have given me so much already Tess—" I began to protest.

"Take the damn envelope," she snapped, as she pulled another cigarette from her pocket.

I reluctantly took the envelope and slowly peeled the back lip open. I had expected to see another voucher or perhaps a pre-paid motel room booking for a few nights, but instead, the envelope was filled with hundred dollar notes. I flicked my fingers through it, astonished.

"There's a cheque in there too," Tess said as she continued drawing on the cigarette, her face averted.

There was indeed a cheque. I pulled it from the envelope to read the details; it was made out in my name for an amount of $60,000.

"Oh my God, Tess! I can't accept this! I only met you a few months ago." I put the cheque and money back into the envelope and handed it back to her.

"Like hell you're not taking it," she said, turning to look straight at me. "Alexandra, you don't have anything but the shirt on your back and technically even that belongs to me. Now, you haven't had one visitor, not even so much as a card or a phone call. You don't have a handbag or purse. You are the definition of alone. You're taking that cheque, getting to the closest bank and banking it. Forget about your family—forget about everything. Get on a bus and keep going until you're a million miles away from this shit hole before it kills you too." She drew another long drag back on the cigarette. "You do what I can't; start your life over and actually live it." She looked around at the hospital in resentment. "I have worked in this hospital for longer than I care to admit, and for what? Alexandra, you have your whole life in front of you. For Christ's sakes, don't throw it away."

"You're not thinking straight Tess; you're upset. People don't just go around handing out thousands of dollars to strangers." I began to protest. "You don't even know me. I might have plenty of money stashed away."

I tried to persuade her to re-claim the money. The truth was, I knew the house I shared with Michael wasn't ours; we'd only rented it. We lived a very simple life without much in the way of material things, so I doubted there would have been much in any bank accounts. Tess was right—all that I had was what she had given me.

I shook my head and looked at my feet. "I can't Tess. I can't take the money, and I can't leave. I'm not ready." I pushed my lips together, trying to hold in my emotions. "I haven't even said goodbye—"

She put her hand on her hip and pointed at me with her cigarette. "Said goodbye to whom? Alexandra, what have you been saying the entire time you've been in the hospital? Your family is dead—gone. If you go to a cemetery, you will see a lump of rock with some words scribed into it, and beneath it—beneath it lies carcasses, rotting carcasses—*not* your loved ones."

"I can't just walk away!" I pressed my hands onto my hips and stared straight at her.

"Yes, you can!" She shook her head. "Right." She put her hand into her other pocket and pulled out a mobile phone. "The deal was I'd sign your discharge papers if you had someone to keep an eye on you when you left; so here you go—call a friend." She held out her phone.

I looked at it but didn't move. I had no one to call. My life had only existed with Michael and Sasha. I didn't need anyone but them. I didn't even know the phone numbers of my neighbours.

"No friends? How about a general acquaintance?" She lifted one eyebrow daring me to take the phone.

I turned away and looked over the city, which today seemed to be emptier than ever.

"You have nothing here, Alexandra. If you stay here, it will kill you. Leave." She stared out over the city with me. "What if it was *you* who died? Would you want them to mourn your absence forever?" Her voice was different now. It wasn't firm and bossy; it was soft and kind.

I looked down at the envelope I held in my left hand. "But Tess—sixty thousand dollars? That's just too much."

"Bullshit! I'd give you more, but the prick moved some money into another account before I could withdraw it from our joint account." She looked me square in the eye. "It will piss him off

to no end when I tell him where his whore money has gone."
She smiled wryly. "I'd pay ten times that amount to think of
him, *my husband*, at the whore house begging to screw one of
the girls and having the card decline over and over again." She
narrowed her eyes as she drew in on the cigarette again. I could
tell she was playing out the scenario in her mind and it was
bringing her great pleasure.

"But won't you use it? I mean it could be a good start for you.
Why don't you get on a bus and go—" I flew my hands around to
the train station, which was nearby.

She shook her head. "Nah, I've got cancer. I'll be lucky to out-
live the year." She answered bluntly and plainly just as though
she had just ordered a hamburger. "I am dying, Alexandra; I am
dying with a failed marriage and a daughter who has disowned
me. I am filled with memories of a career that consumed most
of my life. Let me die knowing I've made a real difference to at
least one person's life—just take the money."

"Oh, Tess." I went to throw my arms around her, to hug her,
to comfort her.

She stepped away from me immediately. "Get off with your
sympathy. If this shit is what is going to take me, that's fine.
But I'm going out in a big way, and quickly." She held up her
now third cigarette. "I've seen cancer patients. I've fed them all
the shit about how it won't be too bad—blah, blah, blah. And if I
do live through the sleepless nights, the shit-stained sheets, the
never-ending pain, what do I have left?" She shook her head and
snuffed out her unfinished cigarette.

She strode towards the hospital. "Send me a postcard from
wherever you end up," she called without looking back. She
walked through the sliding doors and they snapped shut behind
her.

I stood motionless, holding the envelope in my hand as I stared at the closed doors. I was hoping she would change her mind and come back to retrieve the envelope from me, but the doors remained tightly closed.

"Are you coming, Miss ... Miss?" I heard a man call.

I turned to see where the voice had come from. Tess and I had been speaking right next to the bus stop; the bus driver was waiting for me to board.

I looked at him, then looked down to the envelope. Tess had scribbled across the front of it: *'New beginnings - don't screw it up!'*

I swallowed hard. "Yeah, I'm coming."

~ 5 ~

CHAPTER FIVE

I pressed my eyes shut as I sat in a seat at the rear of the bus. I just wanted to be away from everything; I wanted to be free of the pain, the horror, the memories. But I knew no matter how far the bus took me, I would not be able to escape my grief.

A wet droplet landed on the back of my hand. I peeled my eyes open and looked down to it. The sun shone through the window, reflecting on my tear, making it dance. My chest burned as I thought of the times Sasha and I would sit on the riverbank and watch as the sun danced along the water. I would tell her the sparkling sunlight was the fairies fluttering their wings as they danced to the music of the world.

The bus jolted to a start, drawing me from my trance. I looked at the tear on the back of my hand. As I wiped it away, a crushing reality came down on me; never again would the dancing sunlight be a fairy. Now, all a tear would ever be was water.

I stared through the smeared window to the blurring city. Every building, every car, every person just melted together with no meaning or purpose. As I looked at my reflection in the window, red hair cascading over my shoulders, I realised that I, too, had blurred into something unrecognisable, with no purpose.

A woman's voice broke my train of thought. "Looks like we're the only two on the bus today."

I turned to see her leaning across the aisle; I swore she wasn't there a moment ago. Her dark hair was in a tight bun. A light scarf draped around either side of her face and flowed down her shoulders. But it wasn't her clothes that startled me; it was her eyes—they were almost golden. They appeared to be alive as she stared into me.

"Yeah, I guess so," I said slowly, still somewhat transfixed by her unusual eyes.

"But then again, no one much bothers with where we are headed."

"I don't even know where we're going," I said.

"You boarded this bus without knowing its destination?"

I nodded. "I don't care where it's going, so long as it's going." I tore my gaze away from her and stared through the smeared window again.

"Our destination is Central Australia. Hot, sand-filled air to breathe, dry lakes and nothingness as far as the eye can see."

I looked back at her, sensing there was something 'off' about this woman, but not sure what. Looking at her was like looking at a memory only vaguely recalled.

"If it's so horrible, why are you travelling there?" I asked.

She pulled a corner of her lip into a smile, her golden eyes gleaming even brighter. "I never said it was horrible." Her words floated through the air like a silken scarf in a breeze. "Some live for aridity. Tell me—do you believe in destiny and fate?"

"What?" The unexpected question startled me.

"Do you believe in destiny and fate?" she repeated her words, just as silkily as before.

I shrugged. "Yeah, I guess so." I was beginning to regret my decision to board the bus.

She continued to look at me as though my simple answer would not suffice. I cleared my throat. "Yeah, I kind of like the idea that everything is pre-ordained, so no matter what you do, you'll always end up right where you're meant to. It's comforting." I desperately wanted to believe my own words; I wanted to believe that the death of my family had meaning and that I would find a purpose again.

"Yes, I suppose it is," she said slowly, watching me intently.

"What about you? Do you believe in destiny or fate?" I asked.

"Of course. Destiny is a river, forever changing, wild and ferocious. You cannot run from it, and you cannot hide from it."

"So, you could say, build a raft and hold on for dear life?" I half smiled at my analogy.

"Precisely."

"What's your destiny?"

She pondered for a moment. "Perhaps my destiny is to alter yours ..."

"Right... Um, you know, I'm really tired. I'm going to try to get some sleep," I said and turned to face the window.

I wasn't the slightest bit tired, but that woman and that conversation were unnerving, so I feigned the tiredness. It seemed to work as she stopped talking. As I sat with my eyes gently closed, I could feel her eyes watching me for some time before I heard her eventually move to a seat further back.

Hours passed slowly, as I stared out the window. The woman had fallen asleep shortly after our conversation ended, for which I was grateful. I was still feeling unsettled by her manner and her words.

Darkness fell, obscuring the countryside. I looked up to the sky. A million dazzling stars gazed back. There was something about the stars; no matter where I was, or who I was with, just one look at them and I would feel at home. I suppose it's because they're constant. The countryside changes, the oceans are distant, but no matter where you are on this Earth, you can almost always see the stars.

The bus rocked gently, as it glided over the undulating road. My eyelids grew heavier, blurring the night stars and drawing me into the dream world.

I was standing on a raft made of irregularly sized logs, fastened together with thick white rope. The raft was gliding smoothly on a slow moving, black river. Silence. There was no other noise apart from the gentle splashes of water lapping the raft. White fog filled the gaps between the trees and danced along the still, black water.

As the raft floated along the river, the white fog began to lift, revealing long, bare branches entwining themselves around each other as they touched the dark water.

The raft took me through and around the outstretched branches, even deeper into the misty forest. Beyond the fog something was becoming clear—I could begin to see the outline of faces.

"Hello?" I called.

The faces remained motionless.

"Hello? Where am I?" I called again, my voice flat and empty.

The raft moved through the people as though they were nothing more than stagnant parts of the forest. Instantly the mist lifted, revealing the people were, in fact, dead—men, women and children—hanging. Their faces had succumbed to decay and their hair hung as straw by their faces. I tried to pull away from the forest of hanging dead. I desperately wanted the raft to turn back, but it didn't seem to matter what I did—the raft stayed on course, unfaltering in its pace.

The black river flowed directly into an enormous tree growing through the centre of the flowing water; its ancient branches twisted around one another, proudly stretched out over the canopy. The raft spun on the spot. Instead of people hanging from the trees, they levitated above the river with hands outstretched.

"No! No! Go away!" I cried as the hands of one of the hangmen wrapped around my throat.

I could feel its decaying fingers slide across my throat and tighten their grip. The smell of decaying bodies filled my lungs.

"No!" I cried. "Get off me!" I screamed as I tried to pry its fingers from my throat.

"Hey, hey, hey. Wake up!"

I threw my eyes open and sat up abruptly, sweat beading on my forehead.

"You were dreaming," the man said.

I focused my eyes and felt an immediate sense of relief as I realised I was still on the bus and not in the death forest.

I sat back in the seat catching my breath. I rubbed my throat as I tried to breathe deeply. I could still smell the rotting flesh of the hanging dead.

"Sorry to tell ya Miss, but we will be staying here for a bit." The man who had woken me was the bus driver.

He leant over the seat in front. The smell of stale beer flowed into my nostrils. At any other time, I would have been repulsed, but for now, it cloaked the lingering smell of the rotting flesh.

"Just hit a bunch of bloody roos. Surprised the hit didn't wake ya! Anyway if we weren't out in the middle of no-bloody-where, it'd be fixed in no time ... there's a few places to stay, ain't nothin' like what you'd be used ta back in the city, but, it'll just have to do ya. I'll be sure to give ya a yell when the bus is right to get goin'." He smiled. As he did his fat, stubbly chin crinkled.

I couldn't be bothered explaining that I didn't live in the city, or that I was only there because I was laid up in a hospital. I looked out the window to see daylight just creeping over the horizon.

"Where are we?" I asked as I craned my neck, trying to see anything familiar.

"Warrangatta. Home of the nothing," he laughed. "Does have a bloody good pub, though. Best meals you'll get." He winked and nodded his head.

"Is everyone alright?" a man called from the door of the bus. He was a short, plump man with a receding hairline. What remained of his hair was completely white apart from a few black strands that he had positioned carefully across his head.

The driver pushed himself from the seat he was leaning on. "G'day Sam. Yeah, we're alright. Can't say the same for the bus, though. Bloody roos! If it weren't for the bloody tourists, we'd have a cull on the damned things! It's what we need."

"Where's the woman?" I asked, interrupting his rant. I had only just noticed she wasn't sitting in the seat behind me.

"Who? Oh, you mean the old bat, the one with the scarf. Yeah, she got off about a town back." He scratched his chin as he spoke. "Said to give this to ya." He leant across to the seat she had been sitting in and picked up a small parcel wrapped in brown paper tied together with string. 'DRIA' was scribbled across the top of it.

"What is it?" I asked as I inspected it.

He shrugged. "Dunno. Hang on—she said to say somefin', um. What was it? Oh yeah, 'She hopes this will help you find your way'." He shrugged again. "Anyway, as I said, if we weren't in the middle of no-bloody-where we'd be off in no time. Say, Sam. Would you be able to show this lass around? Gotta organise a mechanic to sort this baby out. Bruce still running the garage?"

he asked as he walked back to the driver's seat and sat heavily on it.

"Yes, Bruce still owns the garage. He owned it twenty years ago when I moved here, and I reckon he'll own it for another twenty," Sam joked as he walked towards me, leaning heavily on a brown cane as he went.

"Good morning," he smiled, almost losing his lips under his thick white beard.

"Hi," I answered quickly, still inspecting the parcel.

"Bill says the bus is going to be out of action for some time. I own Warrangatta Books, just across the way." He held up his cane and pointed it towards the main street. "Spend most of my time there. But when I'm not there I'm at home. Until the bus is fixed, you're welcome to join me. I'm not a very exciting seventy-something-year-old, and I can't promise you'll have the most comfortable bed, but it doesn't have mites or smell of urine like the pub." He smiled kindly. "I'm just about to open the store now if you wanted to follow me? I've got coffee. Oh, and you can meet Andy. He's about your age, about twenty-five, nice young fella. He moved here only about two weeks ago. He won't be staying long, but might fill in your time while you wait for the bus to be fixed," he beamed.

He was kind to me, and he seemed genuine. I slipped my hand into my pocket. The envelope Tess had given me still sat in there. I wrapped my fingers around it tightly as I thought of the words across the front: 'New beginnings – don't screw it up.'

I inhaled deeply. "That would be great. Thank you."

"Wonderful!" Sam beamed. "Now, I'll get that for you, while you grab your bag," he said tucking the parcel under his arm. I followed Sam as he shuffled along the aisle and down the steps to the dusty road. "Let's get you settled now. Andy will be delighted to have someone other than me to talk to."

I spent the next several minutes listening to Sam excitedly explain the history of his little town as we made our way to the Warrangatta Book Store, my new home for the next few days. Sam showed me up to my room, which was small but neat and appeared to be clean.

"I'll leave you to settle in. When you're ready, come down. Andy should be in by then, and I can introduce you," he said as he left the room.

I fell back on the bed bemused at my situation. The soft doona hugged me and the mattress was heavenly—nothing like the thin, rubbery thing I slept on in the hospital. I stared at the ceiling thinking about all that had happened in the last 24 hours and wondering how I might fill my time in this small town for the next few days. Before long, sleep had taken me.

*****

I woke to feel something touching my hand. I peeled my eyes open properly, and to my surprise, a beautiful Border Collie pup sat at the edge of my bed. He was nudging my hand as he wagged his tail happily.

"What are you doing here?" I patted behind his ear. "You're a sweetheart, aren't you?"

I sat up and leant over the edge of the bed to search for a collar, as he licked my hand and wrist.

"Come here boy ..." I heard someone call from outside my room. "Come here ... where are you, you stupid dog! Are you in here?"

The door swung open. "Oh, oh! Sorry! I forgot ... Sam said someone was staying here—"

I looked up to see a man standing in the doorway. He was tall and slender with a stubbly beard. He looked to be about my age, twenty-five. "You must be Andy. I'm Alexandra," I said as I continued to pat the dog's head.

He just stared at me, his mouth ajar.

"Is this your dog?" I asked.

He continued to stare at me without saying a thing.

"Hello? You look like you've seen a ghost," I said.

"What?" He blinked several times and ran his hand across the nape of his neck. "Ah, Andy ... yes. Sorry, um, you look ... um ... pretty." He staggered over his words.

"Pretty?" I asked, dubiously. From his strangely surprised expression, I doubted he was thinking about my looks at all. Still, I had just met him, so I didn't want to push the matter. "Thanks. So, is this your dog? He is a bit of a sweetie."

He gave a small shake of his head, as though changing his train of thought. "My dog? No!" Then he smiled. "He's just some stray—and a pain in the ass! Always scavenging through bins. Yesterday he got into the potato bin at the back of the pub ... tipped them everywhere!"

"Did you just?" I looked back to the dog, who was panting vigorously.

"Does he have a name?" I asked.

"Well, people call him plenty of names when they chase him out of their shops, but no, no official name."

I leant in close to the dog, rubbing both his ears as I looked into his eyes. "Potatoes, huh? Spud! I'll call you Spud!"

"What? You're going to keep some stray?" Andy laughed in surprise.

I looked at Spud for a moment and whispered to him, "Something we have in common; we're both strays."

*****

Days turned into weeks as I waited for the bus to be fixed. I got to know Sam and Andy well in that time. Sam told me of his life before Warrangatta. He used to have a small hobby farm until he fell off his horse and damaged his left knee. These days, he had to use a cane to help him walk. He didn't complain, but I could tell it upset him. I think what made him most upset was that three weeks after his knee was damaged his fiancé left him for a Spanish man. She was his entire world. He said he was a broken man for a long time after she left.

I told him of my family. He was wonderful to speak to because he didn't offer any advice or tell me how I should be feeling. He would just sit at his desk at the front of the store and listen.

Andy was entirely different to Sam. He didn't just sit and listen; he poked fun at me from the time we met. When I would tell them my most painful memories, Sam would listen, and Andy would say something ridiculous to make me laugh. I felt comfortable with both of them, so when Sam offered me a job, it was an easy decision to stay in Warrangatta. Using the money Tess had given me, I was able to by a small house on the outskirts of town. It needed a lot of mending—but so did I.

~ 6 ~

CHAPTER SIX

Two Years Later

My long hair fell into my eyes as I was trying to pull my boot on.

"Bloody hair!" I yelled as I threw my hand back, pushing my hair out of the way, only for it to fall back on my face immediately.

The springs on the wood-framed wire door groaned in protest as I pushed the door open to step onto the veranda. It was a challenge in itself to walk across my veranda because many of the boards had rotted through—I knew which ones to step on, so I didn't land in the dirt beneath.

Cylinder wind chimes hung on either side of the veranda and were playing a long, drawn out song as the wind blew hot and slow. Although it was only mid-morning, the skies were dark and ominous.

Spud was sprawled across the veranda, taking advantage of the gaps in the boards where the cool air flowed up from under the house.

"This rapid weather change is gonna be the death of us, Spud," I said to him as I patted him on the head. He licked the back of my hand once and put his head down again to the cool floor.

I whistled loudly, as I walked towards one of the old utes sitting in my desert-like yard.

Bruce and I spent endless hours working on one, and we got it up and running well. The others, however, were more garden ornaments than functioning vehicles. I never intended to have so many utes, but my story quickly spread through Warrangatta and the locals all pitched in to help me get on my feet. I was offered everything from spare furniture, help from tradespeople restore my little house, and spare utes. I don't know how many utes they thought I needed, but the townspeople were so eager to help that I didn't have the heart to refuse.

I had a home once again, and it felt wonderful, but an unfamiliar feeling slowly began to creep inside me—a sense of displacement.

I thought an adventure to Northern Australia might fill the void, and I didn't mess around in organising it. Bruce agreed to look after Spud for me. I bought a swag, cooking stove, hot water system with a shower; just about every cent I earned went to funding this wonderful escapade. I had been so keen to get going, I had forgotten to tell anyone where I was heading to first, which proved to be a big mistake.

I had driven a few hours when my temp gauge fell to cold. "Damn it," I cursed aloud. That could only mean there was no water in the radiator and the engine would overheat at any minute. I pulled over into the nearby trees and popped the bonnet to assess the damage. Sure enough, it was a faulty water pump. My heart fell when I realised my adventure was over before it had even begun. In just about any other climate, I could have driven for a while then stopped to wait for the car to cool again, but not in these outback areas. The engine would have overheated within minutes.

I tried to call for help, but there was no phone reception within hundreds of kilometres in any direction. I sat with my car for a couple of days waiting for someone to come roaring along the dusty road, but no one came.

I was all too aware of the dangers involved in leaving my car, but I was unlikely to be found soon. I had two options: I either stayed with my car hoping that someone would come along, or attempted to walk and prayed I made it to water. Either way, the outlook wasn't good.

I finally decided I would have to try and find help. I filled a backpack with as many water bottles as I could and some non-perishable food. I pushed my car deeper into the low trees, behind an enormous brown rock, and covered the car well with dead branches—I didn't want someone coming along stripping it back to a shell, not that that was very likely out here.

As I stepped away from my now covered car, I noticed an Aboriginal painting on the rock—a picture of the sun. I slowly ran my fingers over it wondering how long the remarkable depiction had been there. I smiled as I thought of all the weather that would have thrashed against it over the years, and yet, there it was, still strong and vibrant. It reminded me of myself; life had beaten me around, but I was still here—strong and vibrant.

I had thought I should be able to walk at least three days with the amount of water I had with me. I didn't want to walk. I knew better than anyone that the temperatures out here could range from negative –6^{0}C overnight, to 50^{0}C in the afternoon.

I set out early in the morning before the sun had peeked over the horizon. It was cool walking along the gravel road; the only noise was the crunch of gravel under my feet as I moved along steadily. I had made good ground before the blazing sun entered the highest part of the sky.

Although I was wearing a hat and every type of sun protection, the sun was radiating off the hot gravel road—the heat was almost unbearable. I kept glancing at my watch and only sipped water every half an hour. But I couldn't keep it up. The amount of water that was being drained from my body wasn't enough to be replenished by the tiny sips I was taking. I knew that I needed to conserve water, but I also had to drink more to stay hydrated. I was feeling light-headed, and a hollow pain had begun just below my chest.

I decided I needed a more substantial drink, so I finished off the small amount remaining in the bottle. I let the relief of the water fill my body as I took my hat off and wiped my forehead clean of sweat and flies.

I looked around again to see if I could see a house in the distance, but all I could see was flat land with small shrub-like plants that were no taller than my ankles. I pulled my phone out of my pocket to check for phone reception again. The little cross at the top of the screen continued to flash. I was beginning to doubt my decision of attempting to walk. All the water I had just drunk had already been absorbed into my body, and I was yearning for more.

I slipped my phone back into my pocket, pulled my backpack back over my shoulders and began to walk again.

I walked for what felt like hours until I found a tree big enough to offer any form of shade. I pulled my backpack off and sat down on a small rock under the tree with my head hanging between my knees. My head was thumping, and my ears were ringing. I looked at my watch; it had been forty-five minutes since I had stopped for my last break.

I pulled a water bottle from my backpack; it was empty. I pulled another one out—empty too. I pulled out every water bottle I had; each one was empty.

"Oh no. No, no, no!" I cried as I looked at what I had done. How could I have drunk all that water already?

"Damn it!" I yelled as I threw the bottles back into my backpack.

It might have been the realisation that my water supply had been completely emptied, or it might have been the feeling that the sun was burning hotter, but I suddenly became aware of how parched my mouth and throat were. I forced myself to stand up, and I swung my backpack back over my shoulder. I walked down the centre of the road with the gravel crunching loudly under my feet. The only thought running through my head was to re-peat 'left, right, left, right' in a desperate attempt at staying on course; but, occasionally I would stumble over my own feet.

I kept a look out for anything that resembled water, but mirages were starting to play havoc. I could see water in the far distance. It appeared to be a lake, but I knew that as soon as I got there, I would find nothing but hot, dry, sandy dirt. Even though I knew they were nothing more than mirages, my mind was also telling me to run for the water. I had to use every ounce of strength to resist running toward the false water.

As I stood confused and wondered what action to take, an uneasy feeling washed over me— the feeling of being watched. I turned on the spot—was there someone there? I saw nothing. *Just your imagination, Alexandra.* I strained my eyes to see any sign of civilisation— a distant camper or a farmhouse that I hadn't noticed—but there was nothing.

A gentle breeze blew up the road. I took my hat off and let it dance around my hair and cool my forehead. I scanned the sky in hopes of rainclouds on the horizon—perfect blue, everywhere.

Another breeze blew, but this time, incoherent whispers travelled with it. My heart pulsated, and my extremities tingled—everything in me wanted to run. *Run where, and from what?* I forced myself to stand still. *It's your imagination, Alexandra; there's no one out here. Get it together,* I scolded myself.

I turned to start walking along the road again, but suddenly a gust of wind blew past me, pushing me to the ground. The dust particles circled me in an upward spiral as the centre of a tornado.

The whispers returned and with them, the eyes; the same eyes that penetrated my mind in the hospital. I stared into the dark blue eyes, and they stared straight back. I scrambled backwards to get away from them, but I wasn't fast enough. The eyes appeared in my mind, pulling memories out. The first memory was sitting with Andy at the bookstore, laughing at one of his jokes. The second was working with Bruce on my ute. Then I saw the lantern hanging from a dark wooden verandah; it was glowing brightly against a midnight background. A deep voice whispered, "I am coming for you..." The eyes released their grip and the tornado dissipated. The gravel burned and grazed my cheek as I lay on my stomach. I wanted to push myself from the ground, but I had no energy left.

"Whatcha doing out here?" I heard a man's voice.

"Yeah, bit of a funny place to be doing yoga," another man laughed.

I saw two pairs of black feet in front of me. I looked up to see whom the feet belonged to, but the blazing sun blinded me. *It can't be real.* I reached my hand out and touched the man's foot. *It was real!*

"Alex, that you?" the first man asked.

I nodded. Relief flooded my body. I was saved.

Hands reached down to help pull me to my feet. I stumbled as they let me go but I managed to stand by myself. My eyes focused on the man standing in front of me. He was wearing only a pair of blue knee-length shorts.

"Pindari?" I rasped.

"Yeah it's me," he smiled. "Warrain's here too," he said with a quick nod indicating Warrain's presence behind me.

If I had any water left inside me, I would have cried. Pindari and Warrain were two Aboriginal locals from a town over from Warrangatta.

"Did you see it, Pindari?" I asked, panicked.

"See what?"

"The tornado! I was just inside a tornado— the eyes! They're back ..." I could feel my heart banging hard against my chest.

"Huh?"

"Yeah, just now! I was inside a bloody tornado! How you could not have seen it?"

"Slow down! You need water," Pindari said.

"No! I need to get away! They're back!" Panic was building in my stomach.

"Alexandra! Stop it! You're bloody dehydrated. You need water," he snapped.

"Right." I tried to calm myself. "Can you get water from those?" I asked as I pointed to the ankle-high shrubs, aware that the indigenous folk understood their environment well to locate water and food.

"Nah." He shook his head. "No water 'round here, mate." He put his hand in the air and caught something. "Comes in bottles, though." He smiled as he handed me the bottle of water that Warrain had just thrown to him.

I snatched the bottle from him, ripped the lid off and drank thirstily.

"Thank you so much, Pindari," I said as I took a second bottle from him, my voice returning slightly.

"You're just bloody lucky Pindari wanted to go to War-rangatta today." Warrain walked beside me and stood next to Pindari. He was wearing green knee-length shorts.

"You guys drive here?" I asked. I couldn't bear having to walk any further.

"Nah, rode our kangaroos... Of course we bloody drove here!" Pindari answered and pointed behind me.

I turned around, and there was a single cab ute with a red bonnet, blue doors and the body too rusted to tell what colour it was originally.

"I could hug you." I opened my arms to hug both of them, but they both took a step back waving their arms.

"Any other day. Alex, you stink." Warrain said, making Pindari laugh.

"Oh," I sniffed my underarm. "I think I'm used to it. I can't smell a thing." I attempted a laugh.

"How'd ya end up half dead along Moorabilli-Warrangatta Road anyway?" Warrain asked.

I shuffled my feet, avoiding the question.

"Ya didn't leave ya car back there did ya?" Pindari folded his arms.

"I know, I know. I thought I could make it. And before you say it, I know I'm an idiot." I threw my hands in the air and walked towards their car.

"Ya a *bloody* idiot." Pindari shook his head. "Ya know how many dead tourists we've found along here? All because the leave their bloody cars!" he yelled at me.

I rolled my head back. "I know. Just take me home—please."

Pindari softened his face. "Do you wanna go back for your car?"

I shook my head. "There's no point now. I need to order in a new water pump. Without it, it's not moving anywhere. I'll come back later on. I might get someone to give me a lift...think I might skip the walk. So you really didn't see anything 'weird'?"

"You mean, apart from you lying on the ground half dead?"

I didn't smile at his joke. If I had started to hallucinate again, it was serious.

"Andy told us about your 'head stuff' and it's like 500 degrees out here. The heat probably got to you."

"Crap!" I slapped my hand to my head in sudden realisation. "The bloody pills are meant to be stored in a *cool*, dry place!"

"Well, you got the dry part sorted!" Warrain laughed and slapped me on the back a couple of times. "Come on, get in the back. We'll drop you home."

I had ordered in the new water pump at the local hardware store, a few days after Warrain and Pindari dropped me at home. But like everything else, it took forever to get anything delivered, so I had to make use of one of the other utes I owned while I waited. I was grateful I had a spare ute, but it was anything but reliable. No matter how many attempts I made to repair it, I could never get it to start without having to turn the key several times. It did, at least, provide me with some transport.

I was running late for work at the bookstore, as usual. I pulled the car door handle. The door groaned open, and I had to hold it firmly so it would not slam back on me. I wore a bruise on my right thigh for making that mistake earlier.

I climbed into the ute and turned the key in the ignition. It took a few turns, but it finally rumbled to a start. As I drove down my long driveway, I pressed 'play' on the cassette player—I had taped my favourite songs from the radio. I sang along in a loud, out-of-tune voice as I drummed my fingers on the steering wheel. I could see Warrangatta in the distance and my heart warmed. When I first arrived, I believed I would be forever tethered to the life I had with Michael and Sasha, and that I'd live my life alone in a world of darkness. But the towns-people welcomed me unconditionally, and the void created by my family's death slowly began to fill. But much as I adored Warrangatta I didn't fit in. I wasn't like the locals, and I didn't think that would change if I moved towns either. I felt like I was meant for more. I felt trapped inside myself with no escape.

The temperature had risen a few degrees in the minutes since I had left my house and the humidity was like nothing I had experienced in Warrangatta.

I rolled down my window and put my hand out, letting the air rush through and around my fingers. I loved feeling the hot, steamy air, flowing in through the window and dancing with my long hair.

I pulled my ute into one of the vacant car parks at the rear of Warrangatta Book Store and dashed out of my car, letting the door slam loudly behind me. Because I was running late, the regular tour guide had already begun her tour of the town and was cluttering the entrance of the bookstore with tourists.

I rolled my eyes and hung my head back in frustration. I hated when I was late and had to listen to her drone on with the same speech. Her name was Julie Walters. She, too, had red hair, but unlike mine, hers had more of an orange hue. Coupled with her home self-tan, she highly resembled a carrot.

She and I conflicted from the moment I arrived in town. Whenever she saw me walking up the alleyway, she would make a point of lingering in front of the store while she rambled on about the history of the town.

"The building behind me was built over one hundred years ago. Its original purpose was a bakery, not as the bookstore it is now. As you can see, it is a double-storey building—the bottom was the shop, and the top was living quarters for the original owners. Now it houses all of Sam's belongings. Sam is the bookstore owner." She spoke in her usual nasally voice and used far too many hand gestures.

The store section had two shop front windows on either side of a washed-out orange door. The top storey was also washed-out orange and had slithers of paint peeling off. No one ever bothered to re-paint it. There was no need to impress the locals of Warrangatta as no one cared about superficial things such as paint. The rest of the stores had similarly faded facades, presenting a run down and 'outback' appearance to the town that the tourists loved.

The bookstore was one of the largest stores in the town, which was fortunate given the astonishing number of books that were squeezed into it. Every first Monday of each month, several vans from the surrounding towns would arrive out the front of the store waiting to collect a month's worth of books for their local schools and return the previous month's loans. Warrangatta was a bit of a hub for these towns, some of which were hundreds of kilometres away and with schools that only had a maximum of twenty children each. "Warrangatta was one of the first 'outback' towns in Australia," Julie continued as she puffed out her chest even more than usual, gloating at having frustrated me by blocking my way into the store. She would count that as yet another victory over me.

I drummed my fingers on my leg as I impatiently waited for the tourists to move along. If the bookstore didn't double as a tourist information centre and souvenir shop, I would have barged passed them. But, as much as they drove me insane, the bookstore relied on them.

"Settlers had planned on planting copious amounts of grains," Julie droned, "but soon found that rain is as scarce as hen's teeth in these parts. So instead, it became a major station for the rail line. It was, and still is, the only town within hundreds of kilometres in every direction." She paused for dramatic effect as the tourists 'oooed' and 'aaahhed' at the thought of such vast distances between the outback communities.

"Warrangatta is well noted for being one of the hottest and driest towns in all of Australia, the hot, red sands lightly coating everything that remains stationary for more than a minute. Over the last week, Warrangatta has been subject to an unprecedented amount of rainfall, which makes it a fantastic time for you to be visiting the area. Warimudga, a waterhole at the base of Barri-Barri Rock, is overflowing now. It's a great place for a dip. I think we might all need one by this afternoon; the humidity is stifling." She fanned her face with her chubby hand. "One of the first additions to Warrangatta was a town pub with accommodation upstairs." She pointed one of her stumpy orange fingers to the pub across from the bookstore. "The pub still stands today, one of the few remarkable buildings that has not been touched; everything is original, except for the owner of course."

And *that* was the exact reason she despised me—jealousy. I had lost count of the number of times the current pub owner had asked me to date him. She wanted him for herself. As far as I was concerned, she could have him. I thought of him as a self-absorbed idiot.

"The carrot holding you up again, is she?" I turned to see Emilee standing next to me. She wore her long blonde hair pulled into a loose, messy ponytail at the back of her head. Her hazel eyes darted across the tourists excitedly, as they always did. She was far smaller than I was. Her entire frame was petite and fragile—all except for her chest, which was out of proportion to the rest of her body. She said she hated having large breasts, but considering the low cut shirts she consistently wore, I had my doubts.

She was one of the first people I had met when I arrived into Warrangatta. Her parents owned one of the largest cattle stations in Australia. As such, they were able to send her to an elite boarding school in France. She had wanted to design perfumes in Europe, but eighteen months into her tuition, she became terribly homesick and decided to return. While in France, she had spent a lot of her time working in coffee shops. When she returned home, she opened her own café offering the most exquisite cakes and coffee. For a long while, the locals exiled her for bringing in something new. They couldn't understand the need for such fancy drinks and cakes. But the tourists loved it, which meant local business boomed.

Tourists would come to Warrangatta saying they wanted to experience the Australian Outback, but none of them would truly give themselves to the land. They wouldn't camp in a swag under the stars by Warimudga waterhole and watch the rivers of stars across the endless night sky. Nor would they climb to the top of Barri-Barri and shower under the stream of water that forever flowed from it. No—they would come into town and feign envy at how simply we lived but then complain at the lack of extremely fast internet that they were used to accessing in the city. They would warn each other not to venture too far from the group as dingoes may attack, and then they would go to Emilee's café and sip gourmet coffee and nibble on fine cakes. To finish their 'outback' experience, they would come into the bookstore and buy a kangaroo teddy or a koala fridge magnet.

"Yes." I put my hands on my hips in frustration, as Julie continued to ramble on about the history of the town. "And it's not as though I can just push through the tourists. Look how many there are!" I waved my hand at the countless tourists who were eagerly snapping their cameras in every direction. "What is so fascinating about Warrangatta? Seriously, we have like a dozen shops. Can't they go 'click' at something else?" I rolled my head back.

"Hey! Don't say that. I need them to buy my coffee," she laughed. "Besides, some of them are *hot!*" She pointed to a tall, good-looking man leaning on the verandah post. "Check him out! Oh yeah, come to Mamma!" she growled only loud enough for me to hear. "He is so checking you out, Alex!" She nudged my ribs.

"He is not." I dismissed her observation. I didn't care if he was looking at me; I wasn't looking at him, or anyone for that matter. It had only been in the last few months that I hadn't woken in the mornings still searching for Michael's warm body next to mine.

"It's so not fair. I absolutely despise you." She held her hands on her hips and paced in a small circle.

"What'd I do?" I snorted.

"All you have to do is stand there, and every guy wants to jump you. The worst part is, you don't even notice."

"Oh, whatever."

"Why do you think carrot hates you?" She looked up at me through her overly mascaraed eyes.

"I dunno, 'cause I don't look like I escaped the '80s yesterday?" I eyed Julie up and down with disgust.

Emilee spat a loud laugh. "True, but no. She's pissed at you because she wants to bang the pub owner, Ben. But he's after you." She leant in towards me. "I heard you and him had a steamy night at Warimudga the other night." She lifted her eyebrows several times.

"What? Not if he was the last man alive. Have you seen his chest? I could plait that hair! Urg!" My body shivered at the thought of him touching me.

"Seriously?" She pushed her hands on her hips. "You told me when Tom asked you to dinner, you could never be attracted to him because he didn't have any hair. You said it would be like dating a child."

"Yeah, well ..." I shrugged.

"Michael's never coming back." She spoke matter-of-factly. She had had that conversation with me many times before but never had she spoken so bluntly. I didn't know if I liked it or not. I knew he was never coming back, but I still wasn't entirely sure I was ready to move on.

"But what if I'm no good? I've only been with Michael," I said quietly, as I looked down to my fidgeting fingers.

"Is that what all this is about?" She threw her hands in the air and turned on the spot.

"Not all, but a part." I shrugged a shoulder. I had never told anyone that Michael was the only man I had ever been with. I just couldn't imagine another man touching me—the thought was repulsive.

"You just need to do it! Once you do, you'll wonder why you spent so long alone."

I cared dearly for Emilee, but she certainly wasn't shy around men. She spent most nights at the pub, and she rarely went home alone, or with the same companion.

She sensed I didn't want to talk about it anymore so she changed the subject.

"Anyway, Julie is super pissed with you now. You know, because you're pregnant with the publican's kid," she said coolly.

"What? I am not!" I folded my arms furiously. "I know she's an idiot, but does she really have to believe that crap?"

"She doesn't believe it; she just likes bagging you out! Like now—she doesn't have to stop in front the bookstore; she just does it to piss you off. Your problem is that you let it happen. Give her a right hook or an uppercut; that'd sort her out—probably make her look better too!" Emilee laughed at her joke.

"But that's it! I haven't done anything to annoy her."

"You exist, darling. She is like the Anti-Christ of you. Everything that you are, she's not and she's jealous."

I rolled my eyes. "Oh yeah, I'm screwed up in the head and my family are all dead. I'm peachy."

"Well, aren't you just a bag full of marshmallows today? Harsh much? But I know what you mean. I dunno—Julie is Julie. She's a self-absorbed, pain in the ass. She wants everybody's attention, all the time. Why do you think she's a bloody tour guide. And you, you're all 'I'm a gorgeous woman from a faraway land with a sad history. Now excuse me while I'm just going to be all mysterious over here.'" Emilee wiggled her fingers and put on a ghostly voice.

"What?" I laughed. "I am not like that!"

She lifted one eyebrow.

"Okay, so I'm not an open book. Still doesn't explain the Anti-Christ up there." I enjoyed using Emilee's analogy of Julie.

Emilee leant in closer to me. "I'll admit it's weird. I've actually never seen Julie hate someone as much as she hates you ... reckon you deserve a trophy or something."

"Oh shut up!"

"Well, anyway everybody's talking about it at the pub—your pregnancy. I think that's the fourth guy you've been pregnant to this year," she teased.

"Why the hell am I the talk of the town? I am the most boring person in the world. I go to work, and I go home. Who can be bothered with all the rumours?" I was bewildered as to how people could be motivated to make up such garbage. "I dunno. But they're fun. Hey, you still keen to go swimming at Warimudga tonight? There's meant to be a wicked storm." She wiggled the top part of her body. Her eyes were alive with excitement.

"Maybe. I'll let you know. But speaking of storms, have you seen the riots going on in Melbourne?"

"No." She shook her head. "What riots?"

"Well, apparently this crazy weather is fairly widespread. Heaps of people believe the Government's to blame and their solution is to block half the cities with rioters. They're saying they won't stop until the Government fixes it."

"Really, how could Governments control the weather? Oh well," she sighed. "At least we don't have to put up with any of that B.S. here. All we need to decide is what to call the four babies you have growing in your belly." She patted my belly jokingly.

"Go away." I playfully hit her hand away. I caught Julie sending a furious look my way as Emilee patted my stomach.

"Oh yeah, I keep forgetting. Bruce wanted me to give you this." She held out my necklace; the one Tess had given me at the hospital. "He said you took it off just before you left on your 'adventure' ... something about you didn't want to get it tangled in some mechanical thing you were fixing on your car. I dunno—I don't get cars. But here you go."

"Thanks, Em. I knew I was missing it, but I couldn't remember where I put it. Funny how you get used to something. I've felt naked without it."

~ 7 ~

CHAPTER SEVEN

"Morning Sam," I said as I hurried through the front door of the bookstore as the last of the tourists moved along. The air conditioner was running inside and offered instant relief from the hot, humid weather outside.

"Morning Alexandra," he answered from where he usually sat, behind his desk at the front of the store.

Sam's desk was made of dark mahogany and in the middle of it sat an old fashioned cash register that you had to hit in the right way to make it work. I had tried to convince him to get a computer, explaining how much easier it would be, but he wouldn't have a bar of it. 'Unreliable heaps of junk' he called them.

In many ways, I was happy for him not to invest in a computer because it meant I had to sit at the desk for longer. I loved sitting there, looking through the huge windows, watching everyone walk by—mostly they were tourists; people who lived their lives in the cities. They didn't share the same practical approach to everything as outback folk. To me, a pair of jeans with holes in them would be set for the rag bag, or at the very least, be shoved behind the seat of my ute for when it broke down on the side of the road and I didn't want to get my good clothes dirty. But so many of the female tourists walked up and down the streets of Warrangatta wearing pants with huge gashes in them—the latest trend—as they fervently texted on their phones.

"What a morning!" I complained as I hung my bag on the rack in the entry. "Took me ages to get my old ute to start and then I had to wait forever for those bloody tourists to move. Jesus, Julie drives me insane!" My jaw clenched as I thought of her. "I swear, her sole purpose for existing is to be a pain in my ass! One day I'm going to snap; I am going to kill her! Her and her fat fingers, carrot hair and nasal voice. I mean really, any wonder no man wants her! Ugh!"

"Oh, go on. You love her. You're just jealous you don't look as awesome as she does," Andy called out, stopping my rant.

Andy was a few inches taller than me, with short brown hair. He often wore a stubbly beard; not because he wanted to look sexy or rough, just because he couldn't be bothered shaving. He spent most of his time behind the 'tech desk' at the side of the store behind the book shelves. His desk was filled with computer gadgets, none of which I had even the simplest understanding. "Yeah, she's a sexy beast," he continued. "It's the hoobs that do it for me."

"Hoobs?" I asked as I screwed my nose up at the thought of anyone finding Julie attractive.

"Yeah, hoobs! It's when your boobs are so saggy they reach your hips, so they are hoobs." He nodded enthusiastically at his terrible joke.

I shook my head in disgust. "Anyway, moving right along from hoobs, I hope that water pump comes in soon because that other ute is terrible," I complained to Sam as I slumped into the swivel chair by his side.

"Ally, why don't you just get a half decent pick-up? One that actually goes?" Andy leant against Sam's desk as he stuffed a cake in his mouth.

"Pick-up? Are we suddenly in America? It's a ute, Andy!" I scowled at him, which I shouldn't have because he only said it to get a reaction from me. "Anyway, weren't you only going to be here for like a week until your new thermostat came in...? About two years ago?" I retorted. "I mean really, why are you here Andy? You spend all your time on computers. Have you ever even read a book?"

"Oh, he's not here for the books." Sam threw me a sideways look as he continued to read his newspaper.

I ignored him. He didn't understand that Andy and I were only friends. We could never be with each other romantically.

"I'm here because I'm bringing Warrangatta into the twentieth century. It is my duty." He stood to his feet and held his hand over his chest as though taking a vow.

"Andy, we are in the *twenty-first* century." Sam pushed his small, half-mooned spectacles up his nose.

"Whoa! Let's not go all crazy! I think just getting Warrangatta to the twentieth century is a feat all in itself. Besides, books? Seriously who needs them? Everything that can be found in a musty old book can be found easier and quicker right here." He tapped his laptop faithfully.

"Not to mention, it's always up to date." He folded his arms and leant back on the desk. "That newspaper for example— yesterday's news."

"Not today it's not," Sam said as he looked up through his glasses.

"And why is that, Old Man?" He blinked his eyes smugly, referring to Sam with the pet name he frequently used, hoping all the time for Sam to rise to the bait and tell him off. Sam, of course, never did.

"Storm took out the wi-fi tower on Barri-Barri. No phones either." Sam lifted his eyebrows at Andy. "You'll have to resort to reading these things." He held up the newspaper.

Andy's manner changed from good humour to agitation immediately. "What?" he groaned. "No! No wi-fi?"

Mobile phones and wi-fi were the only source of communication and internet available in Warrangatta, as no telecommunication company would run cables hundreds of kilometres.

"Yep, Tech Boy. Welcome to the *nineteenth* century." I spun on the swivel chair to see Andy more clearly. "Speaking of the internet, please tell me you ordered more of my medication online before the tower broke?"

Due to the remoteness of Warrangatta and our lack of a pharmacy, my doctor had written a specific prescription for me that allowed me to fill the script online. I barely knew how to turn a computer on, so I had Andy take care of it for me.

"Crap!" He slapped his hand over his mouth. "No, I didn't. Damn it! I'm so sorry Alex."

"Really? Urg," I groaned. "Well, Tech Boy, you have the pleasure of taking me to Poonaburra so that I can fill my script." Poonaburra was larger than Warrangatta, with a few more services and amenities available, but it took about two days' travel to get there, assuming the roads were open. "Oh man, I have to put up with you for four days straight!" He pulled an exaggerated face of pain, then smiled. "Nah, that's fine, we'll take the swags—you can have my old one," he jibed.

"And people say chivalry's dead," I retorted.

"Well, it takes two days to get there. We should head off first thing in the morning. Just my luck I'll get a flat tyre, you'll run out of meds, and I'll be stuck with you seeing flying monkeys.'

"Shut up! Idiot!" I threw a piece of scrunched up paper at him, which he smugly dodged.

"Alright, you two!" Sam interjected. "No one's going anywhere until the forecast storm has passed ... Oh Alexandra, before I forget." He rummaged through a drawer in his desk. "Remember this?" He handed me the parcel I had been given on the bus by the woman with the strange eyes. "I found this under the dresser in the upstairs room when I was cleaning up last night. It must have dropped on the floor or something the day you arrived here. I'm sorry."

"Oh yeah. I completely forgot about that!" I said as I took the parcel from him, trying to remember the circumstances of that day and how I could have forgotten about it.

I scooted forwards on my swivel chair and placed the parcel on the desk. It was still tied together with string with the letters 'DRIA' written across it.

I untied the string, which fell away easily, and pushed back the thick, rough paper. It wasn't like regular paper or anything like what I had seen before.

"What you got there?" Andy asked as he sat on the desk beside me.

"I don't know. There was some crazy woman on the bus with me when I came to Warrangatta. She was really, *really* weird. I had completely forgotten her. Anyway, she left this parcel for me ..."

"Some stranger leaves a parcel for you, and you forget it?" Andy scoffed.

"Yeah, well I kinda had a lot going on, you know, arriving in a strange town after the loss of my family and waking up from a two-year coma ..."

Andy threw his hands in the air to signify surrender. "Calm down! What is it?"

I pulled the item from the paper. "It's a book of some kind. Eew, it feels awful," I said as I ran my fingers across it's black leathery cover. There were several curious symbols pressed into the leather. Unlike the coarse touch of the cover, the symbols felt smooth; almost like silk. "I wonder what language it's in. Sam, do you recognise these symbols?"

Sam pushed his glasses up his nose further and took the book from me. "Hmmm, it does feel odd, doesn't it—like scales. I've never felt anything like this." He slowly turned open the front cover. The leather also covered the inside of the book, but the pages inside were entirely different. They were made of a rigid material that was the colour of ivory. Perfect black writing scrolled across the pages, each character appearing to be pressed into the rigid surface. Sam ran his fingers gently over the pages. "It's like no language I've ever seen before. At first observation, one could be forgiven for thinking it was Arabic, but the writings are more like symbols. And, it doesn't look to be written or printed. Look at these pressed markings ..." Sam's mouth was ajar as he moved his head up and down looking for anything slightly familiar. He stood up and started to pace up and down as he studied the strange book he was holding.

Andy took the book from him and ran his fingers over the cover. "Don't think it's a witch's book do you?" he asked excitedly.

"Oh come on." I rolled my eyes and took the book back. I'd never believed in witches or anything else supernatural. No matter how unbelievable something seems, there's always a logical explanation for it.

"No, I mean it," he insisted. "I'm not saying it's a magical book. But back in the day women believed themselves to be witches, they made books—books of spells." He wiggled his fingers in the air and pulled a ghost-like expression. "There were a few books made of ... human skin," he whispered creepily.

"Human skin? Come on, Andy. You don't believe in that rubbish do you?" I threw him a disapproving look.

"He does, and so should you," Sam said seriously, as he took the book back from Andy and placed it on the desk, tapping the closed cover lightly with his fingers. "Books bound in human skin are not a myth. Although not as common as Andy would have you think, there certainly are a few. Not to burst your bubble Andy, but this is not one of them. Funnily enough, human skin and standard leather feel remarkably similar. This book is not human skin." He stood back, folding his arms as he kept frowning at the book. I could tell it was irritating him not being able to identify it.

"It scares me, Old Man, how you know that. Not planning on having an Andy wallet are you?" Andy asked with one eyebrow lifted.

"I might if you keep calling me Old Man", he retorted as Andy chuckled. Sam took his glasses from his nose and pinched the bridge between his closed eyes. "Andy, I know this because I actually read books. I don't spend all my hours playing floppy duck on the computer," he said exasperated at Andy's nonsense.

"Makes a nice change from playing with his floppy *disc*." I pulled a smile at Andy.

"It's loads of fun to play with. You can come to my place tonight and play with my floppy disc—turn it into a hard drive?" He lifted his eyebrows suggestively.

"I think you're doing enough all on your own. These things are getting huge." I reached across and squeezed his biceps. In the last couple of weeks, they had almost doubled in size.

"Yeah, I know!" He twisted his arms around and flexed his upper arm muscles. "I don't know why. But it's bloody awesome!"

"I didn't think young people used floppy discs anymore. If you enjoy using them I've got a whole box full," Sam said, completely oblivious to our referencing.

Andy put his hand over his mouth as he tried to hold back from laughing, as I responded to Sam in as normal a voice as possible. "No thanks, Sam. If I need a floppy, I'll ask Andy." I patted Andy on the back. He stopped laughing and threw me a dirty look.

As I picked up the book to place it back on the brown paper, I noticed a small inscription written on the inside of the wrapper.

"Hey, look at this." I tapped Sam on the shoulder.

He turned and looked at the wrapper I held in my hand. He slipped his glasses on again and read the inscription:

'Run as you might,
Escape if you may.
Destiny with fate,
Wait shall they lay.'

"What on Earth could this poem be referencing?" Sam scratched the back of his head.

Andy reached across and grabbed the book, along with the wrapper. "Everything is on the net; I'll research it for you as soon as the wi-fi's back." He carefully folded the paper around the book and walked it to his satchel hanging by the front door.

"Yes, I am highly interested in any information you may find about this ..." Sam spoke absentmindedly, as he stared after the book.

"Don't look too hard," I said. "I seriously doubt you'll find anything. The woman who gave it to me was strange. It's probably a book from a cheap city shop." I shrugged. "Well, that's about enough crazy for one morning. I'm going to get myself a coffee before I start the rest of the day. Would you like one too, Sam?" I called over my shoulder as I walked towards the staffroom.

"Better make mine a tea. Doctor says the old ticker isn't in tune." He tapped his chest with a pencil. Sam was fit for his age, and as such, I would often forget he was in his mid-seventies. Every now and then something would happen, like the comment his heart wasn't in the best of shape, and I would be reminded he wouldn't always be there. Such reminders hurt.

"I'll have a hot chocolate, three sugars. Thanks for asking," Andy called after me as I disappeared into the staffroom. I ignored him, but he knew I would reappear holding his drink.

The staffroom was located at the rear of the long and narrow store. It was a reasonable size room with enough space for a small table and a kitchenette. While waiting for the kettle to boil, I noticed the local newspaper opened to the horoscope page. I always thought horoscopes were corny, but I decided to peek at mine. *'Soon you will discover yourself,'* it read. I rolled my eyes—what a load of rubbish!

The kettle clicked off as it reached the boil. I pushed the newspaper away, stood up to the sink and made the drinks. Placing the mugs on a tray, I carefully balanced them as I walked down the two steps to the store. As I turned a corner of one of the aisles, I bumped into a customer, knocking the mugs from my hands and spilling their contents over his shirt.

"On my God! I am sooo sorry!" I exclaimed as I automatically started to wipe the spilt liquid from his shirt using my bare hands. Two black hands gently wrapped themselves around mine, stopping me from touching the shirt.

I looked at his hands around mine. They were the darkest black and felt rough on my soft skin. My eyes lifted to meet his; they were dark brown and full of warmth.

"Do not be concerned. It is okay. I am sure the rain will rinse me well enough." He spoke in a deep African accent.

It took me a moment to process what he said. "Rain? Can't be, it was roasting hot out there just minutes ago."

"Yes. It is raining heavily." He pointed to the front window.

I craned my neck over the bookshelves. Sure enough, the weather had altered—again. The heavens had opened, and rain pelted heavily against the window.

"I can't keep up with this weather." I shook my head as I watched tourists run for shelter in every direction.

I looked back to him. He was very broad and masculine. His hair had been almost completely shaven, and he had a slight shadow of a beard. He was wearing a pair of dark cargo pants with a wide black belt, and a black shirt that outlined the shape of his well-defined body. His dark skin glowed gently under the dimly lit bookstore lights. But it wasn't just his appearance that had me transfixed; it was the smell of his aftershave. It smelled of trees—ancient forests. I had to force myself not to close my eyes as I breathed it in; it was intoxicating.

"Alexandra... Alexandra!" Sam called to me.

"Huh?" I answered vaguely, as I continued to stare at the man.

"Alexandra! There are towels in the staff room." Sam said in a loud whisper.

"Right ... towels." I turned awkwardly on the spot as I realised how ridiculous I must have looked. I quickly bent down and picked up the mugs. "Um ... this way." I beckoned him to the staff room, and he followed without speaking.

Next to the sink was a stack of small hand towels ranging in colour from hideous to horrendous. I pulled the least offensive towel from the centre; it was lime green with a purple border.

"Sorry, usually customers don't see our towels. I'm not in the habit of throwing boiling drinks over complete strangers." I smiled as I handed him the towel and leant against the cabinets.

He took it and folded it in half. "Well, I should feel privileged. I am receiving special treatment." He smiled as he blotted out the dark liquid from his shirt.

There was an awkward silence. I tried to think of something witty or charming to say, but my mind had gone blank.

"Have you always lived in Warrangatta?" he asked, finally breaking the silence.

"No." I cleared my throat. "No, I used to live in New South Wales. I've been here for about two years now." I tucked my hair behind my ears then quickly pulled it out again—I felt gawky either way. "What about you? I'm guessing Africa?" I said, as nonchalantly as possible, as I searched for a position to rest my arms that would not make me appear ungainly, but every position felt unnatural.

"You guess correctly. What was the giveaway?" He smiled widely.

I half laughed, and half tried to speak, which sounded more like a snort. "Are you staying here?" I spoke quickly, trying to hide my ridiculous snort. "I mean, not here in the bookstore, I mean here in Warrangatta." I stumbled over my words, and I could feel my face begin to burn.

"I am travelling through Warrangatta. I am searching for a lost friend," he answered as he continued to blot his shirt.

"Oh, any luck in finding him?" I didn't mean to emphasise the word 'him', but I had said it before I could stop myself.

"Her. And perhaps. Much time has passed, so I am not certain she would recognise me."

The word 'her' struck a nerve, one that I wasn't used to feeling. I had only just met him, but I didn't want him to belong to another.

"I'm sure she would recognise you." How could anyone forget him?

"Perhaps. But she may not want to."

"Ah, ended badly?"

"You could say that, yes." He promptly changed the subject. "New South Wales to Warrangatta? That is quite a change. What caused you to move?" He folded the towel to a clean section and continued to dab his shirt clean. I was getting the impression he was intentionally taking a prolonged time to clean it.

"Yeah it was. I used to live there with my family... but there was a house fire ... I was the only one who made it. So after I got out of the hospital, I jumped on a bus and somehow ended up here. I met Sam, Andy and Emilee. And, well, this is my new home." I fidgeted with my fingers as I spoke.

"You do not appear to have been burned?" His eyes ran over my body, examining me.

I shook my head. "It was more of an explosion. I have a doozy of a scar on my stomach." I pulled my shirt up just enough to expose a long, winding scar that ran from my belly button to just above my pant line.

"Where did you get that scar?" he asked.

"I don't know what exactly happened. I guess something jabbed into me during the explosion. It would have healed while I was in the coma."

"Coma?" His eyes widened with surprise.

"Yeah, after the explosion I was in a hospital for about two years."

"I am sorry. I did not know."

"How could you have known? We've only just met."

"But you are lucky not to have died."

"A lot of people have said that. I'm grateful now that I'm alive. But for a long time I resented the fact that I survived when they hadn't. But, it's getting easier. I mean it doesn't hurt to breathe anymore." I shrugged.

"Death is not easy. I, too, have lost people I love." He looked at me as though he had known me for years. His eyes were warm and soft. They didn't match his hard, masculine body. I had to resist the urge to fall into his arms and beg him to hold me.

"Time is a good healer," he said, drawing me from my dazed state.

I smiled. "Yes, it is. Well, if you need anything else, I'll be on your disc, my disc..." I could feel my face burn hot. "I will be at-my-desk," I said precisely.

He smiled widely. "Thank you."

I nodded once, turned and walked back towards the desk and sat on the swivel chair. I was still trying to catch my breath.

"Hey, Alex," Andy called as he strolled around the corner of the desk.

"Yeah?" I composed myself as he dragged another chair around behind the desk to sit next to me.

"I've searched around for info on that book."

"What? Already? I thought there was no internet."

"Yes, well we're not all snails. And you're right; there's no internet. No phones either, but I was able to connect to Moori-billi's tower just long enough to get a few emails through to a friend of mine in Melbourne. He's got this wickedly fast computer. I mean it's crazy! The processor in it is ..."

"Andy! Get to the point." I interrupted his excitement. I wanted to know what he had discovered, but I was finding it increasingly difficult to keep my eyes from the African man, who was now browsing the books.

"Right, this guy has written his own program. The algorithms are insane!" He saw my raised eyebrow. "Okay, I won't go geek on you. The program essentially scans all images over the internet and is crazy quick." His eyes lit up, as they always did when he was speaking about anything new in the world of technology.

"Is that legal?" I cupped my hand to the side of my mouth in case somebody overheard me, even though the only customer in the store was the African man.

"Well, it depends on which way you look at it. Anyway, he ran the images of the book I sent him through this program. He said he checked everywhere, and—nothing." He pulled his mouth to one side. "I think you might be right. The book's just a fraud. You want it back?"

"No, you keep it." I slunk back in the chair. I was more disappointed than I expected I would be. "It can go with the rest of your weird collection."

Andy had a large assortment of weapons; mainly swords he had collected over time. They hung on his lounge room wall, and at night, the moonlight sleeked through the window and the swords glistened; it was as though they were alive. Being near the swords was unnerving for me, so I tried to avoid visiting his house at all so I wouldn't have to see them. The side of town where he lived was beautiful. His house was surrounded by trees, which were kept alive by water from the underground spring that fed into Warimudga. Ordinarily, I would have been happy to drop in to have a chat or share a meal, but not if it meant being near those swords and listening to him talk about his latest acquisition.

"It's not weird. I've tried to tell you so many times ... they're weapons that were used by some pretty amazing people. They're artefacts," he said defensively.

"Come on; they're junky swords and knives you picked up from the internet. They're probably mass produced in a factory in the middle of China," I chortled. I'd never let him know how the weapons affected me; he'd never let me live it down.

"You know nothing of history." He held a blank face and shook his head.

I sighed and leant my head on my hand. "What about the cover on that book? That material must be something weird, right?" I asked hopefully.

"Alex, I know you are bored and want to believe there is some incredible adventure out there for you, but you're out of luck here. My best guess, a cow and a snake had a wild night and the cover is made with its love child." He slapped the table a couple of times, stood up and walked back to his tech desk, book in hand.

"That's a terrible analogy," I called to him as he disappeared around the book shelf.

I turned back to face the desk to see the African man standing behind it waiting to be served.

"That man, Sam, told me he did not know how to operate the register and to bring the book to you." He shrugged a shoulder.

I looked past him to see Sam leaning heavily on his cane, smiling and nodding enthusiastically at me.

The man smiled a little and handed over a book: *Cake Decorating for All Occasions*. I looked up at him surprised and a little disappointed. I had envisioned him as a soldier or warrior. Without thinking I said, "Cake decorating? Seriously?" As soon as the words came out I wanted to dig a hole and bury myself in it. *You bloody idiot, Alex.*

"Yes. I enjoy cake." The man responded without humour, his eyebrows furrowed.

"Oh I'm sorry … I just wasn't expecting … I shouldn't have … " I stumbled over my words.

He began to laugh, a deep rolling laugh. "I would not know where to begin with cakes. It is for my sister."

"Oh … right." I could feel my face burn again. "Well I have been told it's an excellent book for beginners—not that I'm saying your sister is a beginner, of course. I'm sure she's very experienced … oh, but not like that! I don't mean experienced with men, I mean … cake." I closed my eyes as I said the last words.

He just smiled.

"Well, anyway, that's $15.50 thank you." I mumbled.

"Thank you, Alexandra," he said as he collected his book and walked towards the exit.

His walk was more of a march with each step taken firm and strong. It took me a few moments to realise that he had used my name.

"Sam, how did that man know my name?"

"Oh he was asking me loads of questions about you—very interested he was. Wanted to know your address, phone number, car rego …" he said with a smile as he slowly limped behind the desk. Before I could respond he added, "Or it could be your name tag—that'd be a giveaway!"

He landed his hand on my shoulder for a moment, gave me a wry smile, and walked back into the shop to arrange some new kangaroo merchandise.

I looked out the window in the hope of seeing the man one last time as he walked down the street. The rain had stopped again. Steam was swirling up from the hot road. Across from the bookstore, there were a few female tourists sitting outside Emilee's café. One of the women noticed him walking past where they sat. She nudged her friends, and they leant in eagerly to each other, bantering as he marched past. One of them, a brunette with dark gorgeous skin stood up, adjusted her already low cut floral dress so it was a little more revealing, checked her reflection in the café window and strutted on over to him. Her movements were light and graceful. She quickened her pace a little and in doing so her beautiful hair bounced gently around her soft face. Her dress appeared to swim over her slender body.

I had no idea what she was saying to him, but I was filled with a sudden jealously at the attention he was paying this pretty woman. I felt inadequate against such a woman and it burned deeply.

She smiled as she chatted to him and put her hand on his arm. I glared at her through the panes of glass. I really wasn't that angry at her, rather, at myself. I wanted desperately to look like her and to have the sex appeal and confidence to walk up to a complete stranger and introduce myself with clear intentions of what I wanted.

I could see he was speaking to her, but of course, I couldn't hear even a whisper of it. I knew he would leave with her; who wouldn't? She was beyond stunning. But ... what was happening? Instead of her accompanying him, she instead turned on her pointy high heels and sulkily strode back to where her friends were awaiting a report.

He had just rejected her. Elation filled my body—he didn't accept her! That elation was soon relinquished, however, with the realisation that if he had rejected *her*, what chance did *I* have? Not that I was likely to see him ever again.

I turned back to the store. Two people stood at the counter, a woman and a man. The man was medium height, stocky with short brown hair and had a jagged scar on the side of his face. The woman was of similar height, with wavy black hair that sat neatly by her white marble-like face. Her lips were accentuated by the bright lipstick she wore. She was quite possibly the most beautiful woman I had ever seen, although I was disappointed I couldn't see her eyes behind the darkened sunglasses she was wearing.

"Can I help you?" As taken as I was by her beauty, I was no longer startled by strangely dressed people, as tourists from all over the world flocked to see our outback town, each looking vastly different.

"I am wanting to acquire book." She spoke in a heavy Russian accent. "It is of great importance." Her voice was cool, her demeanour solemn.

"Well, I'll do my best. We do have a lot in stock. But if the book you are looking for isn't in, I'm afraid it will take a fair while to get it," I said as I pulled the list of our stocked books from under the desk.

"The book in which I am referring would be very memorable," she said in a low voice.

"Okay—memorable, how?" I squinted as I tried to recall all books I had recently catalogued.

"Do you recognise me, Alexandra?" She tilted her head slightly.

I must have served her before. All tourists who re-visit Warrangatta expect me to remember them, but I saw so many faces each week, I rarely paid any attention to any of them.

I stepped back to take all of her in. "No, sorry. I serve a lot of people here."

"No matter. Long time has passed." For the first time she pulled a slight smile.

I looked at her again. I had a vague feeling of déjà vu but it floated away before I could register any true memory of having met her.

"Hey Ally, Emilee is run off her feet over at the café. She's asked if I can give her a hand. Sam says it's okay. You're right here for the rest of the day?" Andy asked as he walked behind the desk, putting some books away in a cupboard.

"Yeah, that's fine. I have some paperwork to do after hours tonight so I won't be across to have a coffee with you both. Oh, and I won't be up at Warimudga either. Tell her to bring me my coffee in the morning instead." I smiled a cheesy smile. I had tried to get Emilee to deliver my morning coffee for many months and so far hadn't had any success.

"Ha, ha. I don't like your chances." He lifted his eyebrows and shook his head as he walked around the desk and out the door. I watched him through the window as he wrapped his arms over his head and dashed across the street. He was drenched by the time he reached Emilee's café.

I turned back to the couple who were looking for a memorable book, only to see them both leaving the shop.

I rolled my eyes. Bloody tourists—they're all weird.

~ 8 ~

CHAPTER EIGHT

As the busy day drew to an end, I lay back in the large chair behind the front desk, letting my long hair drape over the back of the chair as I relaxed down into its comfort.

"How can the weather change so many times in one day?" I asked Sam as I watched the rain hit the windows. "It's absolutely freezing now." I could feel the coldness from the outside leach inside through the glass.

"Oh, it's not really that cold I don't suppose," he answered as he neatened the map stand next to the desk. "We're just used to extreme heat. I went to the snow region once. Now, that's cold." He shivered at the thought.

"I'd like to visit the snow one day," I said absentmindedly, as I imagined soft, fluffy snow falling gently.

"Well, you might be sooner than you think. I was reading in the newspaper earlier that a cold front is being pushed up from Tasmania. It is meant to hit later today." He hobbled closer to the desk. "So you make sure you are home and have the heater turned right up before it hits," he instructed as he wagged a finger at me.

"I will be, Sam. I've just got a bit of paperwork to do, and I'll be on my way," I promised him.

"Well, you just make sure that you are. And don't dilly-dally on your way home. You haven't lived in Warrangatta long enough to see a real storm tear through here, and they say the one that's on its way is going to be a real doozy. You don't want to be caught up in it. I would wait with you, but the vet is dropping Vinnie home in twenty minutes and I need to be there for him. That damned dog is costing me a fortune," he complained as he took his coat from the coat rack and slipped it over his arms.

"It's fine, Sam," I smiled at him. I knew although he complained about the vet bill, he would spend any amount of money on that dog.

"Alright, well I might not be in tomorrow. It will depend on Vinnie. I might need to keep an eye on him," he told me as he pulled his cap on and pulled the door open.

"No worries, I'll see you when I see you."

"Right." He gave a quick wave and walked through the door. An icy breeze came rushing through the door the moment it opened. The freezing air danced across my skin, instantly producing goose bumps.

All the other shops were now shut because of the weather. A cold snap like that in Warrangatta was very unusual. The tourists had fled to their accommodation for the night, so the street was deserted. Even the pub across the road had closed its doors.

I only spent about half an hour sorting through the paperwork, when I heard the wind howl down the alley beside the store. The wind thrashed the rain against the window making the glass vibrate. I pushed my chair closer to the window and looked up to the sky. Night had fallen prematurely. The storm

Sam was talking about must have hit. I could feel the temperature plummet even further.

I lived at least fifteen minutes away and I knew if I didn't drop everything and leave now, I probably wouldn't be able to get through on the roads, and I did not want to be stuck on the side of the road during a storm.

I slipped the paperwork back into the folder and placed it in the top drawer of the desk. A clap of thunder sounded. I knew I had to hurry. I quickly switched the lights off and pulled on my coat. It wasn't waterproof, but it was warm.

I pulled the door open and instantly my face felt as though a million tiny needles were hitting it, making me cringe. I pulled the door shut behind me and locked it, which was a challenge in itself because the wild wind was fighting against me.

I began walking to my car with my coat wrapped tightly around me, but it offered no protection as the rain thrashed in every direction, drenching my clothing.

"Alexandra?" I heard a deep, male voice call from behind me.

I turned to see where the voice had come from. There stood the man who had only today purchased the cake decorating book from me. My stomach fluttered at the sight of him. It was the coldest weather I had ever experienced, but I suddenly felt hot.

"Oh, Hi. Not something wrong with the book, is there? We're shut for tonight but we'll be open again at 9 a.m." I had to yell over the rain, which was hitting the tin roofs of the nearby shops. He must have been freezing because he still only wore a shirt with his cargo pants.

"So you remember me?" He asked as he wiped the rain from his face. His upper arm muscles bulged as he bent his arm to his face and his wet shirt pulled taught around his torso showing his sculpted body. My body heat began to soar as I forced myself to look away. "Yeah of course, you bought the cook book earlier." I tugged my coat around my waist further.

A clap of thunder sounded above us, reverberating down the street, making the shop windows shake. It was followed by another gust of wind. The thunder was so explosive, I was certain the buildings were going to crumble around us.

"I've never seen weather like this in Warrangatta. We can't stay out in this," I yelled.

I had no sooner finished speaking when a gust of wind whipped down the street with such force that it lifted a sheet of tin from a shop across the street and sent it hurtling towards us. I could see the sheet of iron coming directly towards me. I wanted to move but my body was frozen. All I was able to do was close my eyes and brace for the hit.

Just before the tin struck me, I felt him grab me and push me against the wall. He threw himself over me as the tin smashed through the glass window, the shattered glass blowing into the street.

He slowly pushed himself from me and took a few steps back. "Are you okay?"

I couldn't answer; I couldn't find any words to speak. I stared at the sheet of tin that lay through the window of the shop—it should have killed me. Another gust tore down the street, ripping several branches off a nearby tree, sending pieces hurtling in every direction. "We need to get out of this," I yelled at him over the howling wind.

The only shelter I had access to was the bookstore. "We'll wait it out in the shop." My voice was barely audible over the pelting rain and ferocious wind.

"Okay," he yelled back.

He wrapped his arm tightly around me as we forced our way through the unyielding wind. The rain was being shot through the air with such velocity it felt like tiny bullets hitting me.

When we reached the door to the bookstore, I slipped the key into the lock and turned the handled, but the door was torn from my hand as the wind slammed it open. Immediately the wind began playing havoc with the books and loose pieces of paper, tossing them through the air. I reached for the door with both of my hands and tried to push it closed but the wind was offering too much resistance. He reached over me and with little effort slammed the door shut. Instantly the pages that had become airborne dropped to the floor, and I fell against the door as I tried to catch my breath.

My coat was soaked through from the rain and hung heavily from me. I unzipped it, threw it over the counter and fell back to the door. All the while, he stood next to me with one hand on the door as though in anticipation of it flying open again.

I felt something drip onto my bare shoulder. As I wiped it away with my hand, I realised it was tainted red. Another drip landed on my shoulder. It was blood! Thinking I had been cut by the flying timber or glass, I felt around my face and head for signs of where a wound might be, but there was no blood on my hands. I looked up to see blood coming from his arm.

"The tin! It must have cut you." There was a cut under his arm. A small pool of blood was forming at the base of his feet as his wound bled steadily.

I knew a moment of panic, understanding the need to stop the bleeding quickly. I raced to the staff room and pulled open the small blue cupboards under the sink. My hands were shaking as I reached for the first aid kit, knocking over several bottles in my haste. I also grabbed a small silver bowl and filled it with warm water; I knew there would be antiseptic in the first aid kit, which I would add to it later. I tucked the first aid kit under my arm, as I balanced the water with as many towels as I could carry and hurried back to where he stood. Although his skin was dark, his face was beginning to pale. I looked down to the floor at his feet. The pool of blood had quadrupled in size.

"There's a couch down the back. Can you make it there?" I was worried he was going to die of blood loss before I was able to tend to him. I hadn't had any medical training but I knew a major artery was located near where his arm was cut.

He smiled. "Yes. But it is not that bad. I have had much worse." His voice was calm.

I, however, was on the brink of having a panic attack. I was certain he was going to die. I had never seen a person bleed as much as he was right now.

He took one of the towels I was holding and pushed it firmly into his cut. It turned red instantly, which made my stomach flip.

"Sit on the couch and I'll wrap it." My voice was pitched higher than usual, and I was breathing faster than I should. I didn't wait for him to respond. I darted for the couch

and carefully placed the water and towels on the nearby coffee table. He sat on the couch casually, with an amused expression.

"How are you not panicking? Your arm is almost sliced in two." I growled at him. I found it annoying that he wasn't concerned for his own safety.

"It will be fine, Alexandra. It looks worse than it is." He almost laughed as he spoke.

"It needs to be cleaned and bandaged!" I insisted. I knelt down next to the table, soaked a towel in the water and squeezed it several times. "That tin was completely rusted. God only knows what other bacteria it had on it. Not to mention any arteries it severed. You really need a hospital, but that's impossible! The closet hospital is hours away! *I* have to tend to it. " My annoyance and panic were growing and he found it amusing, which only aggravated me further.

"Fine," he groaned and rolled his eyes.

He grabbed at the back of his shirt and pulled it over his head. He was careful not to allow the towel to be lowered. I sat back on my heels in awe; I breathed in sharply as I looked at him. He wore several black, raised tattoos across his chest and down each side of his abdomen. Every muscle of his body was perfectly defined. I had only seen men with bodies like that in magazines or movies, never in real life.

"You can take a picture if you like." He sucked his lip in and let it out with a smile.

"What?" I asked dismissively, as I was shocked out of my gaze. I knelt down and busied myself soaking and squeezing the towel in the antiseptic water. I could feel his eyes on me, my face beginning to burn red. I pulled my long hair around my face in the hope of disguising my embarrassment. My hair was wet and cold as it landed around my face.

I held the back of his hand, which he used to support the blood-soaked towel and I readied my clean towel to exchange them quickly. I pulled his hand away and quickly pressed the clean towel to his wound. Blood soaked the clean towel just as quickly as it did the first one. My stomach fell even further. He was going to die because he saved me. The thought made my chest tighten.

"Stitches. It needs stitches." I said frantically, as I held two blood-soaked towels in my hands. "I don't know how to stitch." My hands began to shake again. "We need a doctor." I could feel panic rise higher inside me. "There are no phones. Oh God!"

"Alexandra. Calm down." He placed his clean hand on my shoulder. "I will hold this." He held his hand over the towel under his arm. "Open the first aid kit." He instructed.

I slowly lowered my shaking hands and reached for the first aid kit. I tried to open it but my blood-covered fingers were sliding across the latches. I wiped my hands on my jeans and tugged at the lid again. This time I opened it.

"There should be large gauze pads and bandages. Take them out and unwrap them."

I sifted through the various medical items in the kit until I found the gauze padding. I ripped it from its plastic covering.

He reached across and took the gauze pad from my hand. His movement shifted the air in my direction and with it carried the smell of his aftershave. The scent of ancient forests filled my lungs. As I breathed it in, I could feel my toes curl in my boots. I shook my head slightly to bring myself back to reality.

He removed the blood-soaked towel and replaced it with the gauze. "Can you wrap the bandage?"

I stood quickly with bandage in hand. I leant across him and gingerly begun to wrap the bandage around his arm. My fingers were shaking as I passed the bandage from hand to hand around his arm.

"That doesn't hurt, does it?" I asked as I pulled the bandage firmly into place. I had never wrapped a bandage before, and I was scared I would pull too hard and hurt him.

He laughed. "No."

"Why are you laughing?" I asked sternly, thinking I might be doing something wrong. "You are so worried and there is no need to be." He leant back into the couch as he watched me wrap the bandage up and down his arm.

"You have a huge cut in your arm and lost so much blood. How on Earth are you not concerned?" I couldn't understand his blasé attitude to his injury.

"This is not a lot of blood, Alexandra," he smirked.

"Even so, why aren't you worried?" I frowned as I positioned each cycle of bandage perfectly, laying it over the previous section.

"Why are you?"

I slowed my layering of the bandages. I didn't have an answer for that question. I had no idea why I was so concerned for a complete stranger. I had no inkling as to who he was, yet I felt an urgency to help him, to protect him—to be near him.

"Anyone would be worried ... *you* should be worried," I said impatiently, trying to disguise my irrational attraction.

I tucked the last piece of bandage into itself and checked to ensure no more blood had seeped through. The bandage remained clean. "All done." I said as I inhaled deeply. As I let out my breath it ran from my mouth as fog. Only then did I realise how cold it was. I looked to the large front windows; the corner of them had begun to ice up.

"This cold snap really isn't mucking around, is it?" I said vaguely, as I watched the ice on the windows inch along the glass.

An enormous clap of thunder rolled over the town, shaking the entire building as it went. Instantly the room turned black, making me jump.

I could hear the wind tug and pull at the roof as hailstones pelted against the glass. He stood by my side as we both watched the front windows begin to ice up on the corners. I don't know how it happened, but somehow I found my fingers intertwining themselves with his, and I stepped closer to him. Storms rarely scared me, but this one did. It was by far the most violent storm I had ever experienced.

"The power's out now. It usually doesn't get put back on for days. Everyone has generators, but they're outside ..."

"We are safe in here," he comforted me.

He slipped his hand from mine and gently placed it around my shoulder and pulled me into him. "You are cold, Alexandra." He spun me to face him as he rubbed his hands over my exposed arms. "You are freezing, and your clothes are wet." His voice was rushed and urgent. "Take your clothes off."

"Excuse me?" I wrapped my arms around myself and took several steps backwards.

"The wet clothes will cause your body temperature to fall too quickly. Why do you think I did not put my shirt back on?"

"It's okay. I'll acclimatise," I said. I knew he was right about the wet clothes forcing my body temperature down, but I was not removing any of my clothes while he was with me. Emilee, Andy and I regularly went skinny-dipping at Warimudga. They had both seen me naked more times that I could count, and I didn't care what they thought of me. But I did care what *he* might think.

"I cannot see you; it is pitch black in here. There is no need to be embarrassed. Please, just take your wet clothes off. I have been with people who have suffered from hypothermia, both mild and severe. I do not wish you to experience it." His voice changed; he was no longer amused and easy. He was pleading with me.

I didn't want to take my clothes off, but I knew I couldn't stay in them either. I was already beginning to shiver uncontrollably. I looked out the front windows. The rain continued to beat against the glass with no sign of reprieve, and the thunder continued to roll across the skies.

"Okay," I reluctantly agreed.

I sat on the edge of the couch, pulled a blanket from under it and wrapped it around myself. My eyes were beginning to adjust to the dark room, and I could vaguely see his silhouette. He was looking away from me, towards the staffroom. Although he couldn't see me clearly through the darkness or under the blanket, it made me feel more relaxed that he was looking away. I pulled my clothes from me and threw them on the floor beside the couch, leaving only my underwear on. I hugged the blanket around my almost naked body as I huddled in the corner of the soft couch.

"Are you covered?" he asked as he continued to look away.

"Yes. Thank you. I only just realised, I don't know your name."

He turned back to face me. "My name is Derrek."

"Well, Derrek. I bet you had better plans for tonight than being caught in here with me, with all this ..." I gestured towards the rain and hail crashing into the windows.

He sat at the end of the couch, his elbows resting on his knees with his forearms and hands hanging loosely between his legs.

"You are correct; I did have big plans for tonight."

I couldn't help feeling disappointed at his response, but then he continued, "I had hoped to be eating dinner with you now." He looked across to me, the whites of his eyes gently reflecting the slither of moonlight peering through our windows.

"What?" I breathed.

"That is why I came back tonight, Alexandra. I had hoped to take you to dinner."

"Really? You wanted to take me to dinner?"

"I understand if you would not be interested. I did notice earlier, you and your friend are very close ..."

"You mean Andy? No, no. I mean, he's great. But he's just a friend."

"I am happy to hear that." His upper body shivered as he spoke.

I grabbed the side of the blanket and threw it across him, also.

"No, it is okay," he said and pushed the blanket away.

"You'll freeze. You just told me how bad hypothermia is."

"It is, but I know you are uncomfortable being unclothed. I will add to your discomfort if I share the blanket." He spoke plainly like a soldier giving an order.

"Don't be ridiculous." I dismissed his concern, although he was accurate.

"I have been in far worse conditions than this. I know I will survive." He laughed slightly.

I pushed down all feelings of inadequacy and guilt and the other negative emotions that were flooding my body. I slid across to him, lay my back to his chest and pulled the blanket around the both of us. His body was warm and smooth against my bare skin. My heart raced furiously, and I could feel my face burn as I waited for his response. I could barely breathe as I waited for him to either accept me or reject me. I was expecting him to move away. Instead, he gently put his arm around my shoulder and rested it on my arm.

"Thank you, Alexandra." He spoke quietly. His breath was warm on the side of my neck, sending a shiver through me.

I knew that he was not allowing me to sit like this because he was attracted to me—it was purely a survival technique. I couldn't relax onto him, so I held my body rigid, fighting my emotions.

"I am making you nervous. I do not mean to," he said quietly.

"No. It's just that ... I ..." I swallowed hard. I was reluctant to finish the sentence because I would reveal my true feelings, but before I could stop myself, I was speaking. "I lost my husband about two years ago, and I haven't been ... close with anyone since." After I said it, I realised how it sounded and what it implied. "It just feels strange being so close to someone who isn't him." I quickly added. "I kind of feel like ..."

"You are being unfaithful?" he finished my sentence for me.

"Yes ..." I was surprised he knew how I was feeling.

"I have also been in love." He drew circles on my arm with his thumb as he thought of the woman he had loved.

"What was she like?"

He took a deep breath in. "They say perfection does not exist. But it did in her."

"Michael was perfect too—and Sasha." I hadn't spoken much of her since I arrived in Warrangatta, and even though a couple of years had passed, just the mention of her name tugged strongly at my emotions.

"Sasha? Who is Sasha?" he asked.

I couldn't help it. I tried to hold back any tears that were forming behind my eyes, but I couldn't.

"My daughter." I spluttered. "I'm sorry." I clapped my hand over my mouth.

Just hearing her name aloud pushed thorns through my heart. I held my breath for several seconds as I tried to stop my emotions overflowing.

He wrapped his arm tightly around me and pulled me into him. "It is okay." He pressed his lips against the back of my head as he spoke. His breath was warm as it ran down my neck.

For a split second, I forgot it was him holding me and thought of Michael who used to comfort me in the same way. I twisted myself onto my side and lay my head on his chest. As soon as I had moved, I regretted it. That was more than a survival technique. He would never respond well to that. As I began to push myself from him, both of his arms wrapped themselves around me, pulling me close. I could smell nothing but his aftershave and feel nothing but his warmth. My heart leapt and my stomach tensed. A new warmth flooded my body, a warmth that no heater or blanket could begin to produce. As his warmth flowed into me, my eyes became heavy. I didn't want to sleep; I wanted to talk to him all night. I only closed my eyes for a second but it was long enough for sleep to take me.

~ 9 ~

CHAPTER NINE

"What have you done?" someone yelled, but I was still sleeping, so I incorporated the words into the dream I was having.

I stretched slowly as I peeled my eyes open. I squinted at the bright shining through the windows. Derrek no longer lay there with me on the couch.

"I can explain. It is not how it looks." I heard Derrek speak defensively.

"There's nothing to explain! I can see what you've done!" That was Emilee's voice.

I sprung forward to see Andy and Emilee cornering Derrek—and no wonder! The shop looked like a murder scene. The pool of blood remained at the front door, and the blood-soaked towels hung from the edge of the table. I caught a glimpse of myself in the window reflection; my hair was still windswept and awry; blood smeared my neck and the side of my face.

"Wait!" I called as I jumped to my feet and ran to them.

Emilee's eyes widened as she looked to me and quickly back to him.

"Ally, what has he done?" She was furious and on edge.

"Actually, he saved my life." I looked to him with a shy smile. I wasn't sure if the night we spent together meant anything or if he was only being kind under the circumstances.

Andy looked around the room with furrowed eyebrows. "What did he do? Give you a blood transfusion?"

"Actually, that is my blood ..." He held up his bandaged arm, a small amount of blood had seeped through it overnight.

I stepped closer to Derrek and held up my hand to stop him continuing. It was my place to explain to my friends what had happened. "Last night I got caught in the storm. The sheet of tin that's lying in the next door window almost sliced me in two." I could feel my face turn red as it heated. "He pushed me out of the way, but it caught his arm. We came here to wait out the storm, but the power went out and it was freezing." I looked to the couch. I could feel my face burn even hotter as I remembered his lips touch the back of my head. "Our clothes were wet, and we needed to keep warm."

"Well ..." Emilee pushed her hand into her hip and pulled a sideways smile at me. "Andy told me you wanted your coffee to be delivered this morning." She turned to the desk, picked up a large polystyrene cup and handed it to me. "I didn't expect you to have company, so I only bought three. But you can have mine." She picked another polystyrene cup up and handed it to Derrek. "Be gentle with Warrangatta's finest."

He took a sip of the coffee. "The coffee is delicious," he said with a smile.

"I wasn't talking about the coffee." She looked directly at me and smiled. I knew she thought more had happened than just lying on the couch. I would disappoint her with the truth later.

I suddenly remembered I was only wearing my underwear. I put the coffee back on the desk and ran back to the couch where my clothes lay in a pile. They were still wet and sent cold shivers through my body as I pulled them on.

"Well, while you two were keeping warm," Andy began as he walked to his tech desk, "I was working *my magic fingers* on something else." He threw a sly look at my direction.

I glanced over to Derrek to see if he had heard the remark. He remained by the desk speaking to Emilee as he drank his coffee.

"Andy! Shut up. Nothing happened." I hissed at him.

"Oh yeah, right." He laughed once.

"I mean it. It really was just to keep warm ... I don't think there was anything to it." I could feel my heart sink as I said the words aloud.

"You mean to tell me you were practically naked with him and he didn't try it on?"

"Shh. No. I'm just not his type. I mean, he'd go for girls who wear dresses and matching underwear."

He took a step closer. "You really don't know men, do you? If he didn't like you, he'd at least tried to have sex with you."

"What?" I screwed up my nose, as I finished buttoning my shirt. "That doesn't make any sense."

"If he wasn't into you, he would have tried it on. If you rejected him, well, he'd leave today and forget about it. If he was lucky enough to have 'scored', then he'd leave today and forget about it."

I couldn't help but smile at what Andy said. "You really think so?"

"Stop underselling yourself. You're awesome ... and beautiful; well, usually you are. Today you look like a scarecrow that fell off a tomato truck."

"Oh gee, thanks for the honesty." I folded my arms.

"You're welcome." He pulled a cheesy smile. "Well as I was saying ..." He spoke loudly again. "Last night I spent far too many hours on my computer, and I found this." He took a USB stick from his pocket and slipped it into the back of his laptop. "I was able to connect to the internet for short bursts. The same report was playing over and over."

I sat on the couch and waited for the computer to load. Emilee sat on the swivel chair by the table. She held a smirk firmly on her face as she threw looks in my direction; I knew I would be spending the better half of the day relaying every detail of the happenings of the night before, no matter how hard I protested it.

Derrek walked towards me, and my heart skipped a beat as he approached the couch. He reached across the table, grabbed his shirt and pulled it over his head. Each one of his defined muscles grew as he lifted the shirt and pulled it on. Andy was still speaking, but I wasn't listening to a word he was saying. All I could think of was Derrek's big arms holding me tightly, and his amazing aftershave, which still lingered in the air. I watched him with a smile as he pulled his boots on. He then sat at the opposite end of the couch, looking at the computer. Disappointment flew threw me like a razor—Andy was wrong. I looked to Derrek. He gave no reaction to me at all.

"All ready?" Andy asked sounding far too enthusiastic. He looked at each of us, but none of us responded. "Alrighty then ..." He lifted one eyebrow, pulled his laptop towards him and pressed several keys.

A British female journalist was reporting: "... Experts are speechless. So far we are receiving reports of bizarre weather conditions from almost every corner of the globe. Australia's centre has received almost four years of its annual rainfall in as little as two weeks. Australia's southern states have been subjected to cyclones that would usually present themselves only in the tropics. Russia, which should be experiencing its coldest months, is currently going through an unprecedented heat wave of temperatures never before seen."

The reporter stepped aside as the green screen behind her was filled with a large Russian woman wearing a short dress fanning her face. She was upset and speaking quickly as she pointed to her home, which had a shallow river flowing beside it caused by melted snow.

"And that's only part of this bizarre situation. Parts of Asia have been left devastated as tornados have ripped through cities and destroyed many farming communities, while sections of Africa have experienced snowfall. People have already started rallying in capital cities all around the world demonstrating global warming ..." The news flashed to an image of Melbourne with about hundreds of people waving signs and yelling loudly. "They are blaming governments and large corporations for polluting the world, causing the weather anomaly ..." The laptop screen went black.

"That's all I was able to get before the power went out last night," Andy said as he folded the laptop shut.

"Well, I'm just glad we don't live in a big city. I don't think I could tolerate those activists." I stood to my feet and began to re-pack the first aid kit. "I read in a book somewhere if we condensed the existence of the world into a twenty-four-hour block, humans have been on this earth for no more than thirty seconds. Long before governments and corporations polluted the atmosphere, inland Australia was filled with ocean. In my opinion, nature is a forever changing beast, and no matter what any one person does, nothing can change." I threw my hand towards the blank laptop.

"That's true. But sometimes it's worth saying how you feel. Never know, you might be surprised by their response," Andy said as he looked directly at me.

"But sometimes the answer is blatantly obvious and the person speaking would just look like an idiot." I clipped the first aid kit closed and picked up the clean towels.

"And sometimes they're just being plain stubborn, like they always are." He folded his arms and leant back on his desk.

"Am I missing an entire conversation here?" Emilee waved her hand in the air.

"No! I'm going to clean up this mess before Sam get in," I said and walked to the staff room.

I pulled open the blue cupboards under the sink and pushed the first aid kit in roughly. I was annoyed and angry that I had allowed myself to believe Derrek may have been attracted to me. I put my hand on the edge of the bench and leant heavily on my arms.

"Did something upset you?" Derrek spoke.

I looked up. He was standing in the doorway of the staff room holding the two blood-soaked towels.

"No. I'm fine." I lied unconvincingly. I folded my arms and leant back on the bench. I kept my eyes to the floor; not because I didn't want to look at him—I was scared that if I did, I wouldn't be able to look away.

"Okay," he said as he slowly placed the towels in the sink behind me. "I have to leave for a few days. Would it be okay if I visited you when I return?"

Just as I expected; he was making a polite excuse to get out of here. Emilee spoke about the 'let down' men would give her; only, in her case, she had slept with them before they made all the excuses. Just lying next to me for several hours was enough of a deterrent for Derrek, it seemed.

"You don't have to." I shrugged and continued to look at the floor. I did want him to visit me again, but I knew he was only saying it so he could leave without a fuss.

"You do not want me to?" His voice dropped.

I looked back to him. "I don't want you to feel obligated. I mean last night ... was ..." I knew what I wanted to say, but I couldn't bring myself to say the words. I couldn't bear to hear his outright rejection of me.

"... incredible," he finished for me.

"What?" I was sure I had misheard him.

"Last night was incredible." He stepped forward and slipped his hand up the side of my neck. His rough hands made my skin tingle.

"If I did not have to leave today, I would ask if I could share another night with you." He rubbed his thumb across my cheek.

I closed my eyes as I leant my face into his hand. His free hand found its way around my waist and pulled me gently towards him. His body was touching mine, as he looked down at me.

"I have wanted to do this from the moment I first met you." He pressed his lips to my mouth. His lips were big and soft as they glided across mine. I lost all control of my own lips as they followed his. I could smell nothing but his aftershave and feel nothing but him.

"Keeping warm again?"

I jumped at Andy's voice and took a step backwards from Derrek, as I tried to compose myself.

Andy stood leaning in the doorway. He was holding more blood-stained towels. A large smirk ran across his face, not just because I was obviously happy, but because he had been right.

"I should go. I will be back in about a week." Derrek ran his hand over my cheek and pressed his lips against mine again, only this time it wasn't a passionate kiss. It was short and sweet.

"Okay." I wanted to say so much more, but 'okay' was the only word I was able to speak.

I watched him through a small window in the staff room, as he left the store. Once he had disappeared from sight, Emilee raced into the room.

"Details; I need every tiny, teeny detail." She pulled out a chair, then sat on the table with her feet on the chair, elbows on her knees, ready for a run-down.

"Really, nothing happened. Just now was the first time he kissed me."

She threw her hands to the table. "Seriously? You spent the night alone with that man and you didn't do *anything*?" Her eyes were wide.

I shrugged. "I dunno; I feel fuzzy. Maybe a little tingly."

"Don't worry; they'd have ointment for that," Andy said dryly.

"Shut up! Dingbat!" Emilee threw her hand to Andy's stomach. "Ally, you're falling in love!" She jumped to the floor and wrapped her arms around me. "It's about time!"

I didn't hug her back. I just stood motionless, as I thought of her words. "I can't be. I've only just met him."

"Stop thinking and start feeling!" She pressed her hands over my heart. "Let this guide you, not this." She tapped my head several times.

"But..."

"But nothing! Just let it be. Perhaps Derrek will be the next Michael. Perhaps he'll be your first ever fling. Just embrace it. *Feel* it. Feel alive again. Promise me, when the time comes, you'll feel—not think."

"Okay," I said breathlessly.

~ 10 ~

CHAPTER TEN

Two days later
The night was hot and sticky as I lay back on my veranda swing. It gently rocked me back and forth with the occasional breeze rolling around the corner of the house, cooling me for a moment. As I lay there, I stared up to the stars in the night sky. I thought of Michael, and I wondered if he was up there staring down at me, watching over me. I knew the stars were nothing more than suns for other solar systems, but I took comfort in believing the people I loved most were at peace. I thought of him and my beautiful Sasha often, but the memories were no longer filled with pain and emptiness. Instead of being saddened by their absence, I would smile when a memory passed through my mind.

"You would have liked them, Spud." I patted his head as he lay stretched out under the swing.

As I lay there, I thought of Derrek. I smiled as I remembered how he had gently held my hand. I closed my eyes and drew a deep breath of the night air as I tried to conjure the forest scent that lingered on him. I could almost feel his lips pressing against mine. I did not understand why I had been so drawn to him; perhaps it was my subconscious telling me it was time to move on.

Spud sat up quickly and barked once towards the driveway. The low rumble of a motor and a set of headlights signalled the approach of a car coming down the drive.

"Who's visiting us tonight, Spud?" I remained on the verandah trying to make out who might be driving out here at this time of night. It was dark, so all I could make out was the shadowy vehicle slowly rolling into my front yard before coming to a stop. I heard the car door open and then close. Spud started barking and running in circles, clearly agitated by the arrival. I could hear one pair of feet crunch on the gravel as they walked closer to the house.

"Hello?" A deep voice spoke.

I didn't move. It can't be!

"Hello, Alexandra?" he called again.

I stood at the top of the stairs. His face was revealed as he moved into the glow cast by the verandah light.

"Derrek?" All I could do was stare at him, eyes wide in surprise. "But, I thought you were going to be away for a week?"

Without speaking a word, he walked up the steps to the verandah, took my hand in his and kissed the back of it.

"I had to see you again." He slipped his hand across my cheek and pulled the nape of my neck closer to him.

His lips had almost touched mine, when Spud ran between us, snapping at Derrek's feet. H arching his back and baring his teeth, snapping at Derrek's feet.

"Spud!" I growled at him.

He ignored me, pulling his ears back as he continued to snap at Derrek's feet.

"Spud! That's it!" I grabbed him by the collar and dragged him towards his pen. Spud continued to snarl and bark at Derrek even as I pushed him into the pen and shut the gate.

"I don't know what's gotten into you, but that's enough! Bad dog!" I growled and turned to walk back towards the house. I could hear him barking as he tried to scale the pen. "I am so sorry about that—he's never done that before." I put my hands in my back jeans pockets and walked up the steps to the verandah, where Derrek stood.

"I am a stranger to him. It is wise to fear strangers." He folded his arms as he spoke.

"Well, you're not much more than a stranger to me. Should I take your advice too?"

He pulled a small smile. "I hope to be much more than just a stranger to you."

Within an instant, blood rushed to my face, as my heart bounced at his inference. I stuttered and darted my eyes from him to the ground, hoping he hadn't noticed my awkward blush. "Would ... would you like to come in for a drink, or something?"

"I would like that."

"Okay," I smiled. It had been such a long time since I had felt the sensation of butterflies in my stomach; I welcomed the almost forgotten feeling of excitement that attraction could generate.

He pushed the front door open. "Ladies first," he said as he stood with his arm holding the door wide for me to pass.

"Thanks," I said, trying to sound as calm as possible as I brushed past him to walk into my home.

My front door opened straight into the lounge room. In the centre of the room sat a rustic coffee table that had been made by a local craftsman; on it stood a thick white stone vase. Because I lived alone, the only couch I had was a small, two-seater that ran the length of the window. I didn't spend much time at home, so I never bothered to update my furnishings. The television was more than two decades out of date.

"It's not much, but its home." I put my hands in my pockets and shrugged my shoulders.

"What's that?" He pointed to a crossbow that hung above the television.

"Ha, that's kind of an embarrassing story." I tucked my hair behind my ears.

He lifted his eyebrows as a smile spread across his face. "They are my favourite."

"Right, well about a year or so ago, I watched a movie ... can't remember what it was now ... but anyway, in the movie there was this amazing woman. She went on incredible adventures. She was strong, sexy; men fell over themselves to be with her, and she had a crossbow." I gestured to the one on the wall. "So, one weekend Andy and I went on a road trip and one of the towns we went through had an op shop open. We went in, and I found this behind a heap of junk. I thought of the woman in the movie and decided, 'Yeah! I can be just like her'." I laughed. I felt ridiculous even suggesting it.

"And are you? I mean, can you use it?" he asked with seemingly genuine interest.

"Yeah, but I suck. I can hardly even cock it. Andy has some terrible photos of me attempting to shoot it somewhere. It had just been sitting around in the shed for ages, so I decided to put it on the wall."

"It looks very old and very beautiful," he said with his eyes fixed on the crossbow. "What does that symbol represent?"

"No idea. I mean, I didn't pay very much for it, so I don't think it means anything—just decorative. I can get it down if you would like to have a look?"

"Yes, I would like that," he smiled.

I dragged a dining chair from the adjoining dining room and climbed on it. I gently lifted the bow from its hanger and passed it down to him. "This is an incredible find," he said, slowly taking it from me. His hand hovered above the bow for a moment, as though he was reading the inscription.

"Well, I like it. It came with these too." I pulled open the drawer of the television unit and picked out three silver bolts. The heads on the bolts had tiny engravings delicately scribed on each.

"Why do you not have them together?" he asked as he accepted the bolts from me.

"What do you mean?" I frowned.

"They fit in here." He slid one after another into a small casing attached to the back of the bow.

"Oh my God! How could have I not seen that?" I took the bow from him and looked at the back of the crossbow; there were five perfectly shaped notches, designed to hold one bolt each. "I wonder where the other two bolts are," I said as I ran my fingers over the smooth, empty notches.

"You do not know?" He seemed surprised.

I shook my head. "No, it only came with three. Andy ordered some bolts for me off the internet. The plan was to use the cheap bolts until I was a good enough shot to use these ones. And there's a reason they still look new." I smiled as I put the crossbow on the coffee table.

"You have never looked into the origins of the bow?" he asked, not taking his eyes off it.

"Well, kind of. Andy took photos and scanned them to his computer. He scoured the internet for some ungodly number of hours but didn't find anything. As I said, I didn't pay much for it. My best guess is that it's nowhere near as old as it looks; I would say someone who had a lot of time on their hands made it." My nerves slowly began to subside as we conversed. "Anyway, I was getting you a drink." I turned to walk towards the kitchen.

As I went to move past him, I felt his hand clasp mine. His touch was cold; not like when we held hands back at the shop. Perhaps he was as nervous as I was.

"I lied." He ran his hand up my arm and pulled me closer to him.

"About what?" I swallowed hard as I tried to steady my breath.

"I do not want a drink."

He slid his hands up either side of my face and pulled me into him. His cool lips touched mine, his hands slipping around my body and resting on the small of my back. My hands found their own way to his hips; I could feel the definition of every muscle under my fingertips, as I traced along the top of his belt line. His hands moved lower. My heart beat furiously with desire as his hands wrapped themselves around my hips. In one swift movement, he lifted me from the ground. I entangled my legs around his hips, while my lips danced passionately with his. His strong lips were dictating where mine moved, and I gave into them. I peeled my eyes open slightly. His eyes were closed and relaxed—he was enjoying kissing me. I pressed my eyes closed again as I drowned into him, his big arms closing tightly around me as he kissed me deeply. His lips moved from mine and slowly kissed their way down my neck to the centre of my chest. I tilted my head back as his cool, smooth lips moved along my skin. I breathed in deeply wanting to be consumed by the smell of his aftershave—of ancient forests. To my disappointment my nose wasn't filled with the intoxicating smell of trees. He wore a different aftershave; an aftershave that could only be described as exotic islands. As I breathed it in I could almost hear distant drums beating and almost feel waterfalls cascading across my naked skin.

His hands slipped up my back as he slowly lowered me to the couch. He grabbed the bottom of his shirt, pulled it over his head and threw it on the floor. I hadn't noticed in the bookstore, but in the centre of his chest, across his heart, was a scar of an X. He gently lowered himself onto me. I could no longer tell if my heart was beating furiously or had stopped entirely. I lifted my hand and gently ran my fingers across his scar. It felt smoother than his skin and was slightly indented. He took my fingers in his hand and kissed the ends of them gently.

The scar tattoos that covered his arms appeared to be engraved into his skin, but as I ran my fingers over them, I was surprised to feel only his smooth skin. They were not engraved as I had expected.

He leaned in and kissed my neck. Shivers ran through my body making my toes curl and my back arch. His lips moved down the front of my neck and slipped lower down my chest until his lips met my shirt. A moan slipped through my lips as he unbuttoned my shirt and pushed it aside. His lips kissed slowly down my stomach. He wrapped his fingers around the top of my pants and pulled them slowly down my legs, kissing every part of me as he went. My body was in such a state of ecstasy that I could think of nothing but his touch. He pushed my legs apart and slowly lowered himself on top of me. I ran my fingers down his back until I felt his belt, followed it to his buckle and began to twist it open. He leant heavily on me as he pulled his pants off. A feeling of deep desire spread through me, something I had not felt in such a long time.

"You are the most beautiful woman I have ever seen," he said quietly as he tucked my hair behind my ear.

A feeling if intense guilt struck me; Michael would tuck my hair behind my ear and whisper the exact same thing to me. I closed my eyes and tried to put Michael out of my mind; he was dead and no matter what I did or didn't do, nothing would ever bring him back.

Derrek was kissing my body, but instead of pleasure, I felt disgusted with myself. I covered my hands over my face.

"I'm sorry Derrek. I can't do this," I said quietly. I was both furious and embarrassed at myself.

"Did I displease you?" he asked as he pushed himself from me, frowning.

"No, not at all." I touched his beautiful face. "I just can't."

"But why?" he asked confused.

"I can't stop thinking of my late husband." I stroked his face. "I am sorry."

"Alexandra, he would want you to be happy?" he asked as he kissed my forehead.

"Yes." I knew Michael would want me to find someone who made me just as happy as he had.

"You need to allow yourself to be happy." He smiled as he leaned in and kissed my neck again.

I closed my eyes. I tried to drift into him again, but his lips over my skin no longer made my body tingle; they felt intrusive. I could feel him press against me—he was ready to enter me. I desperately wanted the desire to overwhelm me again. I closed my eyes and thought of Derrek in the staff room, trying to recall how much I had wanted to touch him. I forced Emilee's words back into my head; I promised her I wouldn't think—that I would only feel. But as much as I tried, all I could think of was Michael.

"I'm sorry, I just can't. Not yet," I said.

He didn't stop.

"Derrek. Stop." I said clearly, expecting him to lean back apologetically, but he didn't.

"Derrek! Get off me!" I yelled at him. He was beginning to scare me.

His hand moved from behind my head to my collarbone. I tried to sit up but he pushed me harder into the couch. I reached my hands to his chest, trying to push him off me, but he grabbed both my hands with one of his hands and held them down above my head. I could feel him trying to put himself inside me. I kicked my legs violently as I tried to escape but he had completely overpowered me.

"Stop!" I cried. "Why are you doing this to me?" I screamed as tears flooded down my face. "Please ... stop!" I screamed again as he forced himself inside me. "You're hurting me!" I cried; the pain was excruciating.

"Shut up!" He wrapped both his hands around my throat and squeezed, ensuring I was no longer able to scream.

I couldn't fight him off—he was too strong. It felt like he was burning the inside of me, and his hands were pushing so hard on my throat I was certain he was going to snap my neck.

"You and I are meant to be together. You will always belong to me," he whispered in my ear. His breath made my insides crawl.

As he forced himself further into me, I knew I had only one opportunity; I opened my mouth and clamped my teeth down on his ear. Blood sprayed over my body, and I felt part of his ear give way into my mouth—I had bitten off his ear lobe.

He lifted his hand and hit me with full force across my face. The blow left me dazed, and blackness crept along the side of my eyes. Grabbing the back of my hair, he dragged me from the couch and across the floor. He lifted me up and forced me over the coffee table, slamming my head down to the table with such force I thought I would pass out. I pressed my palms against the edge of the table as I desperately tried to push myself from its surface. My attempts were in vain. I was completely overpowered by his size and strength. My eyes pinched shut as I cried out loudly. I had no option but to acquiesce or risk greater injury.

Suddenly, he let go with a yell and fell backwards to the floor. I struggled to sit up. Spud had somehow managed to escape his pen and sunk his teeth into Derrek's leg, shaking it violently. I grabbed the vase standing on the coffee table, and hit Derrek as hard as I could over the head. It wasn't enough to knock him out but he did fall to the floor, disorientated and groaning. Without a second thought, I reached for my crossbow and my bag that had fallen to the floor in the struggle, and ran out the front door. I grabbed the verandah pole, swung off the edge and threw myself under the deck. I tried to calm my breathing so I wouldn't give my position away, and slowly slid further under the deck ensuring I was well hidden from the gaps between the steps. A moment later, I heard the wire door groan open.

"Alexandra!" he called unaware he was standing above me, as I crouched under the boards of the verandah.

I froze. I pressed my eyes closed as I prayed for him to move away so I could make a run for my ute. I had to get to the ute; it was my only means of escape. "Alexandra. I am sorry. Please, Alexandra," he called loudly as he staggered down the steps and onto the gravel. "Alexandra, I did not mean to hurt you. I am sorry."

I held my breath as I listened to his crunching footsteps as he moved close to the front steps. *Please don't let him see me. Please.*

"There is nowhere you can hide Alexandra! I will find you, I will always find you!" His calm ruse was quickly replaced with his angered urgency to find me.

He was so close to me; the moon cast his shadow as he moved across the ground near the steps.

"I know everything about you, Alexandra! I know about Michael, your daughter, the little house you used to live in. I know everything about you!" He began to walk away from where I was silently hiding. "We are meant for each other, Alexandra. And we will be together again. I will always come for you!" he shouted, his voice filled with malice.

His words shot through my body. How does he know about me? Who is he? How did he find me? What did he want from me? I shook my head to clear it—I had to get out of here. The questions could wait. *Focus Alexandra!*

I could hear his footsteps fading as he walked away, towards the rear of the house. I carefully lifted my head and peered out—clear. I waddled awkwardly to get clear from my hiding spot and then, in a low crouch, moved as quickly as I could to my ute. The window was still down, so I threw my belongings on the seat and lifted myself through the window. My body hurt, but I was too terrified to register the pain.

I slid down the seat. I knew the slightest wrong move would mark the end of my life. With shaking hands, I grabbed for my bag and rummaged through it, trying to find my keys. I could hear the crunching of his feet on the gravel as he walked along the far side of the driveway in search of me. My hands were trembling as I tried more than once to put the key into the ignition.

Spud, where are you? I silently pushed myself back into the seat and chanced a look out the window; I could see Derrek sleeking his way around the corner of my house. The tiniest sensation of relief crept into my body as I watched him disappear behind another shed.

I held my breath as I twisted my hand on the key and prayed it would start first time. I turned the key in the ignition but only a whirring noise came from the engine. I turned it again but the same whirring noise came.

"Come on you heap of shit!" I yelled at my car.

I knew that my position had been given away; I knew it would be a matter of seconds before he would pull my unlockable door open and drag me from my car.

Tears poured from my eyes. "Please!" I pleaded to the universe. I turned it again, and it rumbled to a start. "Spud!" I screamed, as I looked in my rear view mirror. Derrek was running towards my car as Spud ran around him and leapt into the back of the ute.

slammed my foot on the accelerator and sped down the driveway; Derrek gave chase for the first part but slowed to a halt as I sped away from him.

I slid open the small window that separated the tray to the cab and Spud crawled in and sat on the passenger seat, staring up at me. My hands were shaking uncontrollably, jeopardising my ability to steer accurately. I knew I needed to calm myself. *Focus, focus!* I could not afford to crash. He would be in his car by now, and if I slowed at all, he'd be on me instantly. I didn't have a destination in mind but somehow I ended up pulling in at Andy's yellow weatherboard house. I drove down the driveway and into his back yard. I stumbled from the ute to his back door, bashing on it loudly.

"Andy!" I screamed as I looked around, praying Derrek hadn't followed me. "Andy! Let me in!"

Andy pulled the door open; he was wearing his long black robe and wiping his sleepy eyes.

"Alex? What the...?" He took a step back in shock as he saw the state I was in; I had arrived at his house in the middle of the night completely naked.

"Andy... help," I sobbed frantically.

"Jesus Christ, Alex. What the hell is going on? Get in here!" He slapped his hand to my shoulder and dragged me inside.

Inside his house was just as dark as it was out, and I could see very little apart from the swords; they shone under the moonlight just as they always did. The unrest stirred in my gut again as I stood in their presence.

"Why the hell are you naked?" he asked as he switched the light on, snapping me back to reality.

I wrapped my arms around my broken body as I stood in the middle of his lounge room. I couldn't answer.

His breath caught, and he took a step back as he looked at me. "Alex. What is going on?" He gingerly reached out and touched my arm. I looked down at my body; it was covered in blood, and patches of skin had begun to turn green and purple with bruising.

He grabbed a blanket from the couch and threw it around me, settling his hands gently on my shoulders.

"What happened to you?" His eyes were wide with alarm.

I couldn't answer—I was frozen. My mind was fixed on Derrek's face as he forced himself onto me; the smell of his aftershave, his threatening words. How could he be so kind one day and a monster the next?

"Alex! What happened?" he repeated, gently shaking my shoulders, trying to break through my trance-like state.

I looked at Andy, unable to gather my thoughts to tell him what had just happened. I couldn't form any words. All I could see was Derrek on top of me, and I could still feel him inside me. I put my hands to my throat, still stinging from his brutal assault, in hopes I could draw breathe more easily.

"Ally! What happened?" Andy's voice dropped, as he looked at the bruising on my neck.

"He wouldn't stop ... he wouldn't ... it hurt," I stammered.

"Who?" Andy demanded. "*Who*? Who did this to you?"

"Derrek." I closed my eyes as tears rolled from them.

Andy wrapped his arms around me and held me, while I cried loudly into his shoulder.

"You're safe now. You're here with me. You're safe."

He took a step backwards, holding one hand on my arm. "I am going to run a shower for you. Just wait here ..."

"No, no, no, don't leave me.' I panicked.

"Okay, okay. I won't. I'm here," he told me calmly.

He gently lifted my arm and draped it around his shoulders. He wrapped his free hand around my waist as he half carried me to his bathroom. Each step we took shot waves of pain through my body.

Andy leant in to the shower, and turned the taps on, adjusting the temperature of the water. He turned back to me, gently lifted the blanket from me, and helped me step into the shower. As he did, I caught my reflection in the mirror that hung crookedly on the wall. My forehead wore a long rectangular lump, which was beginning to bruise. Around my neck were two distinct bruises in the shape of fingers, a cut where my necklace has sliced into me, and my arms and legs had large patches of bruising; blood smeared my body. But it wasn't the blood or the bruising that scared me the most. I looked fragile—I didn't look like me.

"You're okay now," Andy whispered.

I nodded once and stepped into the shower; instantly the shower base turned red from my blood. I stood motionless as I watched the blood swirl down the drain.

"Here's some soap. You probably should avoid any open skin; it'll hurt like hell." He looked at my bruising body. His facial expression was one I had never seen on him before. He was always so easygoing and laconic, a smile never leaving his eyes; now there was only fury.

He was breathing heavily, and I could tell he wanted to show far more emotion than he was displaying but was forcing those emotions down for my sake. I appreciated it more than he would ever know.

"Do you want me to stay?" he asked quietly, his eyes focused on the floor.

I didn't care what he did. I didn't know what to do or what to say. I wanted to scream, I wanted to cry, I wanted to run and hide forever.

"Spud." I finally said. I had forgotten he was still in my car. "Spud's out in the ute. Can you check on him?"

I knew I was speaking. I knew I was standing in his shower, but I felt as though I was watching someone else. Other people get raped—people on midday talk shows talk about it. It can't have happened to *me*.

"Sure," he said as he began to walk towards the bathroom door.

"Andy, there's some clothes and boots behind the driver's seat." I added.

He nodded as he turned the door handle.

"And Andy ..." He looked back at me. "Thank you."

He half smiled and gave a quick nod, then disappeared out the door.

I pressed against the shower wall, letting the water flow freely over my body. I watched as the warm water continued to wash blood down the swirling drain. Tipping my head under the showerhead, I opened my lips just enough for the water to flow in and around my mouth, washing away the taste of his blood from my mouth. I felt naked—not just in the physical form. Everything had been stripped from me. I no longer belonged to me.

I took the soap, meaning to wash myself with it. It smelled of pretty flowers. Andy used soap that smelled of pretty flowers. How ridiculous! Before I could stop myself, I threw the soap at the shower wall as hard as I could. I screamed through my teeth and punched the hard tiles with the sides of my fists. Spurts of cries came from me as I slowed my hits against the hard tiles. I fell back against the wall. The tiles were cold against my skin. I slid down the wall and wrapped my arms around my legs, burying my face into my knees, sobbing.

The bathroom door opened and Andy walked in. He wasn't wearing his robe anymore. Instead he wore a pair of jeans, a T-shirt and a pair of dark black work boots. In his right hand he was holding my crossbow, handbag and clothes, and in his left, he held Spud by the collar.

As soon as Spud saw me, he pulled away from Andy and ran to me, laying down in front of the shower, wagging his tail slowly. I reached out of the shower and patted his head; he lapped the dripping water from my hand.

"You're a good boy, Spud." I said quietly. He wagged his tail faster, but made small whimpering noises and licked the back of my hand, sensing my distress.

Andy closed the door quietly and took a few silent steps into the bathroom. Instantly, I knew something was wrong.

"I don't want to scare you, but I could see headlights coming down the road when I got your stuff," he said as he gently put my belongings on the floor.

"What?" I breathed, my heart thumping. I sat forward on the balls of my feet, ready to jump to a stand and run in any direction he told me.

He leant in the shower and turned the taps off.

"It's going to be alright. We don't even know who it is," he reassured me as he handed me a towel and helped me to stand. "Can you dry and dress yourself?" he whispered.

"Yeah. Are you expecting anybody?" I whispered so quietly it was barely audible.

He didn't answer but threw me a look that screamed 'no' as he darted out the door once more. I dried myself as quickly as I could. Every inch of me hurt to an intensity like none I had ever felt, but I forced myself to ignore it. I pulled on my torn denim shorts and sleeveless flannelette shirt. They weren't much, but these clothes belonged to me—it was all that belonged to me.

As I was pulling on my boots, Andy reappeared holding a big backpack filled with his belongings.

"We're getting out of here. I'm not an idiot. I can't take that guy. He'd kill me with one swing! And you're in no shape to even consider fighting. There isn't a police station within hundreds of kilometres and the phones are de..." He stopped short. We both heard it; a car drove slowly past Andy's house.

"Andy! It's him! Oh God. He's found me. He'll see my car!" I said in a panicked whisper, as I looked around the room for an escape.

"Shh, shh, shh. No he won't. You can barely see my house from the road, and your car is out the back. We're leaving now, out the back door. We're taking *my* car." Even though his voice was no louder than a whisper, he spoke with authority.

I nodded and went to pick up my bag.

"No, you just worry about walking without making any noise. Follow me exactly," he instructed as he picked up my belongings and swung his backpack over his shoulder.

Such a simple instruction; follow him. But I couldn't move. I was struggling to control my breathing. I could feel Derrek searching for me. *I will find yo; I will always find you. You belong to me.* And he *had* found me. I could feel his hands around my neck and his sticky breath in my ear, the island smell. He had found me, and this time I knew he wouldn't let me go.

"I can't, Andy. I can't. He's going to find me no matter what we do. He promised he would." The image of Derrek's face would not leave me—it was burned into my mind. I could feel him; he was coming for me.

"Hey, Ally." He stepped close to me and placed his hands on my hips. "Remember the first time we went swimming at Warimudga with Emilee? It was night time and we were all standing on the top of Barri-Barri. Remember how Emilee just stripped her clothes off and dived in? You and I stared at each other for ages, not knowing what we should do next?"

A mute nod was all I could manage.

"Remember how we just did it? We didn't need to discuss it with each other. We didn't need to worry about what we thought, or if it would be appropriate. We just jumped right in. We trusted each other."

Tears were filling in my eyes and rolling down my cheeks. I remembered that night well. It was the first moment I didn't think of Michael and Sasha. That exact moment he described was the instant I began to recover from their deaths. But I had no idea why he was bringing it up now.

"Yes."

"Remember when you felt something under your feet and you were positive it was a croc?"

"Yes. I panicked and almost drowned. But you swam out and saved me." I don't know if my words were coherent as I choked them out.

"That's right. I told you to calm down and just go with me. Well, this is exactly the same as that night. I am swimming out to save you. All you have to do is calm down and follow me. I am going to save you. I didn't let you drown then, and I am not going to let you drown now—I promise," he said as he lowered his hands.

I nodded quickly and wiped the tears from my cheeks as Spud nuzzled his nose into my leg and wagged his tail slowly.

Andy slowly opened the bathroom door as wide as it would go. He turned back to me and gave me a reassuring nod. *Just follow Andy. Think of nothing else, just follow Andy.* He took a large step over two floorboards as he stepped into the hallway. I held my breath as I copied his light and agile foot placements to his back door.

The back door was a half-light door with clear glass. He squatted down next to it and waited for me to squat down by his side. He slowly lifted himself up to peer out the window and quickly sat back down.

"He's out there," he mouthed to me.

My heart pulsated with such ferocity it echoed in my ears. Andy pulled a remote-type gadget from his pocket and with only breath he said, "When this goes off, we run."

I nodded. I had no idea what 'this' was or what would happen when it 'goes off'. All I knew was I didn't want to be around when it did. I balanced on the balls of my feet as I readied myself to run. He held up three fingers and folded them down one by one until he pushed the button. A door slammed at the front of the house, and I heard Derrek run from the back of the house towards the front. Andy quickly but silently pushed open the back door and peered around ensuring we were alone. He bounced to his feet and sprinted to his four-wheel drive wagon with Spud and me in close pursuit. The short stretch to his car seemed to take an eternity with the gravel beneath our feet crunching loudly with every step we took, the sound echoing through the night air. I knew it would only be a matter of seconds before Derrek came for me again. *You belong to me; I will always come for you.*

We got to Andy's car, but as I reached my hand to the door handle, something stopped me; a gentle breeze blew past us and upon it was carried the smell of exotic islands. I lowered my outstretched hand and slowly turned to face the intoxicating smell. I could almost feel gentle waterfalls trickle across my naked skin and taste the smell of islands.

"Alexandra!" Andy hissed.

But Andy wasn't really there. He was only a person I met in a dream of a dream, long ago.

"Alexandra! Get in the bloody car!" he yelled at me, but it was a distant yell, not one that I had to respond to.

I closed my eyes as I drew in the islands. I could hear the beating of the drums and feel the dancers dancing around a tall fire. That was where I belonged; I was being called home.

I could feel someone's arms around my body, their warmth kind against my skin.

"Get in the bloody car!" Andy yelled at me again as he threw me into the front passenger seat.

The sudden jolt snapped me back to reality. He slammed the door closed as he darted around the front of the car and into the driver's seat. Unlike my ute, his car started instantly as he turned the key in the ignition. Without a moment's hesitation he sped out the driveway, past Derrek's ute, which sat lifeless at the front of the house with no sign of Derrek.

"Are you okay?" Andy asked loudly as we raced down the road.

"Huh?" I vaguely answered. I felt as though I had just woken from an eternal dream.

"Are you okay? he demanded again. "What the friggin' hell just happened back there?"

"I don't know." I ran my hands across my face and through my hair. "I was drawn to him."

"What do you mean, you were 'drawn to him'?" he snapped as he kept his eyes fixed on the road ahead, turning several corners.

"I don't know. It was like reality just fell away ..." I suddenly remembered how we had managed to escape. "The door slammed ... was there someone else in your house? What if he finds them?" I began to panic.

"Calm down! It was just a sound effect. For Christ's sake, put your bloody seat belt on. That's all we need, for me to have to take you to a hospital." He shook his head.

I pushed myself back into the seat and pulled at the seatbelt several times until it finally came freely and clicked it into the buckle.

"I was bored one weekend," he continued, "and downloaded a heap of sound effects on my phone. All I did was connect it to the stereo system—it's all that I could think of to give us a little time to escape. Is he following?"

I turned and squinted out the rear window. "No, I can't see anybody ..." My voice was noticeably high pitched and shaking. The sound of it scared me; it wasn't mine.

"Good. I can't drive too fast. Just our luck we'll run into a camel. It's unlikely Derrek would be able to follow us—took me six months to figure out these back roads." He looked up through the windscreen. "It's a full moon tonight, which will give us enough light. I'll be able to drive slower; less chance of being seen." He flicked the headlights off. I jumped with the sudden atmosphere change. My nervousness didn't go unnoticed.

"Alexandra." He said my full name; he never said my full name. "It's okay. You're safe; you're with me, Andy."

"I know," I said. My voice was thick, as I tried to hold back emotion, but I couldn't.

Tears burst from my eyes and I sobbed loudly. I hugged my arms around my waist and looked out the window; I didn't want Andy to see me like that.

"It's okay to cry, you know," he said. "Jesus, Alex. You were just raped! You wouldn't be human if you weren't upset." He gently placed his hand on the back of mine. "It's me."

I looked across at him. His eyes were warm and compassionate, but they were also the same eyes that only minutes ago had seen me naked and bare. Andy seeing me physically naked didn't bother me. He, Emilee and I had swum in Warrimudgi late at night plenty of times, but tonight he had seen me stripped back to nothing.

"Alexandra, talk to me."

"I'm so ashamed," I blabbered before I was able to stop myself. Once I began to speak it was as though a dam wall had been smashed; the words kept pouring out. "I'm so ashamed and pathetic. It was my fault. I shouldn't have ..." I sobbed loudly as I wiped my cheeks.

Andy slowed the car and pulled over to the side of the road.

He turned in his seat. "Look at me," he instructed.

I pushed my hair from my face and tucked it behind my ear as I looked at him. He took my hands in his hands.

"You have nothing to be ashamed of. Do you hear me? Nothing!"

"I shouldn't have come to your house. You didn't need to see me like that." Tears began to flow from my eyes again.

"What, naked?" He choked a laugh. "I've seen you naked lots of times."

"That's different ... I wasn't pathetic those times."

"Look at me." He held his hands on either side of my face. "You are not pathetic. Do you hear me? What that prick did to you was not your fault. Jesus, he's twice the size of you and you're saying that you're pathetic because he overpowered you? He's the one who's pathetic." His tone wasn't sympathetic or soft; it was furious. "And as for you coming to my house and me seeing you the way I did, not for one second did I think you were pathetic or weak. I saw you the way I always see you—you're strong, so strong. You got away from him, Alex." He lowered his hands. "I love you, you know that?"

I looked to him with widened eyes. How could he possibly be confessing his love to me here, now?

"You fill a hole inside." He patted his chest. "You are my best friend. I don't care what your problem is. If you need me I will always be there." A smile tugged at either side of his mouth. "Pretty sure there's a song about that."

A smile crept to my face. "Thanks, Andy." Although I meant it wholeheartedly, the words didn't seem to be strong enough. "I'm scared. I don't know what that was ... that was insane."

He inhaled deeply and bit his bottom lip.

"Look, Alex. There's a lot I need to tell you," he said in a low, ominous voice, looking through the windows as though he was expecting someone to appear.

"What is it?" I asked in a low voice also. His behaviour was making me even more anxious than I already was.

"We are a few hours away from a motel. We'll stay there tonight and I'll explain everything," he promised.

"What? We're staying at a motel, hours away? No. We need to go to Mooribilli. I need to call the police and tell them what he did!" I slapped my hands over my mouth. I suddenly realised I had had a shower. "Andy! The shower! The DNA is washed away."

I couldn't believe I had been so stupid. There would be absolutely no evidence of the attack. "The police won't be able to arrest him without any evidence!" I could hardly breathe as I thought of his words: *You belong to me; I will always find you.* "He told me he would find me, always. And he will. There'll be nothing to stop him."

My chest tightened with fear at the surety of his promise.

"Calm down!" Andy waved his hands in a downward motion. "Don't you think I've already thought of that? We aren't going to the police because they won't be able to help us." He continued to speak in a low voice as though someone may be able to hear him. He edged closer to me as he darted another glance out the rear window. "Look, there is so much more going on here. I barely understand it myself. All I do know is it's too dangerous to be discussing anything while we are in the open like this." He leant in even closer to me and held my hand. "You need to trust me."

I did trust him, more than anyone else I knew. But it felt wrong. My instincts were screaming at me to go to the police, to let them handle it. Even though his DNA wasn't in me any-more, there would have been small amounts of it at my house. Even if they weren't able to arrest him, they would be able to protect me.

"I'm so scared, Andy. When I was in the hospital and I had hallucinations, they felt so real. And just now, I was drawn to him ... it's insane. What if my hallucinations are getting worse?" I wrapped my arms around my stomach and rocked forward.

"They're not." He grabbed the steering wheel and began to drive along the highway again, this time with his headlights off. "Remember that book—the one that I told you was bogus?" he asked. He was leaning over the steering wheel as he drove, scanning the road for any wildlife.

"Yeah, of course. What does that book have anything to do with this?" I snapped. I couldn't understand why he would bring up such a trivial topic.

"It's not 'some cheap city book' as you thought." He looked at me for only a second. But in that second I saw his ominous expression.

"Andy ...?"

"It glowed."

"What?"

"The book glowed, but only when I touched it. And it burned me." He held his left hand out. His fingertips were burned and had blistered.

"My book did this to you; the one with in the wrapper with DRIA written across it?" I stared at his hand in disbelief.

He nodded.

"What? That's impossible. It must have been something else. Books don't glow and they certainly don't burn people." I shook my head. What he was suggesting was completely ridiculous. I knew he wasn't lying to trying to trick me, but there had to be a rational explanation.

"Where's my book now?"

"It's safe. It's just in the top of my backpack." He threw his thumb over his left shoulder.

I spun around in my seat and reached for his backpack, which was lying across the back seat. I tugged at the zipper and drew it open. As he said, my book sat at the very top.

"It's not glowing," I said.

"You have to touch it."

I reached across and grabbed it with my hand. As soon as my fingers lay on it, the five symbols began to glow an intense red. I sat back around with it on my lap and stared at it in awe; the light that was being emitted was the most beautiful colour of red. I ran my fingers across the symbols. They were still soft and silk-like to touch.

"How are you not being burned?" he queried.

"I don't know—it's not hot."

I gingerly opened the front cover. The writings that filled the ivory pages within the book remained perfectly black as they scrolled along the pages. I touched one of the symbols on the first ivory page and instantly the black writing turned to blinding gold.

"It's beautiful." I spoke in complete awe of its splendour. "Perhaps you burned your fingers on something else and you just thought it was the book." I picked it up and turned it over, inspecting every inch of the cover. "Do you think its battery operated?"

He spat a loud laugh.

"What? Do you have a better explanation?" I snapped. "One that's not filled with goblins and witches."

I loved Andy dearly, but so often his imagination would carry him away, just as it obviously had with the supposed burning book. There would always be a rational explanation but he would never look for it. He would linger in the realm of the fantastic for as long as he could.

"Witches and goblins are nothing compared to what I found. And before you try to defame my findings, they come from a government site ... We are still a couple of hours away from where we'll be staying tonight. You should try to sleep."

"What? You're not serious? After what just happened you're not going to explain everything to me now? He said I belonged to him. Andy, he knew everything about me." I needed answers, and I couldn't believe Andy would consider not telling me all that he knew.

"Ally, we need to get to Melbourne ASAP, which means you'll have to drive while I sleep. So please, just sleep now. I need you to be at your sharpest. You are going to have to accept a lot of stuff that you'd normally laugh off."

"Melbourne? You never said anything about Melbourne. We can't go there! It's thousands of kilometres away. Not to mention Sam will think we've dropped off the side of the Earth. What if Derrek attacks someone else? What if he attacks Emilee?" I threw my hands over my mouth.

Emilee was so small and petite, she'd never be able to fight him off. He would kill her.

"Calm down. Yes, we have to go to Melbourne. No, nobody— and I mean nobody—needs to know we are going there. Sam will just think we've gone to the city to get your meds, which before you freak out about them too, I found a packet at my house. You must have left them there at some stage; it's not a full packet but it will give you some more time. And as for Emilee, he isn't going to attack her," he said with assuredness as he threw his eyes to the rear view mirror again.

"What do you mean he isn't going to attack her?" I scowled at him. If given the opportunity I had no doubt he would.

"Because he will be too busy chasing us. We have something he wants ..." He looked to my lap. "He wants that book."

~ 11 ~

CHAPTER ELEVEN

I awoke to Andy gently shaking my shoulder. I slowly brought my eyes into focus and looked around at the clock in the centre of the dashboard. Three, almost four hours had passed since he had suggested I sleep.

"We're here." He was standing on the side step, with one arm leaning on the open passenger door and the other on the car roof.

"Where's 'here'?" I yawned and looked through the window to our night's accommodation.

The motel was literally a rectangular box comprising twelve rooms. It was run down, and most of the paint had faded or peeled away.

"I dunno. I don't even think this place has a name." He looked around at the barren landscape, which was dimly lit by the moon. "Anyway, while you were sleeping I booked a room. We have the same room—with two single beds," he quickly added.

He didn't give me the option to object to sleeping in the same room. Usually, someone else making decisions for me would infuriate me, and I would want to do the opposite just to spite them, but not today; today, I was happy to simply follow.

"We are parked around the back of the motel ... didn't want the car to be easily spotted from the highway. As it is, I want to be out of here by 6 a.m. at the absolute latest," he said as he pulled his bulky backpack from the boot of the car and swung it awkwardly over his shoulder.

"Spud's asleep in the back. He should be alright for a few hours," he said as he helped me out of the car.

I had almost forgotten how badly Derrek had hurt me until I began to move; my bruises throbbed, and I could feel my forehead had swollen. As I stood by the car, I looked through the back window. Spud had sprawled across the back seat and was sleeping soundly.

"You know, that dog saved my life tonight," I said quietly, as I shook my head. "I should never have put myself in that situation. God! I'm so *angry* at myself. It's just so stupid. Who does that? Who just meets someone then invites them into their home?"

"Almost everyone I know." He looked directly at me. "Just remember, not all us blokes are pigs. Are you alright to walk to the room or do you need me to carry you?"

"I'll be right to walk." I was going to hold on to that much of my dignity.

The motel room was befitting to its external appearance. The ceiling was lined with polystyrene that had broken up in parts. There were two single beds sitting alongside each other. Both beds were covered in deep maroon bedspreads, which were stained.

Andy sat on the edge of his bed, across from where I sat, and dropped his backpack on the floor by his side. I was glad I had managed a little sleep on the drive; my mind was a lot clearer.

"I doubt that you noticed, but tonight, my backpack was already packed."

I shook my head. Honestly, a pink elephant could have walked past us, and I doubt I would have noticed. I was too consumed with the need to escape Derrek.

"It was already packed because I was heading to Melbourne tomorrow—well today, now." He looked at his watch; it had just ticked past 3 a.m. "You know what I want to do right now? I want to pack our swags and take you camping somewhere— anywhere! Watch you try to fish, or eat some of that damper you cook. Just hang out with you and pretend none of this happened." His face fell. "But I can't. I can't take you away from this, Alex. You've had a hell of a night, and I wish I didn't have to make it worse. But I have to tell you this—you *need* to know. There's no easy way to say this, Ally." He rubbed his forehead with his fingertips. "So I'm just going to say it. But before I do, know that I had absolutely no idea he would do this to you. If I had any inkling, I would have gotten you out."

"I know you would have, Andy. But there was no way you could have known. None of this is your fault. If it wasn't for you ..." I stumbled over my words. "Andy if it wasn't for you, God knows where I'd be now."

"Alex, you're missing the point ..." He unzipped the side of his bag and pulled out a long bottle of Vodka. He pulled the top from the bottle and took a large swig, pulling a face as the alcohol burned.

"Here," he said in a thick voice and passed the bottle to me. "Just take this and listen."

"You're really starting to make me nervous now," I said.

"You should be ..." He dug back into the backpack again, this time pulling out his laptop. "Remember how I had my friend scour the internet to see what language the book was written in, and I told you the book was bogus?"

He spoke quietly, as though someone may overhear him, although the motel was completely deserted apart from us and the owner, who I saw briefly as we walked to our room.

"Yes, of course." I leant in towards Andy.

"It suddenly came to me—your crossbow has strange markings as well. I pulled out a photo I have of you holding it the day we bought it and compared it to the book. They're in the same language."

"What?" I almost dropped the Vodka bottle. "How the hell can they be the same language? Those scribbles on my bow are just decorations." He didn't answer me; he just placed his laptop on the side table between the beds and flipped it open.

"I don't know what made me do it, but I pulled the security footage of the bookstore." He stood and began to pace the small room. "I can't believe I didn't think of it before!"

"Andy, you're not making sense.

"They're the same!" he blurted.

"What? The same what? You just told me the book and the bow are in the same language. Andy, calm down."

He took a couple of deep breaths to calm himself. "Ever since you were given that book, I've been running a program to scan images from everywhere."

"To find a match for the symbols?"

"That's right." He paused. "The computer found a match in the security footage. God! I'm so pissed off at myself!" He began pacing the room furiously again. "If I had just made the connection I could have prevented ... this ..." He gestured towards me. "I don't know what the friggin' hell we've walked into, Alex. It's not good."

Andy's demeanour had me worried. He was never like this; he was always calm and easy going.

"Look." He pressed a button on the laptop and turned the screen to me. An image of a shirtless Derrek filled the screen, captured the morning after we had spent the night at the shop.

My stomach clenched the instant I saw him. I pressed my eyes closed as I attempted to block him from my mind. But he was still too real. I could not forget his scent, the smell of exotic islands. I took a large gulp of Vodka. The burn made me splutter, but it did manage to dull the memory of his scent.

"I told you you'd want it." He took the bottle from me and shot another mouthful. "This is only going to get harder. You want me to keep going?" he said, looking at me carefully.

I snatched the bottle from him and took another shot—a smaller one. It still burned as it went down. "Yep." I put the back of my hand to my lips as I swallowed.

"Every symbol on his body matches the language in the book and the one on the bow."

"That's not possible," I said in disbelief. "There's no way they could be connected ..."

"They are. Alex, he's not human."

"*What?*"

"I know, I know," he said. "Don't say anything till you hear the rest. Pass your bow here," he instructed as he began to type quickly on the laptop. "I want you to see this." I bent down to pick up the bow, and as I wrapped my fingers around it, the engraved symbols began to glow a deep, intense red, just as the book had done.

"Andy ..." He wasn't looking at me—he was still typing on his laptop. "Andy! What the hell?"

He turned back to see me holding the illuminated bow in both hands.

"Whoa! The book *and* the bow ... hmm. That would make sense. They're both in the same language, so they must both be responsive to human touch," he said as he looked closely at the engravings. "I wonder if I can still touch the bow."

I was not convinced yet that the book actually burned him, so without thinking, I threw the bow across to him. He caught it with his arms and screamed loudly, as he threw it away. It landed on the floor and immediately stopped glowing. I ran to the bathroom, to get a towel, and soaked it in cold water, wringing some of the liquid from it before returning to him. Even in the time it took to do that, the burns had begun to blister. I slowly lowered the cool towel to his arms.

"I am so sorry, Andy. I don't understand. I could touch it ..."

"I know you don't believe in the supernatural, but you're just going to have to," he snapped as he winced.

"Okay. I'm sorry," I said as I stared at the bow lying on the floor. "How can this be happening?" I whimpered. "I keep hearing Derrek's voice in my head ... the way he said it! He's going to find me, Andy, I know he is." I slumped next to him on the bed and burst into tears. "It's one thing to have a psycho hunting me, but now you're telling me he's not human! And somehow my bow and that crazy book are both connected to him? Andy, how am I meant to deal with this? I don't want to believe that he's not human because that's just too much right now. But, the way he *controls* me. It's like he sucks me into a trance—I know no human could do that. What does he want with me? Andy, he's going to find me—he promised!"

Andy moved closer, dropped the wet towel, and gingerly wrapped his burned arm around me.

"Stop!" he demanded, giving me a slight shake. "If he does find you, I will protect you. Do you hear me? He's never going to hurt you again. Do you understand?" He pulled me closer to a full embrace.

"Yes," I spluttered into his shoulder.

"Now, I need you just to sit here and listen. Can you do that?" he asked as he loosened his arms and picked up the towel. He wrapped it around his arm and then slid back to his laptop.

I nodded, "Yes."

"Okay, don't try to think it through. Just sit and listen; we'll process it all later. His name is not Derrek. In fact, I don't think he has a name." Andy paused, watching me closely to measure my response. I just sat still and listened.

"Have that bottle ready 'cause you're going to need it." He hit another key on the laptop.

An image of a painting filled the screen; a painting of Derrek.

"But ... but ... look at the date—it's ..."

"... painted in 1769." Andy finished for me. "Yeah I read the date on the painting too. And yes, that is definitely him. And so are these ..."

He pressed a key on the keyboard several times, each time pulling up a different image of Derrek. Each photograph was of him in a different era, as though he had passed through the centuries with only his clothing changing. At the bottom, right-hand corner of each image appeared 'The Aztec' and the date it was painted.

"This is impossible," I said, incredulous at the countless images of him. "What is he? Like a ... a ... a vampire or something?" I could hardly believe the words that were coming from my mouth.

"I'll admit that vampire was the first thing that came to my mind. But he is Aztec—The Aztec." Andy shrugged his shoulder as he answered.

"What? Like the ancient Mexicans?" I lifted one eyebrow, dubiously. "He doesn't look very Mexican."

"No, they share no similarities, apart from their name. I'll show you what I found."

He moved the laptop to the side table so he could type quickly, and so we could both see the screen. A document appeared that included a photograph.

"That's ..." I pointed at the picture, stunned.

"... your 'cheap city book'," Andy interjected. "It's called *The Book of Narveere*."

I shifted the laptop screen slightly towards me, so I could read out loud the text that was sitting below the image of the book:

In the mid-twentieth century, four aspiring historians took it upon themselves to explore extensively into the history of The Book of Narveere—the true origins of the myth and what purpose it served in cultural development.

Their intention was not to retrieve the Book, for they firmly believed the true existence of the Book was false. Their hypothesis: "The Book was to ancient societies as religions are today; a way to explain the inexplicable." Rose and Jonah Persival; head of 'The Narveere Expedition'.

They did not uncover the Book, but they did find scrolls.

The scrolls were written in a sophisticated language for their time, and almost indecipherable to all linguists asked to translate.

The language did not consist of letters or characters, but rather, unique symbols that acted as a code; a code that was never intended to be broken.

All linguists agreed, if the language could be deciphered, the scrolls would be invaluable to discovering vital pieces of human history.

Amongst the scrolls were two that were written in another language. Linguists were only able to vaguely translate from a small portion of these two badly damaged scrolls.

If one should fall,
They each will fade.
Darkness will come,
Not one will evade.

The scrolls do not reveal who 'they' are, or what the 'darkness' could signify. Many prophets foresaw the collapse of the greatest leaders— perhaps this poem was little more than a prophecy.

It is said that The Book of Narveere belonged to an ancient man known as The Aztec (it must be noted: after extensive research, it has been discovered that the ancient civilization of Aztec (which existed in Mexico) is unrelated to 'The Aztec.' As to why they share a name remains unclear).

The Aztec is described as an ancient warrior of epic proportions. He is described as being of African descent, and as having unique markings across his body; markings that are also found on The Book of Narveere.

The scrolls reference The Black Sword several times, and each time the writer emphasises the incredible need for the Book to remain hidden from The Black Sword. However, the scrolls do not explain the urgency of this permanent separation.

(Veronika and Boris (see images 2.3, 2.4 and 2.8) are said to have once belonged to a society of people known as 'The Black Sword.' The Book of Narveere supposedly referenced them several times, but no other evidence has ever been discovered to hold any validity to this society ever having existed. It should also be noted that the scrolls do not say, or even imply that The Book of Narveere should remain with The Aztec.

The second scroll was in considerably better condition, but it con-sisted of painting, rather than writing."

As Andy continued to scroll past the painting of The Aztec, the image of a woman appeared. It was only a small picture, and I had to squint to try and make out any details. She had pale skin and black hair that was pulled up into a messy bun. She wore a medieval red and black dress, resembling a wedding dress, which draped over the red velvet chair on which she was sitting. I wasn't able to see her face clearly, although I could tell she was a beautiful woman. She seemed familiar somehow.

At the bottom of the painting, the name *'Veronika'* was inked perfectly across the page. The name did not mean anything to me. I stared at the image with envy and fear. She was beautiful, yes, but there was something about her—something cruel.

Andy continued to scroll to the last image. The name on this painting was 'Boris'. It was of a short, stocky man with light brown hair. His face was marked with an undisguisable jagged scar that ran from the side of his nose, down to his jaw. I took a quick, sharp breath in shock ... that *scar!*

"Oh my God! Andy, scroll up—back to the woman." I edged forward on the bed so I could see the screen better. "I've seen her before. I've seen *him* before!" I said as I recollected the brief encounter at the bookstore.

"What? When?" Andy asked quickly.

I stood up quickly, almost falling as the room seemed to spin. It was either the alcohol I had consumed or shock—maybe both. I paced the small room and pushed my fingers through my hair.

"Oh my God! They were in the bookstore. Don't you remember? She asked for a book! She said it would be 'very memorable'." I could feel my heart begin to pound as I remembered them standing within inches of me.

Andy stared at me for a moment, his brows furrowed.

"And you didn't think she might have been referring to this book? Why didn't you tell me?"

"I thought they were weird tourists! We get a dozen of them a week! I wasn't even thinking about the book at that stage because you told me it was bogus, so why would I think anything of it?" I could feel my stomach turn on itself. "What else does it say?" I asked, desperate for more information.

"Nothing. There's only one more painting," he said as he scrolled down.

The next painting was of an image of Veronika's face in close-up.

"Oh my God!" I screamed. "Her eyes! They are exactly the eyes I saw in my hallucinations." I wrapped my arms around my waist and backed up to the wall.

It couldn't be possible. I had been taking medication for years to stop the hallucinations. That's all they were—hallucinations.

"Oh my God! Oh my God! It was all planned." Past events flooded my mind. I moved to sit back on the bed. I slumped my head into my hands, rocking back and forth; it was all too much.

"What? Slow down. Calm down Alex," he said soothingly. He threw the towel to the floor as he sat by my side. "What are you talking about?"

"Her eyes are exactly the eyes I saw in my hallucinations. Not similar, or nearly alike, they are identical—everything was planned."

"What was planned? Alexandra, make sense!" he demanded.

I turned to face him. "Weeks ago, when I broke down along Mooribilli-Warrangatta Road, the medication stopped working because I became severely dehydrated with the heat ... and I *hallucinated* again." I ran my hands over the sides of my face. Even though this whole thing seemed like complete insanity, it was now actually beginning to make sense to me. What I thought had been random and unrelated events weren't at all.

"Yeah, you had a head trauma, I know. Hallucinations were to be expected."

"You don't get it. The eyes are *real*. They're not hallucinations."

Andy rolled his head back. "Ally, have you stopped taking your meds?"

"No! Just listen!" I yelled. "For years I had convinced myself that I was crazy, that what I was seeing and feeling wasn't real;

but I never truly believed that Andy. When the eyes appear they don't just flash in my mind—I can feel them searching through my memories." I could hear my own words; if I was listening to someone else talk like this, I would consider them insane.

His eyebrows were furrowed as he considered what I was saying.

I edged closer to him. "Look ..." I held up one finger. "First, within mere weeks of the Mooribilli-Warrangatta Road incident, and having those eyes searching through me, The Aztec arrives —out of nowhere." I held up a second finger. "Then, Veronika and Boris just *happened* to be wandering through Warrangatta at exactly the same time The Aztec decides to visit me."

Andy blinked quickly, as he processed everything I was telling him. I could tell he, too, was beginning to piece together the puzzle.

"And," my third finger went up, "when Derrek—The Aztec— visited my house, the very first thing he asked about was the bow. I took it off the wall, but he didn't take it straight away, he just studied it." I snapped my fingers as a thought suddenly occurred to me. "He must have been waiting to see if it was going to glow." I sat, shaking my head as I tried to comprehend it all. The entire scenario was preposterous.

"If what you're saying is true, why didn't he just do what he wanted the night you stayed at the shop?"

I leant my arms on my knees as I thought. Andy was right. Why didn't he just kidnap me that night? He could have done whatever he liked, and no one would have ever known.

"He wanted the Book *and* the bow?" I suggested. "You said so yourself ..."

"You never lock your windows or doors, Alex. Why not just break in and steal it?"

I scratched the back of my head. "Because ... I hadn't invited him in yet?"

"What? *You're* actually going along with vampire mythology now ... that he can't enter someone's house without first being invited?" he asked sceptically.

"I don't know." I slumped back down, leaning my arms on my knees again. Any credibility to my hypothesis was debunked when he put it like that. I didn't believe in vampires or were-wolves and other such creatures of the dark side.

"You said he knew *everything* about you?" he asked slowly.

"Yes." I closed my eyes as the memory of Derrek's words filled my head: *there is nowhere to hide. I will find you. I will always find you.* "Everything. Even from before the accident."

He took a couple of paces away, rubbing his chin thoughtfully, before turning back to me and pointing. "*You* would have to be one of the hardest people to stalk. You don't have a computer, so he couldn't hack into your life. You don't go out to pubs or socialize, and anything that anyone *knows* about you in Warrangatta is a bullshit rumour. The only people who know anything about you are me, Emilee and Sam and I'm sure as hell none of us were helping him ... so your theory of the eyes is making more sense. What if she really could see your memories?"

"This is *crazy*. For all we know these documents you found on the internet are fakes. Perhaps they're actors. Maybe all this is just an elaborate setup, you know, like that prank TV show. Or ..." I desperately wanted to believe my own words.

"Alexandra! Enough! Alright, this is happening. This is real. Now get a grip because we need to get a handle on it all!" Andy snapped his fingers as he paced up and down the small room. "Right, you told me you hadn't hallucinated since you'd been in Warrangatta. You said it only happened to you while you were in the hospital?"

"Yes, that's right. I didn't lie to you. The only reason it happened in the desert was because the meds don't work in extreme heat. I just didn't think about that before I left—I wasn't planning on breaking down in the desert."

He held is hand mid-air to stop me as he continued to place together the puzzle pieces.

"What if the meds you're on make your mind impenetrable?"

I looked at him for a prolonged time. I hadn't considered that, but it could make sense.

He continued his train of thought. "When they stopped working in the heat this Veronika was able to flick through your memories. That would explain how Derrek knew everything about you, where'd you'd be ... what they'd have to do to gain your trust. They must be working together. It's the only explanation."

I ran my hand across my forehead as though to wipe all this information from my brain because it was too much to take in.

"You're right. She was wearing sunglasses when she came into the store because she knew I would recognise her as soon as I saw her eyes. I hadn't opened the parcel prior to my trip along Mooribilli-Warrangatta Road, so I didn't know about the Book. That's why she was asking me about a 'memorable book'; she was gauging my reaction. She must have had some inclination I was in possession of it, but she couldn't have known for sure." I sat back on my bed, exhausted from the mental effort. There was too much evidence to try to deny the validity of the documents Andy had found.

He frowned. "It can't just be the Book. You hadn't received it when she first looked into you at the hospital. What else happened at the hospital?"

"I dunno. Um ... nothing. I woke up. All the doctors were astonished at how fast I recovered—apparently it's unheard of."

"Okay, what about visitors? Anyone, anyone at all?"

"No, no one."

"What about anything strange, odd, out of sorts? Anything?"

"No, nothing."

"There must have been something. Come on, think!" he snapped.

"Andy! I had just woken from a coma to find my family had died."

"What about your things? A bag, a phone ... anything unusual about them?"

I paused as something occurred to me. "My necklace!"

"What about it?"

"Tess, my nurse, gave it to me. Apparently, it was in my file. I didn't have any other possessions."

"But that's your necklace, right?"

"Well, it is now." I picked it up with my thumb and looked down at it. "I think it was meant for another patient, but they insisted it was mine."

"Hmm ..."

"What's 'hmm'? It's a necklace."

"No, I know that. It's just a bit odd. You are given a necklace and then receive this 'all powerful' book. Your crossbow is now glowing, and your necklace is also a bow."

"What? Do you think they're somehow connected? It's just a necklace. The crossbow, well it was just pure chance I came across it. I found it in an op-shop. Anyone could have found it. I know the necklace is a bow—I just don't understand how they could be connected, though."

"Yeah, you're probably right," he answered. "Hey, I wonder ..." He sat up straight and leant in towards me.

"What are you doing?"

"I can't touch the bow or the Book, but what about your necklace?" He moved towards me, leant closer and gingerly touched the tip of his finger on the necklace, quickly pulling back in case it burned. Nothing happened, so he tried touching it again—still nothing. "Hmm, maybe it needs to touch the Book or something to kind of activate it?"

"Activate it?" I raised one eyebrow.

"Well, I don't know! Just bloody try it!"

I pulled the necklace over my head and moved to the Book and bow. Pain thrashed through my body as I moved, but I kept from crying out.

After trying various ways of touching the necklace against the Book and bow, I sat back on the bed. "Nothing. It's just a necklace."

"I'm still not so sure. Why don't you give it to me for a while, just until we're out of Melbourne?" He held out his hand. Every inch of me was screaming not to pass it over. "Alex? Hand it over."

The fact that I didn't want to part with it only made me realise how important it was for me to separate with it. I pressed my eyes closed and dropped it into his hand. I didn't feel better with it gone. Perhaps it was because the necklace was my first possession after I woke from the coma, but I felt vulnerable without it.

"I have a contact in Melbourne who I hope can answer a lot of our questions."

"There are a lot of questions. You think your contact will be able to answer them all?"

"Nope. I think there are only two people on this Earth who will be able to do that, and they are Jonah and Rose Persival. I found some more information on them; nothing really interesting except it's as though they've disappeared. There is absolutely no trace of them anywhere that I can find."

"This contact we're going to see—is he a better computer person than you? Could he find them if you can't?" I asked dubiously.

I knew little about computers, but I couldn't believe anyone could be better than Andy.

"She—and she has skills that I'll never have."

"What if The Aztec finds us before we get there?" It was all too much. I didn't mean to cry, but tears flowed from my eyes before I could stop them. "I'm so scared ,Andy." I sobbed loudly.

He slid along the bed to my side and wrapped his arms around me. "You're meant to be scared, Ally. You don't need to be strong every second of your life. He attacked you!"

"It's not just that." I wiped my cheeks. "I was drawn to him. He's done something to me. I feel like I need to be by his side."

"What do you mean?" He took my shaking hand in his.

"I feel like I love him. Ever since he first walked into the bookstore, he's all I can think about. To begin with, I thought I was just falling for him; I thought I was beginning to move on from Michael ... but now, when there is no possible reason as to why I would ever love him, I think I do. I know it's not a rational love; it can't be. I am scared of him finding me, but I am even more scared of what I'll do. If it weren't for you at your house, he would have taken me again." I could feel my stomach knot and turn again and again.

Andy held me tighter as tears flowed from me.

"It will take less than a week to get to Melbourne. We'll take all the back roads. We don't even need to go to a servo or buy food or water. I've got enough of all that in the back of my car. No one knows where we're going, and if our theory's correct, you are essentially invisible to them because you are on your meds."

"What about Sam? He'll know something's amiss when we don't show up to work."

"Nope. Remember, we were going to the city for your meds ... suppose we still are, just a different city."

~ 12 ~

CHAPTER TWELVE

We left the motel at first light and quickly diverted from the main highway to the back roads. Although the back roads were made of dirt, the rain had dampened any dust that would have given away our location. Each evening, we camped in thick bushland or behind large rocks; anything we could tuck the car behind so it couldn't be seen from the road. And each night we took it in shifts to sleep while the other kept watch. Only, when it was my turn to sleep, I didn't sleep; my mind was plagued with nothing but The Aztec. Each night the same dream played in my mind.

In my dream, I would wake to be standing barefoot on thick, dark green grass, in front of a hut surrounded by tall trees that filled the atmosphere with their mesmerising scent. The ground was soft and comforting beneath my feet. I could feel the forest flow through my veins with every breath I took.

In the distance, I could hear the sound of gently running streams, or the occasional snap of a stick from the many forest animals that moved freely amongst the trees. As I stared through the lightly misted trees, a figure was beginning to emerge from the dense forest, his shape becoming more defined with each step he took; it was him. He was wearing only his dark cargo pants, his taut, masculine body beautifully defined by the sun as it fanned across his dark skin. I held my arms out for him to come to me, as though I had known him for eternity and I was welcoming him home after a long absence. I was wearing a long, flowing, white gown, made of silk that hung gently from my body. My dark red hair flowed across the dress as blood would through milk.

He ran towards me, but instead of throwing himself into me, he seized my hand and pulled me deeper into the dense forest. He let go of my hand and gently pushed me on without saying a word. I knew he wanted me to continue running deeper in the mystical forest. As I ran deeper into the forest, I became aware that we were fleeing someone or something. I repeatedly turned to face him, to ask him what it was that we were trying to escape. Each time as he grew closer to me, he pointed away from me and yelled for me to run faster, only no sound came from him mouth, and each time I turned back to run faster and further into the never-ending trees. The last time I turned to ask him who we were running from, a tree root became wrapped around my foot, and I fell slowly to my back. I lay there for a moment, staring up through the tree canopy, watching the sun as it gently danced between the tree tops, its rays licking my skin.

Instantly the sun disappeared, as it was blocked by him. His beautiful face was staring down at me, his naked body as perfect as I remembered it. His engraved tattoos caught my eye and I desperately wanted to touch them. I wanted to touch his skin; I wanted to feel him under my skin, around and in my body. I wanted to immerse myself into him. I slowly reached my hand out to touch his chest, but just before my hand rested on him, he leant in and pressed his firm lips against mine; I melted into his embracing arms. His legs slipped themselves between mine, as he slid my dress up to my hips with his hand, lifting me onto his hips as he kissed my neck. I tilted my head back as his lips sent shivers through my body. I wrapped myself around him as he lifted me from the ground. The instant he stood to his feet, he pulled his hands from under me, and I fell through the Earth, down a never-ending black tunnel. I reached my arms out for him to save me, but he just stood at the top of the tunnel and stared through empty eyes.

And that's the exact point in the dream I would wake up. For the first seconds after waking, I would forget he was hunting me, I would forget what he had done to me, and I would wish that he was here with me. For a few seconds, I remembered his warm, gentle touch against my skin when we slept on the couch, and I could almost feel his lips press against mine when he kissed me in the staff room. But then my mind would draw up the memory of him forcing himself on me and my stomach would knot up. I was being consumed by him, and I wanted to know why. I needed to know so much more about all the things Andy and I had discovered. I needed to know how The Aztec and my yearning for him related to Veronika and Boris, the bow and The Book of Narveere. So many questions ...

I was impatient to meet with Andy's contact. She might be my only hope of finding the answers I needed.

*****

It came as a great relief to finally arrive at Andy's family home early on Monday morning. Andy was right—the food he had packed kept us alive and ensured we received all the nutrition our bodies required, but it did little to fill our stomachs. So, not only were we exhausted, we were famished.

His family lived in a blue terrace, which adjoined five other identical terraces. Each one had a narrow concrete path that led from a set of wrought iron gates to a concrete step under a verandah. A large willow tree stood proudly on the nature strip, shading the six terraces from the sun, which was just peeking over the neighbouring buildings.

"Well, this is it," Andy sighed as we approached the wrought iron gates. "Let's go meet the folks." He lifted both his eyebrows and inhaled deeply.

As soon as Andy pushed open the gate, a small yelping dog began to scratch at the inside of the front door. At the same time, a little boy's face peered from behind the heavy white curtains.

"Andy! Andy's home! Mum! Dad! Andy's home!" the excited child called. We could hear the soft thud of his feet as he ran up and down the hallway calling out loudly.

Finally, we heard the key unlock from the inside. The door opened, and as it did, an older man's voice spoke in a low, disappointed manner, "See Leroy, you're just imagining things again. Andy's not ..."

Before the man could finish his sentence, the boy pushed open the door and ran down the concrete path towards Andy.

"Andy! Andy! Andy!" he cried.

Andy swung his backpack off his shoulder and landed it on the ground as he scooped up the little boy.

"Hi, Leroy. It's good to see you again, buddy," he said as he wrapped his arms around the excited child.

"I knew you'd come back." Leroy spoke with a lisp as he squeezed Andy tightly. "Are you staying forever?" he asked hopefully.

Andy carefully put Leroy back down on the path, and knelt down to look at him. "Only for a little while, then I have to take Alexandra home."

Leroy looked up at me through thick round glasses. His eyes were the same deep brown as Andy's, but his were cross-eyed, and he wore a hearing aid in each ear.

"Oh. Is she your girlfriend?" Leroy asked with a cheeky smile.

"No, she's just my friend," he smiled kindly.

Leroy frowned and thought for a moment as he studied me. He looked back to Andy and whispered, "She should be your girlfriend. She's pretty. She looks like glitter."

A bubble of warmth brewed in the centre of me. He was such a beautiful little boy.

Andy choked a laugh. "Glitter, who's ...?"

"What's going on out here?" a woman's voice called from inside the door. She pushed past the man, who was still standing in the doorway.

She was a short, plump woman. Her jet black hair was cut in a bob that sat just under her jawline. She stopped suddenly and put both of her hands over her heart.

"Oh my, Andy!" she cried as she ran to him with open arms. She threw her arms around him and held him tight for a moment.

"Hi Mum," Andy said, as he slowly placed his hands around her back.

A moment passed until Andy spoke again. "This is Alexandra."

His mother slowly loosened her embrace and stepped away from him, keeping her hands on either of his arms. She looked around to me.

"Hello. Sorry, I've lost all of my manners. I'm Alice, and this is Joe." She turned to where the tall, balding man stood. His eyes were welling at the sight of Andy.

"Come here, my boy!" He walked down the path with his arms abreast and wrapped them around Andy. "Ahh, it's good to see you again." He slapped Andy several times on the back.

"You too, Dad." Andy threw his arms around his father. "Is it okay if Alexandra and I stay a few days?"

Joe lowered his arms and clapped his hands to either side of Andy's upper arms. "You can stay as long as you want, my boy!" He turned to face me and extended his hand. "Welcome, Alexandra." I accepted it and shook it.

"Thank you very much," I smiled.

His eyes were wide and full of warmth, just as Andy's always were.

"We've heard so much about you. Andy speaks so highly of you when he calls home," Alice said gleefully. "You do look like you've been through the wars, my dear. Is everything alright?" She slid her finger along my chin, inspecting my bruises.

"Car accident," Andy answered quickly. "A bunch of kangaroos jumped out in front of Alex's car before we left. That's why we're in my car." He spoke calmly. He was so believable; I had to remind myself that it was a lie.

"Oh my! That would have been frightening." She clasped one of her hands over her mouth.

"Yes. It was." I spoke stiffly. I knew I wasn't nearly as convincing as Andy. I needed to act calmer, just as he did. "Kangaroos are everywhere in Warrangatta. Kind of just get used to hitting them. Guess I hit them a little too hard." I shrugged.

"Is that a dog?" Leroy cried as he ran to the side of Andy's car, and looked in at Spud who licked the window and wagged his tail excitedly.

"Yes. That's my dog, Spud," I said, relieved the conversation had moved from the origins of my bruising. "Would you like to play with him?"

"Yes! Yes! Yes!" He bounced and clapped his hands.

Spud bounded out as soon as I opened the door, and ran circles around me.

"Spud—sit," I said firmly. He sat back with his tongue hanging from the side of his mouth, his tail still wagging. "Shake hands," I told him. He instantly sat back on his hindquarters and lifted his paw into the air. "There you go," I gestured to Leroy.

His eyes widened as he took a few steps forward and shook Spud's paw.

"Mum, can I play with him? He knows commands! Please Mum?" he pleaded to Alice.

"Spud's not my dog. You'll have to ask Alexandra," she smiled at him.

"That's fine. He knows loads of other commands. Try 'play dead', 'talk' and 'roll over'." I suggested.

"Come on, Spud," Leroy called as he ran through the house to their backyard.

"Well, you've certainly made someone happy," Joe laughed, as he also walked back into the house.

It was touching to see Leroy play with Spud. Michael and I hadn't had a dog, but I imagined Sasha would have been just as excited. Warmth filled my belly as I thought of my baby girl.

"Well, come on in, you two. I'll show you to your room. Don't want to stand out here for too long—it will probably start snowing. Melbourne's weather has been absurd!" Alice beckoned with her whole arm, as she walked along the concrete path into the terrace. I watched until she disappeared into the house and tapped Andy on the shoulder.

"Are you sure I should stay here? I mean I'm putting your family in danger. What if he finds me here—not to mention Veronika and Boris! I don't know what they're capable of ... Andy, your little brother ..." I could barely speak as panic rose from the pit of my stomach.

He put his hand on my shoulder and looked into me. "Assuming they even know we're in Melbourne—Melbourne is huge.

The likelihood of them ever finding us here is slim. She hasn't looked into you since your car broke down, and you've never visited here before; they would have no inkling we'd be here." He turned his head from side to side, ensuring he couldn't be overheard. "Besides, I don't plan on being here for long. I want us to see my contact, tonight."

"Tonight?"

"Yes. She lives across the other side of Melbourne, so it's best we take public transport." He rubbed his chin with his index finger and his thumb. I hadn't noticed until then, but he hadn't shaved in the week that it took us to drive to Melbourne, and he had almost grown a complete beard. It looked good on him; made him look strong. "I think we'll leave my car and Spud here," he said, pointing to the ground as he began to walk into the terrace.

I thought for a moment as I followed him. "Yeah, okay. We'll be back tonight, and I think Leroy will keep Spud entertained."

Through the front door of the terrace was a long, narrow hallway. The floors were polished boards, and ornate cornice ran the perimeter of the white ceiling. Alice stood at the end of the hallway and gestured to one of the rooms.

"It's so nice to have you at home, Andy," she beamed as we walked into the bedroom.

"Ahh, it's nice to be home," Andy said, as he swung his backpack on the bed.

The bedroom was a small room with a queen-sized bed, which took up most of the space. A bulky brown wardrobe was squashed into the back corner.

"Have you spent much time in Melbourne, Alexandra?" Alice asked.

I shook my head. "No, I've never visited Melbourne before." I forced a smile. She was a lovely woman, but I was in no mood to be social. I was exhausted and hungry, and my thoughts were only of The Aztec, Veronika and Boris. I wondered how Alice would have received me if she had known the danger I brought with me.

"Well," she clapped her hands, "Andy, you must take her out, show her around Melbourne's nightlife. Alexandra, you will love it here! Oh Andy, take her to the theatre. There are some great performances showing ..."

Andy cut her off before she was able to finish. "We are planning on going out for dinner tonight." He threw a quick sideways look at me.

Instantly, I knew he had no intentions of going to dinner; that would be ludicrous. As much as he loved visiting his family, and as much as I enjoyed meeting them, it was only being used as a via point; a place to rest and recuperate before we embarked on the next stage of the journey.

"Just hoping we could use the amenities before we do. It's been a long, hot drive from Warrangatta to here, and we could both do with a wash." He half laughed as he looked down at the filthy clothes we were wearing. "And a sleep. As comfortable as my car is, it is a car."

"Of course you can ..." Alice started, before Joe called from the lounge room, "Alice, honey. A phone call for you. It's Janine, something about the bake fair at Leroy's school." She smiled apologetically. "I have to take this. Andy, you know where everything is. Get Alexandra a towel ... make yourselves at home," she said promptly, as she hurried out the door.

As soon as she had left the room, I fell back onto the bed; it was soft and smelt of freshly washed linen. I meant only to lie there for a moment—to rest my eyes for just a second—but the moment my eyes closed, sleep took me.

****

Something woke me. It might have been Leroy calling out, or it might have been my imagination. Andy lay next to me, sleeping. He had pulled his shirt off during his sleep, and it lay across the bed. One of his arms was draped around me, and as I began to move, he tightened his grip. The bedroom door opened. I looked past Andy's resting body to see that it was Alice, holding a stack of clothes.

"Oh! I'm sorry. I didn't mean to wake you. Only, I noticed you didn't have any clothes with you, Alexandra. Here are some spares that should fit," she said as she sat them on the end of the bed.

Andy snored loudly, waking himself. He yawned as he wiggled around to his back.

"Mum? Jesus Christ!" he yelled loudly. "You enjoy watching people while they sleep? Scared me half to death," he griped as he rubbed his eyes.

"I'm sorry, dear. I was only bringing in some clean clothes for Alexandra ... I didn't mean to interrupt anything," she beamed, her eyes darting from him to me. "I'll leave you two alone." She almost skipped from the room.

"What is she talking about?" he asked as he rubbed his eyes.

"I think it has something to do with the fact you're half naked, and you had thrown yourself over me," I said as I stretched. "That was the best sleep I've had since we've left Warrangatta. I was too tired to dream."

"Yeah, well I had the weirdest dream! We were running through mountains and sailing across oceans; the whole thing was trippy. Oh, God!" he complained as he hung his arm over his eyes.

"What is it?"

"She thinks we're together!" he groaned. "She's going to be all 'cute' the entire time we're here now. She'll do everything but bring us breakfast in bed."

"I wouldn't complain about breakfast. Anything but those gross protein bars you fed me."

I had no sooner finished speaking when a knock came from the bedroom door. Alice pushed the door open and walked in, holding a large tray. On it were two glasses of orange juice and four pieces of toast.

"I know it's not breakfast time; I just thought you two might be hungry," she cooed, as she unfolded the legs under the tray and sat it across him.

I put my hand over my mouth as I tried not to laugh. Andy's face had turned bright red.

"Now, if there's anything else you two need, all you need to do is ask," she said sweetly.

I was too hungry to wait for her to leave the room. I leant across and took a piece of toast; it was only toast, but it was delicious.

"This is beautiful. Thank you, Alice," I said as I took a mouthful of orange juice.

"Anything at all," she continued. "If you need us to leave the house, we will—grandchildren would be wonderful." She clapped her hands together in front of her chest.

I couldn't help but half choke on my juice.

"Mum!" Andy complained.

"Alright, alright. I'll leave you two alone," she beamed as she swanned from the room.

"I'm sorry, Alex. She wouldn't have said anything like that if she knew what you've been through."

I didn't say anything. I just put my glass on the table and stared at it.

"Ally? Hey, are you okay?" he asked.

"Andy. He raped me." Suddenly, the gravity of what had happened hit me.

"Yes," he said with a flat voice. He lifted the table and put it on the floor by the side of the bed and turned back to face me.

"He *raped* me." The words slipped out before I could stop them. They felt foreign coming from me. Water began to burn behind my eyes.

"I know," he whispered.

"I don't how I should be feeling." I wrapped my arms around my stomach and hunched over; it was too much. "I'm pissed off mainly—at him ... at myself!"

He reached across and rubbed my back. "Keep going. You were so quiet in the car; I just figured you didn't want to talk about it, or anything else for that matter."

"I feel so humiliated." I could feel my throat tighten as the tide of unexpressed emotions welled within me, searching for release.

"Oh, Alex. Come here." He wrapped his arms around me and held me close.

I wasn't scared or uncomfortable in his arms—his embrace gave me strength and reassurance. I trusted Andy more than anybody in the world. "You have nothing to be humiliated about! Talk if you need to. I'm listening."

We lay there for a long time; Andy did listen without interruption. I spoke about everything—about how I was feeling at that moment and everything leading up to that moment.

"Are you feeling any better now?" he asked.

"I don't know if 'better' is the right word. I feel stronger. I can't really explain it. Thanks for listening."

"Ally, I'll be honest with you. When I opened my front door and saw you standing there like that ..." He paused for a moment as though memory pained him. "Ally, if I see him again, I am going to kill him. I don't know how, but he has to die." He spoke the words with such conviction there was no room for doubt. But how Andy could take on a man like Derrek, I didn't know.

"I know." I felt conflicted at the thought of Derrek being killed. I was sickened by what he had done to me; but, at the same time, I could not take any joy in the thought of him being dead.

"You're looking better. And the bruising has faded a fair bit." He gestured to my throat.

"Good. I'll take your word for it. I don't want to look at it. Anyway, your Mum said something about a shower?"

"I'll grab you a towel." He swung his legs over the bed and slowly stood to his feet. His body had broadened again.

"You've gotten bigger again." As I looked at him, I knew I should have been scared or, at the very least, intimidated by a half-naked man. I've heard that rape victims are often terrified of being in the same room as another man. I couldn't understand why I wasn't. Just thinking of The Aztec made my stomach knot, but that was where my fear ended; with him—The Aztec.

He looked down at himself. "Yeah I know. I don't know why. But I'm not complaining."

I lifted my arm to push my hair behind my ear.

"What is that?" Andy exclaimed.

"What is what?"

"Under your sleeve." He reached across and pulled back my sleeve.

"Oh my God!" I cried as I tried to scratch off a mark that looked like a tattoo. "It won't come off!"

He sat on the bed next to me, grabbed my arm and inspected it carefully.

"Stop scratching at it!" He pulled my hand away from the tattoo.

We sat in silence looking at the image that had appeared on my arm, before a sudden realisation hit me—I had seen this before. I looked up to Andy and said in a flat voice, "This mark is one of the symbols he has on the left side of his chest."

"It's okay, Alex. Don't be scared ..." Andy began, but I cut him short. It felt like a wave washed over me, taking all sense of fear from me.

"I'm not scared, Andy."

"What?"

"Right now, as we sit here, I am not scared. I was shocked to see the tattoo, mark, or whatever it is, but I'm not scared. Why aren't I scared? I should be terrified." Every word was true. It was like a switch had been flicked inside me. I felt more alert and alive than I had in a long time. "What's happening?"

He stared at me for a moment. "I don't know. What I do know is we can't stay here any longer. But if we just run out the door Mum and Dad will have a meltdown; they'll know something's up. So we'll have a shower, have something more to eat and then we'll leave—nice and casual. But Alex, casual is just the guise; we need to hurry!"

~ 13 ~

CHAPTER THIRTEEN

Our destination was on the fringe of Melbourne's central business district, which meant we had to pass through the heart of Melbourne. As such, we needed to switch trams four times until we got to where we needed to be. I had never seen trams before; they were a cross between a bus and a train. They had to run along their own tracks, and they each had a specific route to follow throughout the city and its outskirts. It was a 'simple' task of hopping on one until you reached the next tram stop for your interconnecting tram. I had never used public transport before and had no knowledge of Melbourne, so I just relied on Andy to ensure we made the right connections.

Our tram slowed as it approached our final stop just outside the main square in the heart of the busy central business area. The tram doors opened, and I stared in awe; thousands of rioters had taken over the square, their voices distorted as they yelled, desperately wanting to be heard above rivals.

"This is our stop." Andy spoke with reluctance. He didn't want to face the rioters either.

"How far away are we?" I was beginning to grow anxious the longer I watched the rioters.

"Just have to weave through these idiots and we'll be there," he said as he swung his backpack on his back.

I had intended carrying my bow through Melbourne, until Andy reminded me that carrying a deadly weapon through a capital city wouldn't go unnoticed, much less a city already on edge with rioters. So it sat almost completely hidden in his back-pack. Only the very edge was visible through the zipper, but it wasn't enough to identify it as a weapon. The Book, however, was strapped tightly to my stomach under the clean jeans and purple shirt Alice had given me.

As we stepped off the tram, the rioters' voices became audible; they were still proclaiming the cause of the sudden weather anomaly was of the government's making. I had seen brief news reports of the riots on television, but I hadn't expected anything like this. People littered the CBD waving signs and screaming obscenities. In the centre of the rioters, was a man standing on the top of a car, his long brown dreadlocks pulled back with a red rag. He was yelling to the adoring crowd about how nature must be preserved and how it was humans who were responsible for destroying the world.

"This way!" Andy yelled at me across the deafening roars of the rioters and pointed towards something.

I craned my neck and stood on my toes as I tried to see where he was heading, but I was too short. He was only a few inches taller than me, but it was enough to give him the advantage of being able to navigate through the sea of people. I reached out and clasped his hand tightly; I didn't want to become sepa-rated. As we pushed through the screaming rioters, I accidently stepped on several sets of bare feet. I stopped to apologise, but none of them reacted as they continued to yell and wave their banners in every direction.

"We're almost there," Andy breathed heavily, his brows were furrowed as he pulled me into an opening of a lane; a lane rioters hadn't yet filled.

I couldn't help but gasp as I turned to face the lane. It was lined with irregularly sized bluestone blocks and was pinched between two tall, dark, windowless buildings. I would normally never choose to walk through a lane such as this one.

"Come on," Andy said, as he adjusted his backpack on his back and began to walk down the ominously dark lane.

As I took several steps behind him, I glanced back to the square. The rioters were still screaming and waving their signs, but their voices didn't carry down the laneway. It was as though their voices were being caught by an invisible curtain at the entrance of the lane.

"What is this place?" I asked him, my voice sounding flat and empty.

He was already metres in front of me. I walked quickly to catch him, each footstep echoing down the dark, narrow lane. "Andy! Where are we?" I demanded, as I pulled his shoulder around to make him face me.

"We're here." Andy spoke softly.

We had reached a dark timber door, nestled within a solemn building. As he held his hand up to knock on the door, it swung open. A black-skinned woman stood in the doorway. She wore a bright orange scarf tied tightly around her head. A large round golden earring hung from each of her earlobes. Her dress was a combination of bright orange and pink—the colours flowed together majestically as the fabric twisted around her curvaceous body.

"You bring with you a great danger." She spoke with an accent, one I recognised instantly. And then I saw them—her eyes. Golden eyes.

"*You!* It's you!" I yelled. My body tingled with anger and shock. I couldn't believe who I was looking at. "This is all your fault!"

I lunged at her, but Andy pulled me back and pressed me against the bluestone wall. "What the hell, Alex?"

"It's her! She's the woman from the bus—the woman who gave me the Book!"

His face registered his shock. "No. It can't be."

I pushed him aside and strode toward her. "It is, isn't it? You're her? I will never forget those eyes and that voice. Why did you do this to me?"

"I asked you if you believed in destiny. You said yes." Her voice was as silky and disturbing as I remember it had been on the bus. "I also told you that my destiny was to alter yours."

"So you decide to give me a book that leaves a wake of devastation in its path? Because of you, I was raped. *Raped!* I had to run from my home!" A ball of anger was boiling in my chest.

"Raped? How is this possible? Andy, you were sent to protect her." Her golden eyes moved to Andy, who now stood by my side.

"Sent?" I turned to face him. His gaze was locked onto his feet. "Sent? Andy, what is she talking about?"

"You did not tell her?" the woman asked.

He put his hand into his pocket and pulled out a piece of paper. It was obvious that it had been folded and unfolded many times; it was dog-eared and crumpled. "Abde," he gestured to the woman in the doorway, "gave me this. She drew it. She told me you'd need my help, and it was imperative that *I* be the one to be there for you." His voice was shaking as he spoke. "Alexandra, I didn't tell you because, well ... how was I meant to?"

I took the paper from him and stared at it. My stomach knotted as nervousness began to bubble. "This is a drawing of me. It's dated before I arrived in Warrangatta." I paused as memories flooded back. "The first time we met, you acted strangely. You recognised me ..."

"Yes," he said in a flat tone.

"How could you keep this from me?" I demanded as I took a step backwards. It felt like the world around me was crumbling. The only person I trusted had been lying to me. "What else have you lied about?"

"Nothing! I swear to you." His eyes were wide, and his voice was thick with emotion.

"I *trusted* you!"

"Ally ..." He reached for my arm, but I pulled it away. I couldn't stand the thought of him touching me.

"You lied to me. Even after everything, you still lied to me! I'm not going anywhere with you." I turned to walk away.

"Alexandra! Wait!" he called from behind me. "Honestly, what would have you done if I had shown you this?"

I stopped and turned to face him, the ball of anger in my chest ready to explode.

"Really, Ally. Imagine if, just a day after you'd arrived in Warrangatta, I'd shown you this. You don't believe in the supernatural, Ally! You'd have thought I was a stalker or, or crazy, or something. And, I didn't really understand it myself ... I'm having trouble making sense of all this too. How do you think I feel? All I'm told is that I'm meant to help you, or save you, or something! I thought I'd go to Warrangatta, hang out there for a month or so and come home—I went there for a holiday. And when I saw you lying on the bed—you were real! I was on edge for so long! Every day I was on the lookout for something that might hurt you, but I had no idea what. And I missed it! He was right there! I could have stopped it all, but I missed it!" His voice had become thick with emotion. "You know me, Alexandra! Not just the 'big' things, you know every tiny thing about me. If you honestly think I'd be capable of hurting you ..." He couldn't finish his sentence.

"You could have told me a year after. You could have told me last night." I said. I was still too angry to fully appreciate his defence.

"Would you have come here?" His voice was cool and calm, unlike mine.

"Of course not!" I yelled before I could stop myself. My words hung in the air.

"Now, you have to see why I didn't tell you. We need to be here to find out what's going on."

Before I could respond, Abde grabbed my arm and pulled me through the door. "Come," she commanded.

"Let go of me!" I yelled as she dragged me through a room that was dark and cluttered. I was struck by the strong smell of incense in the air. Objects hung from the walls and ceiling, but it was impossible to distinguish what they were in the dim light. There was only a hint of moonlight sneaking through the tiny window in the door. Through the darkness, things moved in cages, and glistening eyes watched us as we moved further inside.

"Get off me!" I demanded again and tried to free my arm.

"Do you know who hunts you?" she asked as she turned on the spot. Her eyes were alive, to each their own soul.

"Yes." I feigned courage as I answered.

"Do you know what your hunters are capable of?" she whispered as she ran a long fingernail along the side of her face.

"Considering he raped me, yes, I have a fairly good idea." The words sprung from my mouth before I could stop them. It was like someone else was speaking for me.

She laughed loudly. "That is nothing, child. Those that hunt you are not human. They are capable of unspeakable acts.

"Why did you give me that book?" This time I couldn't disguise my shaking voice.

"'*Run as you might, escape if you may. Destiny with fate, wait shall they lay.*' You cannot escape who you are, Alexandra."

"And who is that?" I whispered, losing all volume to my voice.

"The only one who can stop them." She dropped my arm and walked through a wall of hanging beads. I followed her into a smaller room that was bathed in a dull yellow light cast by the small candles that ran the perimeter of the room. Skulls sat between each of the candles—most were animals, but several were undeniably human skulls. Variously coloured strips of materials covered the ceiling. The walls were covered in tapestries, their images flickering under the influence of the candlelight, giving the illusion they were alive.

I had to remind myself I didn't believe in witchcraft or anything supernatural.

Abde sat behind a round table draped in a white lace table cloth that spread across the top and fell to the ground. A deck of tarot cards lay fanned across the front of the table. In the centre of the table sat an opaque glass ball delicately balanced upon a brass stand of three legs.

"We have little time, child. Sit," she instructed.

"You're a fortune teller?" I scoffed as I looked around the room. "For a minute there I was actually worried, but you're just a con artist. You know I don't have any money to pay you?"

"Money? You will soon learn, nothing is without a price and those of monetary value are most insignificant of all. I do not want your money," she said as she began to shuffle the tarot cards.

The beaded curtain sounded as Andy entered the room. I was so conflicted as I looked at him. I trusted him above everyone, but he kept a secret like this from me. Deep down, I knew his reasoning was justified, but still, I couldn't shake the feeling of betrayal. For the moment, I ignored him and continued to push Abde. I could have it out with Andy later.

"No, then what do you want?" I folded my arms in defiance.

The candlelight reflected in her golden eyes. "Veronika, The Aztec ... they must be stopped."

"Yeah, that's great. How? I can't look at The Aztec without falling into a trance, and as for Veronika and Boris, I know nothing about them." I panted loudly. "Why would you give me that book? Of all the people in all the world, why me?"

She glared at me for a moment, her golden eyes alive as she studied me. "It is your destiny."

"Destiny? What destiny? To get killed?" I raised my voice higher than I intended.

She pulled a sideways smirk and reached an arm around either side of the glass ball to spread the cards face down across the table once again. Her actions were controlled and confident like she had faith in what she was doing.

"Take a card." She waved her hands across the cards, her long orange fingernails skimming over each one.

I tried to remind myself that I didn't believe in her supernatural nonsense, but felt compelled to go along with her request. I reached out to take a card when I heard his voice. I spun quickly, almost falling over the table as I searched through the darkness for him.

"What is it, child?" Abde stood to her feet as she looked through the darkness with me.

He said he would always find me and he would. I could feel him calling to me.

"It's him," I said in an uneven breath. I clasped my hand over my mouth as tears welled in my eyes. "He promised me he'd always find me." The new-found strength I thought I had, left me the moment I heard his voice.

She grabbed my arm, turned it over and pushed my sleeve up to my elbow to reveal the black, engraved tattoo.

"When did this appear?" she demanded. Her face was flat and stern as she traced her fingers along the tattoo.

"This morning." Panic was beginning to rise from my stomach and fill me entirely. "What's happening?" I pleaded.

"You are being taken." She released my arm and stepped back to her seat behind the table.

"Taken! What are you talking about?" Andy demanded.

Pain flashed through my head. I clapped my hand to my forehead and screamed as I lurched forwards. Andy grabbed me by my waist with both of his arms to stop me from falling. I wrapped my fingers around his arms as I waited for the pain to subside. I knew I was digging my nails into him, but I couldn't stop; the pain was too intense. The eyes appeared, staring at me. I knew it would be only seconds until they started filing through my memories again. Veronika would learn where I was. But they didn't. It took me a moment to realise that although her eyes were present in my mind, I was invisible to her. Then, just as quickly as they appeared, they disappeared. I lost all strength in my legs and fell towards the floor. Andy still had his arms wrapped around me, stopping me from hitting the floor. He put me on a chair and sat in the one next to me.

"What happened? Was it the eyes again?" he asked urgently, as he patted his hands over my body, checking for any anomalies.

"Yes. But she didn't see me. I'm still taking my meds but I think she's getting stronger." I knew she was getting stronger.

It wouldn't be long until she would have unrestricted access to my memories.

"Abde, you have to help." Andy turned to her.

She shook her head. "She is becoming his."

"Please! There has to be something ..." he pleaded with her.

Andy laced his fingers together and placed them on the top of his forehead. Blood was running down the sides of his arms from where my fingernails had ripped into his skin. A stabbing pain shot through my heart as I looked at him standing there pleading with Abde on my behalf.

Abde looked quickly from Andy to me, the whites of her eyes shining under the candlelight. "I need a drop of your blood," she told me. There was something sinister behind her golden eyes.

"Why?" I asked.

"Wait, why do you need her blood? You can have mine." Andy held up his bleeding arm. She held my eyes with her gaze. "It is in your blood where your darkest secrets are re-lived. Your blood passes through your heart; it knows of your deepest love and the hatred that lingers there. It passes through your mind, it knows the thoughts you hide in the darkness, the thoughts you would have no one else see, the thoughts you would hide from yourself. And it knows of your deepest lusting desires. The desires you would only dare indulge in your darkest, wildest dreams. It is in your blood where I will find the answers that you seek, Alexandra," she said as she pulled a long, pointed dagger from under the cloaked table.

She held the tip of the dagger to her index finger and held the handle in the palm of her other hand.

I flinched at the sight of the dagger. I hated knives and swords; almost everything with a blade made me shudder.

"Is there a problem?" she asked.

"No. No problem," I answered as I gingerly held out my hand.

"Not from your hand," she said slowly. "From your throat."

"My throat?" I asked, stunned. I didn't have to be a fortune teller to be able to predict what would happen if my throat was cut.

"I need the blood from your throat because it is there your words slip past. But I cannot take your blood; it must be taken by someone you love and who loves you equally in return." Abde spun the dagger in her hand to hold the blade in her fingers. Her eyes moved from me to Andy.

His eyes widened as he looked to the dagger and back to her. "What? You want me to cut her throat? There's no way! I'll kill her!" He waved his hands across each other in refusal.

"It is the only way," she told him, her arm remaining outstretched, holding the dagger.

He looked to me, his eyes welling up. "Alexandra, there is no way I am doing this. We will figure something else out. We'll find someone else." He pushed his chair out and stood.

I grabbed his hand. "There's no time, Andy. I can feel him calling me. I can see her searching for me. Andy, please, you don't have to cut deep, just a little nick."

"No. No. I won't do it. Alexandra, I could kill you." Tears were running down his cheeks. I had never seen him cry before.

I reached out and took both his hands in mine; his palms were sweating. "I love you. You've told me before, but I've never told you ... I trust you more than anyone on this Earth. You brought me here because you knew Abde could help us. You trust her. Please, do this."

"Ally, don't ask me to. If I slip ..." His hands tightened around mine.

"You won't." I sat back in my seat.

My long hair hung around my shoulders and flowed down my chest. I pulled it away and draped it over the back of my seat.

Andy took the dagger from Abde and looked to her for re-assurance. "Once her blood covers the blade, you must give the dagger to me immediately." She touched the back of his hand and gave a slow nod.

He stood behind me. As I leant my head on his belt line, I could feel his hard, metallic, buckle press against the back of my head. I looked up to his face, which showed the tension and fear the task held for him. I drew a smile across my face; if it were anyone else holding that dagger, I would have been terrified, but not with Andy. My anger at him had passed. I knew with certainty I could trust Andy, despite his well-intentioned deception.

He cupped his hand under my chin and pushed my head further into his belt. His hand was sweating, but his fingertips were cold. He slowly raised his other hand with the dagger. He looked at me one more time. I had seen that same face before; it was the face I saw when Tess had walked back into the hospital, when I was praying for her to change her mind. This time it was him praying for me to change mine, but there was no way I was going to. I couldn't live a life of hiding in fear. I spread a smile across my face again and gave a small nod. I closed my eyes and waited for the dagger blade to touch my throat. I heard him suck in his breath and then push it out quickly, steeling himself for what he was about to do. Then I felt it; the blade was cold against my skin. I dug my fingers into the seat and pinched my eyes closed as the blade dragged across my throat. I could feel the warm blood begin to run down my neck as the blade slipped along my skin.

"There," he said, as he pulled the dagger away from me. "That's it."

I opened my eyes and sat forward, then took the white cloth Abde held out to me and placed it gently against my throat. I looked down at my body, expecting it to be covered in blood, but there was none. Andy had cut me just beneath the skin.

"Give it to me," Abde told Andy, as she held out her hand for the dagger.

Andy passed it to her then sat back down heavily on his seat, his face drained of colour. I leant across, rubbed the back of his hand and mouthed the words, "I'm fine."

I looked back to watch Abde. She pinched the blade with her fingers and thumb, slipping the blood from the blade and landing it on the glass ball that sat in the centre of the table. The blood fell through the top of the ball and stopped in the centre, levitating. Countless drops followed, all falling through the glass and stopping in the centre of the ball. I lurched forward, gasping as the last of my blood fell through the glass. I felt my body change; it was alive but being controlled by someone other than me.

"Alexandra!" Andy jumped from his seat and reached out to me.

"Do not touch her!" I heard Abde order.

He looked to her and back to me, before slowly retracting his hands from me and sitting down again.

"I see you, Alexandra." Abde ran her fingers over the glass ball, her fingernails scratching the glass lightly. I could feel her dragging my blood through my veins. There was no pain, but it felt uncomfortable; like a dull and persistent ache.

Inside the ball, an image appeared. It was him—The Aztec. He was wearing black cargo pants and a tight black shirt, exposing his defined body. His face was firm and unfaltering; his stride was purposeful and strong. In his left hand, he held a Nimcha sword.

The image twisted and vanished into swirling smoke and turned into Veronika and Boris before dissipating. Then, just as quickly, the smoke returned to reveal Veronika and Boris again. Veronika wore a long, red leather jacket over dark clothes and high black boots. Boris wore loose brown pants and a white shirt.

I could feel Abde pulling my blood past my heart. "Your heart does not worry for Veronika or Boris who *do* hunt you avidly. Nor does it hold concern for the Book that you hold to your body. It longs for only one. You are in love, Alexandra," Abde cooed.

I was immobile, unable to speak, but a vivid image of Michael filled my mind. I would always love him.

"It is true; you will always love Michael. But your love for him is a dying fire; only warm coals remain. You are in love with another, and this love burns wildly; it is uncontrollable." Her eyes widened as she spoke.

The swirling smoke cleared revealing him kissing me in the staff room. As I watched it, I could feel his lips press against mine. I could feel his rough hands run over my body. The scent of him flowed in my nose and consumed my lungs. I could feel him calling to me, drawing me to him.

"He is hunting you. He *will* he find you; he will claim you as his own, and through the endless struggle to escape him, you will love him. You will love him until you draw your single last breath." She looked up to me, her eyes shining under the candlelight.

"What do they want? Why are they hunting her? Is it just because of the Book? We'll give it to them if that's all they want." Andy pleaded.

"You do not wish for them to come into possession of The Book of Narveere, nor the Bow of Dria. Yes ... The bow and the Book are one and the same. They have come together in you, Alexandra. Perhaps this is by chance, or perhaps it is your pre-ordained destiny. This is why they hunt you. All that lives within the Book and the bow is flowing into you. This is why you can touch them without becoming burned. This is why Veronika so desperately wants you. She wishes to separate you from the Book and the bow. Should the ones who hunt you come into possession of these items, all that you hold dear will be destroyed. With the Book *and* the bow, the wielder can obtain absolute power."

"Once they figure out Alex has the bow and the Book, they'll just come and take it. How are we meant to stop them?" Andy cried.

"These objects cannot be taken. They must be given."

"So we just don't give them!" Andy argued.

Her golden eyes fixated on Andy. "The power of these objects cannot exist within a mere human. These objects will kill Alexandra. You must sever the connection."

A pair of blue eyes appeared in the ball—Veronika's eyes. I looked into them, and they looked straight back. This time I was not invisible to her. I could feel her trying to reach me. She wanted to know where I was. I tried to pull away but could not. I tried to close my eyes against her, but could not.

A gust of wind burst through the door and swirled through the room, extinguishing the candles, leaving the room in almost complete darkness. I slumped into my seat, no longer frozen. Abde's hold on me had ended.

Abde jumped to her feet and threw a cloak over the ball. "You must leave now." She scribbled something on a small piece of paper.

"How do I stop them? How do I sever the connection?" I asked, as I too jumped to my feet.

"Death is the only separator," she told me as she passed the folded piece of paper to me. I took the paper and stuffed it in my jeans' pocket.

"Where do we go now?" I pleaded with her. "What do we do now? How can we hide?"

"There is no time!" She landed her hands on either of my shoulders. "You must leave here—they have found you." She moved across to one of the tapestries and pulled it aside, revealing the small door that was concealed behind it.

"Quickly! This will lead you to the square. Become hidden as soon as you can."

"Thank you, Abde." I said as I walked towards the door. "I'm sorry that I didn't believe you ..." I didn't get to finish my sentence before she pushed me through the door.

A second later Andy stood by my side in the square. The rioters hadn't let up; they still dominated the square. My mind was a blur with all that had happened, but my body was fuelled by adrenaline as it responded to my instinct to flee. All I wanted to do was run; run in any direction. Andy started to speak to me, but I wasn't listening. A gentle breeze had blown past, carrying a faint smell. I was still disorientated and couldn't focus on where I recognised it from. I looked up for a moment, trying to gain a stronger smell of the scent. It brought back an anxious feeling, but I couldn't pinpoint what it was. I squinted as I tried to recall the faint aroma. Another breeze rolled past with the same fragrance. I turned my head to the air and took in a deep breath. It hit me—the memory came flooding back; the smell was of him when he was in my home. I stood completely still and stared across the far side of the square; on the other side of the rioters stood The Aztec, staring straight back at me. My eyes were wide and watery as I watched him staring at me. I closed my eyes as I replayed his words in my head. *I will find you; I will always find you. You belong to me.* He had found me. A tear rolled down my cheek, as I watched him start to push through the sea of people. His eyes were fixed on me. He had found me, and this time he would ensure I did not escape.

I grabbed at Andy's shirt, pulling it several times. "Andy," I whispered.

"What?"

"The Aztec." I don't know if I spoke his name or if I only thought it.

It was too late. He had taken me. I could feel the smell of exotic islands fill my lungs and flow through my veins. I tried to pull away from him, but he had consumed me. I could see nothing but him, feel nothing but him. The square faded away, as did the rioters. The only audible noises were running waterfalls and distant dancing. I could feel the spray of the waterfalls hit my hot skin, as excitement danced through the night air. I knew he had taken me. I tried to scream at myself that I was still standing in the square, that what I was seeing and feeling wasn't real, but my voice of reason was subdued by the burning desire to be taken by him. Abde was right—I loved him.

"Alexandra!" Andy yelled, as his face appeared in front of mine, blocking my view of The Aztec and severing the connection between him and me temporarily.

My eyes came back into focus; I was standing in the square again. I knew I had only seconds to flee whilst the connection was severed. I turned and ran down a nearby alley, which had begun to fill with people. Andy was right behind me. I could hear him throwing tables and chairs to the ground in hopes of hindering The Aztec's pursuit.

"What the bloody hell's happening?" Andy yelled as we ran through the slender path between the tables that lined both sides of the alley.

"The Aztec! Just run!" I cried, as I pushed a man to the ground as I ran past him. I didn't stop to see if he was hurt—I just kept running.

"Where? I don't see him," Andy called back.

"Just keep running! He's there!"

Andy pulled me into an alcove. "Put this on," he demanded as he pulled his jacket off and threw it at me.

"What? Why?"

"Quickly!" he snapped.

I pulled on his jacket.

"And this!" He slapped his cap on my head and pulled the jacket hood over my head. "Aim for the red warehouse on the other side of the square."

"What warehouse? What are you talking about?"

"If you saw him, he saw us. He'll be on the lookout for us—together. Not to mention your red hair is that noticeable you might as well have a neon light flashing above your head. There's a red warehouse on the other side of the square; I'll meet you there." He peered out from the alcove. "Straight through the middle, Alex. Just blend in."

"No, you can't leave me!" I felt like a child begging a parent to stay. "He'll take me ..."

"This *is* the only way. You'll be fine." He kissed my cheek and disappeared around the corner.

I pressed my hand to my face. I could still feel his stubble on my skin.

Just as I was about to step out, a flash of blue whirled in front of my eyes. I knew in an instant what was coming next, and I had no way of stopping it. I fell to my knees and braced myself for the searing pain that would follow. Her eyes appeared, and they looked straight into me. There was no veil protecting me from her, so she could see whatever she pleased. But she drew up one memory—my current location. And in an instant, she was gone.

~ 14 ~

CHAPTER FOURTEEN

As the pain subsided, I stumbled to my feet and out from the alcove. There was no sign of The Aztec, and Andy was lost to the crowd, but it was imperative he be warned. Veronika and Boris knew our location! Rioters still filled the square, obscuring any chance of me seeing Andy.

"Andy!" I screamed, but my voice disappeared through the yelling rioters. "Andy! Where are you?" I screamed again, hoping my voice would miraculously travel over the chaotic noise.

I spun on the spot, desperately trying to find him. He had to be alive; he had to be unharmed. Just the thought of him being dead was too much to bear. I knew it was foolish, but I did it before I could stop myself—I stood on the top of a car next to me. I knew as I climbed to the top, I was doing little but giving away my location, but I had to see Andy. I had to scour the square for him. He could not be dead while I lived.

I scanned the people with squinted eyes. Everybody looked the same in the dimly lit square.

"Alexandra! What are you doing? Get down, you friggin' idiot!"

I looked down. Andy was pulling at my legs for me to climb down from the car.

I jumped down and landed awkwardly next to him. I was bursting with emotion as I threw my arms around him. "They're here!" I cried.

"Who? Who's here?"

"Veronika and Boris! She looked into my mind again."

"We need to get out of here. Come on!" He grabbed my hand and began to push through the rioters.

As we pushed further through the crowd, we passed two policemen who were talking on their radios. Apparently, another riot on the other side of Melbourne had gotten out of control and rioters had stormed buildings, leaving many injured or dead.

An explosion sounded from behind us, shaking the ground and instantly filling the air with dust. We both spun around, trying to see the source of the explosion, but our view was obstructed completely as people began to scream and run in all directions.

Police, holding riot shields and armed with batons, forced themselves through the panicking crowds, trying to direct the crowd away from the explosion site. They were yelling instructions, but no one was obeying.

Andy tightened his grip on my hand as we pushed through the crowd. People had fallen to the ground and were being trampled. I went to bend down to help them up, but Andy pulled my arm hard. "Don't! You'll go down yourself," he yelled.

I watched as the people who were lying on the ground slowly stopped moving as countless numbers of feet crushed them.

"That red warehouse!" He pointed to the other side of the square. "If we split up, meet there!"

Another explosion sent a shockwave through the square, throwing both Andy and I back on the hard cement. Our hands slipped apart from each other, but I could still see him. He was pushing himself back to a standing position before he was crushed by another stampede of people. I pushed myself up off the ground, trying to regain balance.

"Andy!" I screamed. I turned frantically trying to see him, but the sea of people swallowed him. "Andy!" I cried again, but it was useless. I could barely hear my own voice, much less someone a distance away.

I pushed through people who were still dazed from the explosion. I saw something red in my peripheral vision. I stopped and turned toward it. Veronika and Boris! I stared at them, and they stared straight back. I turned and ran faster through the crowd, now not caring if I pushed other people to the ground. I glanced back to see if they were in pursuit. To my relief, they had disappeared. I closed my eyes for a second and breathed deeply. When I opened them again, Veronika stood directly in front of me with Boris by her side. I stopped running only inches before I collided with her. Her eyes were just as cold and as empty as they were when they ploughed through my mind.

"Do you recognise me now, Alexandra?" She pursed her lips victoriously.

"Yes. You're Veronika." I swallowed hard. I had played out countless scenarios of my reaction when I finally met her, but I was so stricken with fear that I lost each and every one of them.

"What do you want?" I could feel tears form behind my eyes as I struggled now with my predicament and prayed that Andy was somewhere—alive. A group of rioters smashed their way between me, Veronika and Boris. I made a dash for the opening. As soon as I did, the gap was once again closed with people. I still had no idea where Andy was, but we had agreed on a meeting spot if we did get separated, so I ran towards the warehouse. I didn't allow myself to think of the possibility of him being dead.

I had almost made it across the square when I felt something burn my shoulder, and the person in front was sprayed with blood. I wasn't sure what had happened until another burning sensation raced through my other shoulder. I looked down to see blood pouring from each of my shoulders.

I turned to see who the shooter was. Veronika stood with her arms folded; Boris held a gun, which he was still pointing at me. I stumbled backwards as they approached. Veronika reached out and swiftly pushed my chest, causing me to fall on the hard cement.

"Hold her," she instructed Boris.

He walked behind me and pushed his big hands onto my shoulders sending paralysing pain through my body. He wrapped his hands under my arms and pulled me to a standing position.

Veronika was holding a knife. It, too, had unfamiliar engravings along the long, slender blade. The handle had two curved pieces of metal that contoured her hand perfectly. She held the blade to the side of my face. The scar on my throat caught her attention. With the end of the knife, she traced the line of the shallow cut along my throat. I closed my eyes as I felt the edge of the blade touch my skin. Knives to me were like spiders to arachnophobes.

"Where did cut come from?" she asked, her eyes focused firmly on my throat.

I didn't answer. I didn't want them to hurt Abde, but mostly I didn't want them learning anything more. Veronika pulled a small bag from inside her jacket. It was made of black leather. She held it dangling from her forefinger.

"A gift to you." She angled her head as she spoke. "I want to make clear our relationship." She pulled her red lipstick-covered lips to a half smile and handed me the small bag.

I slowly reached my arm out to take it, but pain surged through my shoulders. I bit the inside of my lip to stop from crying out.

"Open it," she smiled.

I looked down at the small black leather bag. She couldn't possibly think a trinket could forgive what she had done. I opened the drawstring and slipped my hand inside the bag; the contents were round and slippery. I pulled them from the bag. In my hand were two golden eyes—Abde's eyes.

Veronika took another step closer to me. "Now, you understand?" She lifted one eyebrow. "Do not stand between me and what I want. If you do, all you care for shall die." She lifted the knife to the side of my face and stabbed the very tip into my cheek. I could feel my warm blood trickle down the side of my face.

"Give to me The Book of Narveere," she hissed.

"I don't have it!" I spat at her. I had no idea of the Book's purpose, but one thing had become irrefutably clear; the Book must *not* come to be in her possession.

She curled her lip and gave Boris a nod. He squeezed my shoulders, causing searing pain to run through my arms and down my body. I lurched forward as my knees gave way to the pain. Veronika laughed as she watched me grimacing as I tried to hold back from crying.

"What purpose does Book serve to you? Give Book to me and you and your Andy can live long life with many children," she cooed.

"I don't have the Book you psycho bitch." I snarled through gritted teeth. I refused to let them see me cry. "And even if I knew where it was, I'd never give it to you." I don't know where the words came from—they weren't my words. I'd never antagonise someone like Veronika. Something changed inside me. Something 'clicked.' A fury began to burn somewhere deep inside me.

She pointed the knife directly beneath my chin. "You are beautiful woman, Alexandra. Boris loves to play with beautiful women."

Boris pressed his face against my face, breathing heavily in my ear, his foul breath sliding past my cheek to my nose. My stomach knotted as I thought of The Aztec forcing himself on me.

"Boris is very obedient. Give Book to me and I tell him to stop ..." She stopped as she suddenly gasped and lowered her knife. She took a step back and looked toward her stomach; a crossbow bolt had been buried deep into her back and protruded through her stomach.

Andy!

Veronika stumbled backwards a few steps, and for a moment I felt victorious thinking she had been defeated—until she looked up through her dark blue eyes and smiled with one side of her mouth. She wrapped both her hands around the head of the bolt, and in a swift manoeuver, pulled the bolt from her body. She held the blood-covered bolt in one hand and studied it. It wasn't a bolt that came with my bow; it was a broad head that Andy had ordered from the internet. Those bolts are designed for maximum damage. It should have killed her.

"You are going to have to do better, my sweet." She turned to face Andy. He had wrapped his shirt around the bow to avoid being burned and held the bow poised directly at her.

She swung her knife around her fingers as she marched toward him. He let another bolt fly towards her, but her body came apart and flew as a hundred black crows and reassembled instantly; the bolt had completely passed through her and she remained unharmed. Andy lowered the bow, his mouth agape.

The bolt that had passed through Veronika had stabbed through the Book that still sat neatly at my stomach. I gingerly looked up to Boris; his eyes were fixed on Veronika as he held a victorious smirk across his face. He hadn't noticed the bolt that protruded from me. I slowly inched my fingers closer and closer to the bolt. I bit my tongue hard to stop from crying out in pain as I moved my arms. I wrapped my fingers around the end of the bolt and pulled it from the Book. I paused a moment to ensure Boris didn't become suspicious. I looked up to Veronika and Andy. He still held the crossbow poised at her as she moved her way closer to him. I twisted the bolt in my hand and stabbed it through Boris's thick neck. He instantly let go of me, and without thinking I grabbed the gun that hung from his belt, aimed it at Veronika and prayed I hit her somewhere.

"Andy, run!" I screamed as loudly as I could.

Without a moment's hesitation he threw himself from the bullet's trajectory, and I pulled the trigger. The bullet flew through the air with immense velocity and hit her in the head with her blood covering a nearby wall. Neither of us waited to see if that had killed her. Andy and I both ran into the red warehouse, slamming the door behind us. I fell against the tall, rickety wooden doors. My shoulders drew heavily on my body, as my arms hung limp by my side.

"What now?" I asked. We had eluded them once; they would not allow it twice.

"I dunno," Andy panted loudly.

He was still without a shirt; he had wrapped it around his hands so he could touch my crossbow. I had seen how easily the bow burned his skin, and I wanted to take the bow from him, but I could barely support my own weight, much less wield a crossbow.

I lay heavily against the doors, looking around the empty warehouse for anything that could be used either as a hiding spot or a weapon; the warehouse was completely empty. I did have a clear advantage, though—I still held Boris's gun in my blood-soaked hand.

We both heard a tram ringing its bell as it rumbled along the tracks behind the warehouse. That was to be our escape.

"Can you make it?" Andy asked breathlessly.

I nodded. I needed to make it to the tram. If I didn't, death would be only minutes away. I had no idea whether the bullet had claimed Veronika's life, and after what we had just witnessed, I was doubtful. Regardless of Veronika's life status, one thing was certain—Boris would not stop hunting us.

Andy bent to his knees and pulled his shirt over the bow to disguise the weapon. The last thing we needed was to be arrested for carrying weapons on public transport, especially with all the rioters who were still storming the city.

"Here, put this in your backpack." I held out the gun to him. He put out his hand to take it from me but stopped and retracted his hand.

"What's wrong?"

"It's got symbols on it. God only knows what those symbols will do to me." He swung his back pack off, unzipped it and I tossed the gun in the bag.

The tram rang its bell again to tell all passengers it was about to leave.

"Come on! We can't miss it!" I yelled. Although I was speaking to Andy, I was more yelling at myself. I had no option but to make it to the tram.

The tram had begun to close its doors just as we reached it. Andy forced himself through the doors, levering them open again. He reached for my arm and pulled me inside as the tram rumbled to speed. The action caused excruciating pain. "Get down!" Andy pulled at my side, making me fall to the floor. "Stay here! They didn't see us get on the tram," he hissed. I tried to nod my head but I wasn't sure if I achieved it or not.

Other commuters, who were already on edge, made no attempt to hide their suspicion at the arrival of two people throwing themselves onto the tram, one with blood pouring from her shoulders and the other half naked. I sat with my back against one of the walls of the tram, barely able to hold my consciousness, as blood continued to spill from my shoulders. Andy sat next to me and gently pulled my shirt from my shoulders to examine the extent of my wounds.

"We're not on our usual route, past the hospital, son." The tram driver called from the front of the tram. "We're on clear evacuation instructions. This is the final tram out of the city."

"Fine. Just go!" he yelled to the driver. He turned back to me and whispered, "Shit! You really do need a hospital."

"Young man, why don't you just call an ambulance?" a small, elderly lady called from a few seats down. She was leaning forward on her seat, clutching her handbag tightly.

Andy shook his head. "We can't, the riots are out of control ..."

"You're one of the rioters?" a middle-aged man with a long white beard and a pot belly asked furiously.

Andy shook his head again. "No. We're not from Melbourne; we're from Warrangatta and had no idea what we were walking into. The rioters—they've gone insane—we were just trying to get to a friend's house and the only way through was through the city centre, where the riots are. We heard police on radios saying the rioters had gotten out of control; I don't even know how this tram got through—the entire city has gone into lock down. So even if we did call an ambulance they'd never be able to get here; but, she does need a hospital"

I shook my head and whispered, "I can't. Even if we somehow made it to one, they will find us there—you know that."

He bit his bottom lip nervously as he looked at me. "There's a lot of blood, Ally."

"I know." I closed my eyes. They were too heavy to keep open.

"Alexandra!" He shook my body.

I sprung my eyes open and looked around panicked. I thought we had been found.

He sat back against the wall. "Don't do that," he breathed. "I thought you were dying."

I took his hand in mine, blood quickly running down my hand and soaking his. "Nah, it's just a flesh wound." I laughed. "Just like on all the movies. There's always a doctor nearby where the main character gets hurt."

His eyes lit up. "That's it. Is there a doctor here?" he yelled loudly as he wrapped his arms around me and lifted me to a nearby seat.

"What are you doing? Are you mad?" I hissed at him. How could we begin to explain how I suffered these injuries?

"My friend, she was caught in the crossfire back at the riots. Please, can someone help?"

Such a simple alibi, but it hadn't crossed my mind.

A young Asian woman stood up. "I medical student," she said shyly.

Andy moved to her. "My friend, she's been shot in both shoulders. I can't see how bad it is." He pointed towards me.

She pushed past Andy and moved to sit next to me.

"Suravi." She pointed to herself.

"Hi Suravi. I'm Alexandra." I slowly patted my chest.

"I look?" She hovered her hands over my shoulders, as she waited for me to accept her.

I nodded as best as I could, every movement exhausting.

She pulled back the sides of my shirt and inspected the wounds. I could feel her cool fingers as they gently pressed against my exposed flesh. I clenched my teeth together and squeezed my fingers in a tight fist to try to stop from screaming out. She held up her fingers in a circle and pushed another of her fingers through, indicating the bullets had gone straight through.

Andy bounced on his feet as he nervously deciphered her movements. "Um, bullets gone right through? Is that a good thing?"

"Yes. Good," she nodded.

"Good." He intertwined his fingers and ran his hands over his head as he paced on the spot.

The Asian woman stood up and spoke loudly in her language, looked around the tram and spoke again. No one responded. She turned to Andy as she mimicked the action of sewing. Andy was quick to understand. "Stitches!" he said.

He turned to the passengers. "Does anyone here have anything she could use to stitch my friend's shoulders?"

All I could do was watch, as he walked quickly up and down the tram, pleading with the passengers for any form of thread that could be used. The elderly woman, who had questioned our reasoning for not attending a hospital, opened her large bag and pulled out a small floral case.

"Young man?" She called him over. "There might be something in here."

He snatched the case from her and frantically searched through it, a moment passing before he pulled out a needle and roll of thread.

"Thank you! Thank you!" he cried as he moved back to where I lay. "This will work, won't it?" he pleaded with the Suravi, as he handed her the open floral case.

She frowned as she pulled a needle from the case, inspecting it carefully. She looked up at Andy and imitated moving of smoking.

"What! You want a cigarette?"

She rolled her eyes and pushed him backwards as she stood up. Clearly she had little patience for his inability to understand what she was trying to communicate.

The man standing nearby, pulled out a cigarette packet from his pocket. Suravi moved towards him, pointed to the packet and made a clicking sign with her fingers. The man quickly understood she wanted a lighter. She nodded and took the lighter he offered. She came back to sit next to me and then used the flame of the lighter to sterilize the needle. She clicked the lighter a few times until a flame erupted and held the needle above it.

"Sterilize! Of course." Andy ran his hand over his face, furious at himself that he wasn't able to decipher her meaning quickly.

She pulled the thread from the case and inspected each of them carefully. She mimed she had no way of sterilizing the thread.

"Just stop her from bleeding to death. We'll deal with infection later."

An enormous sound roared through the tram, making it shake on the tracks. Initially I thought it was a huge roaring clap of thunder, but as I looked out the window a layer of thick dust billowed into the street, obscuring any vision of the outside world.

"Another explosion! It was only a couple of blocks from here!" one of the passengers yelled. He was a boy, no older than fifteen, sixteen at the most. He clutched a school bag tightly as he crouched by the window, peering out of it.

"Holy shit! Everyone, make sure you're seated. I can hardly see through this," the driver yelled.

Several people clasped their hands to their chests as they prayed quietly to themselves. For the first time, I wished I had a God to pray to.

"Alex. Look at me," Andy said.

I think his voice was clear and stern, but it became muffled as it flowed into my ears.

He grabbed either side of my head and tilted it towards him. "Alex can you hear me?"

I reached my hand out and touched the side of his face. "Your eyes are brown. They're beautiful," I said as I ran my thumb along his cheek.

"What? Ally, stay with me. Don't start talking like that." Although his voice was muffled, I could hear the panic in it.

I looked at him as I tried to understand his fear. I wasn't scared anymore. I felt warm and my extremities tingled. And somewhere deep within me, I knew it was only moments until I would see Michael again.

"I'm going to see Sasha. Do you think she's grown up?" I smiled as I stared vaguely into nothingness.

"What? Alexandra! Look at me!" he demanded. "Look at me!" He shook my head as he spoke.

I tried to speak to him, but I couldn't. My head felt light and fuzzy. I could feel the darkness beginning to take me. Andy was screaming at me but his voice was silent.

He grabbed each side of my face and yelled at me. "You listen to me! You got me into this shit. You are not going to leave me to clean up *your* mess!" I saw him turn to Suravi. "Just get it done! Don't worry about being neat or careful. Just stop her from bleeding!" he demanded of her.

Suravi's face appeared above my own, and poised herself with the needle in hand. I closed my eyes and tried to think of anywhere else. I brought to mind me sitting on the top of Barri-

Barri, staring out at the sky. I could feel her push my wound together, her fingers slipping across my skin from the blood. I forced myself to remember the gentle water of Warrimudga flowing over my naked body as I stood beneath the waterfalls. Andy's hands pressed harder into me, stopping my body from moving, as Suravi pulled the needle through my skin. His hands pushed so hard on my chest I could hardly breathe. Before I could stop it, a cry of pain flew from my mouth, and my sight blurred in and out.

Andy eventually pulled his hands from me, while she pulled my shirt back across my chest. I went to sit forward but was met with painful resistance. Not only did my wounds hurt, the stitches pulled aggressively at my skin. Andy quickly slipped his hands around my back and took my weight as I sat forward.

She tucked the needle into the side of the roll of thread and handed it to me. I bent my elbow just enough so I could take it from her. An overwhelming realisation flooded me; the injuries I wore at that moment were only the beginning of what was to come. I would need to use the thread again, or perhaps I wouldn't, because the next injury I sustained might be my last. I laid my head back on the head rest. "Thank you," I said quietly to Suravi. She nodded once without smiling, collected the small floral bag and walked back to her seat, handing the elderly lady back her bag as she passed.

Andy sat beside me as the tram rumbled along the tracks. "How do you feel?"

"Tired. I know I should be scared, but I'm too tired to feel anything."

"Any wonder with the amount of blood you lost." He stopped short and whispered, "She—Veronika—turned into hundreds of crows when I shot her."

"You saw that too? I thought I must have been imagining it!"

He stared at the back of the seat in front. "What the hell are we dealing with, Alex?"

"I dunno." Such a pathetic answer, but it's all I could muster.

"Abde confirmed our theories, and back there with Veronika, there's no way you can say there's logical answer ... this shit is supernatural. We need to go back to Abde. She could tell us where to go from here. But, I'm not sure the best way to get there; it's not safe."

"Abde's dead ...Veronika," I said. There was no easy way to tell Andy, and I had no energy to break it to him gently.

He took a quick breath in at the shock. I expected him to speak, ask how or what happened, but he didn't; he just continued to stare at the back of the seat with a blank expression.

I couldn't look at him anymore. She was dead because of me. How many more people might die because of me? I rolled my head on the head rest to look out the window. Melbourne was crumbling. Rioters had stormed most of the city leaving a path of devastation in their wake. Cars that had been left parked on the road side had been vandalised, and shops had their windows smashed with much of their merchandise stolen. I knew it wasn't just the rioters. They were just demonstrating against something they felt strongly about. It was other people who were using them as a ploy to pillage the city.

"Hey, Andy. I think we should make this our stop," I said quietly, not wanting to raise alarm with the other passengers.

"No. We should get as far from the CBD as possible. We'll circle back to my parent's house, get my car and Spud. We'll figure out where to go from there."

"Andy. Look around. There isn't anyone out there." I whispered so quietly I hardly moved my lips. "It means we shouldn't be here. I bet there's going to be a blockade up ahead, which means they'll want us to go somewhere 'safe.' That means they'll have to search us ..."

"They'll see the bow and the Book." He finished my sentence for me. "Not something we can explain, exactly. They'll confiscate them for sure."

"We need to get off the tram."

"Then what?" he asked, as he craned his neck to look through the windows to the collapsing city.

I bit my lip as I considered our options. "You once told me that anyone can be found on the internet."

"Yes, that's right." He frowned.

"The Persivals—Abde couldn't help us with our next move, but I bet they will be able to."

"I've searched for them. I told you that."

"Yes, but you also said you have a friend in Melbourne, that same one you sent the pictures of the Book to. You said he had some super fantastic computer."

"The speed of a computer doesn't alter the content on the internet, Alex."

"No," I said quickly. "I mean you two are hockers. Between you, surely you could come up with something."

He smiled a gentle smile at me. "Hackers, not hockers. And yeah, but I just think it's a waste of time. I've looked."

"Give me a better suggestion then," I sighed.

He bit the end of this thumb as he thought of any other solution. Eventually he stood up and reached for the cord that ran the length of the tram to the driver's cab. "We're here," he called out to the driver as he pulled on the cord to tell the driver to stop.

"Are you bloody mad?" the driver called out.

Andy didn't say anything as he just pulled on the cord twice more. The passengers held mixed emotions on their faces—some appeared relieved at our departure. Suravi frowned with worry as we stepped towards the tram door.

Once the tram was stationary, Andy helped me down the steps to the tram stop. The driver watched us for a moment, ensuring we didn't change our mind. Once he was satisfied we weren't getting back on the tram, he shook his head in disapproval and pressed the button to close the tram doors. We stood by the rails of the tram stop as we watched the tram disappear through the haze of dust. The street was deserted apart from the tram that rumbled down the tracks. On either side of the road were brick buildings, just visible through the dust. They were covered in graffiti and flyers advertising upcoming events around Melbourne. Some of the flyers had fallen off and were rolling down the desolate street.

"Where the hell is everyone?" I asked, as I scanned the road, looking for any signs of movement.

"No idea. Can you walk by yourself?" he asked, as he slowly released his hands from my waist. I could feel the stitches pulling against my skin, and my shoulders hurt so much. I didn't think I could tolerate any more pain.

"I'm good," I lied. My head was still fuzzy. I needed him to be as alert as possible, so having him worry about my welfare was not an option.

"Henry, the 'hocker', is a fair way from here." He looked at his watch and up to the streets. "We'll get out of view while the dust is still covering us. Then we'll discuss our game plan." He looked up and down the street again, searching for any signs of movement. The street was silent and still. I had never visited Melbourne before but I knew this level of stillness didn't bode well. There was an ominous feeling about the place.

"Come on, across to that café." He pointed across the street.

It was the only shop along the desolated street that hadn't been completely destroyed. It had a verandah with white wrought-iron lattice work. Under the verandah sat several sets of white wrought-iron tables and chairs. The image of the neat white café against the cataclysmic surroundings was ghostly.

Just as I stepped from the tram stop onto the road, a deafening noise sounded from the direction the tram had just travelled.

"Andy! Run!" I screamed at him, as I pushed him towards the footpath; however, we were too late to be completely clear of the explosion we had just heard. The tram was thrown into the air from the enormous force of the blast, and flames spewed from the ground. I braced myself as the shockwave rippled through the street, shattering windows and pouring glass into the street as it passed. I lifted my arm over my face as the wave hit me, throwing me backwards, landing me onto the bonnet of an empty car.

~ 15 ~

CHAPTER FIFTEEN

"Michael?" I tried to call, my voice breaking. I could not take a clean breath through the thick dust that filled the air around me. A high-pitched ringing resonated in my ears. There was such pain in my shoulders—hot searing pain. I reached up to rub my eyes into focus, but the movement caused so much pain in my arms I could not hold back a loud groan. I lay still waiting for the pain to pass.

I was lying on hard bitumen. What had happened? I tried to roll over and push myself up onto my hands and knees, but my shoulders burned, so I stilled all movement. I wanted to lie here and cry. I pressed my eyes closed hoping it would all just end. Too much pain ... just let go ...

My fingers fell to the bitumen surface, and I turned my head. I was lying on the roadway next to a car. I wasn't in the front yard of my home. I blinked—what had happened? Stitches, a tram ... Andy! He had been next to me, and there was an explosion; not the one at my home—another! Where's Andy? I think I screamed his name.

Despite the pain, I pulled myself to my feet and leant on the car until I could achieve some sort of balance, the high-pitched ringing still sounding loudly in my ears. Through the thick dust, I could see glowing red flames flicker from pieces of debris that were alight from the blast. I desperately scanned the vicinity for Andy. A part of my brain was trying to prepare me for the real possibility that my best friend hand been blown up, and that in moments, I would be finding his scattered remains. I pushed that part away; I wouldn't allow myself to entertain the possibility of Andy being dead.

I staggered towards the tram that now lay on its side amongst burning piles of rubble and debris. The flames of the burning piles illuminated the dust, showing me the true extent of damage from the blast: buildings had crumbled, spilling their bricks onto the street; shop signs lay bent and crushed along the roadway, and people ... I gasped as I clapped my hand over my mouth. Bodies lay in pieces scattered amongst the debris. The smell of burning human flesh made my stomach convulse. I fell to my hands and knees as I vomited over the bitumen, my arms shaking as I tried to hold my body weight.

I heard a person cry through the wreckage. I pushed myself to my feet and stumbled towards the sound. All I could think of was Andy's face, burned and cut, his body broken and dismembered ...

"Hello?" I called hoarsely, and strained my eyes through the thick dust, searching for any sign of movement.

Another cry came from behind the tangled remnants of the tram. I quickened my pace as I carefully edged myself around debris and broken bodies to the side of the tram. I could see someone waving their arm in the air. I knew instantly, it wasn't Andy; the person's arm was too petite to be his. I clambered over burning rocks and pieces of scolding tram until I reached the person—it was Suravi. A piece of metal tubing had been blown apart and had become lodged in her lower abdomen. I fell to my knees and wrapped my shaking hands around it with intentions of pulling it from her. She shook her head weakly. I pulled my shaking hands away from the tubing and looked down to the rest of her body; one side of her was nothing but charred flesh. I pressed my hands to either side of my face as I looked at her. She was shivering in agony. I wanted to help her, just as she had done for me, but I knew she was beyond any help I could give.

A gurgling noise came from deep within her throat as she gasped for air. I wrapped my hands around her hand—the one that still had skin attached. I wanted to tell her it would be okay, that she was going to be alright, but I knew she would not survive. All I could do was to stay with and not let her die alone. She looked at me, and her lips pulled at the sides into a small smile. She squeezed my hand gently as her lips fell and her eyes dropped. I felt her hand go limp in mine. Her eyes no longer looked at me with any emotion; they were empty. I had never witnessed anyone die before. I had always held my doubts as to whether we do have a soul or spirit within us, but after seeing the light leave her eyes, I believed it was true.

I leant across and gently pushed her eyelids closed. She looked to be sleeping; she wasn't. She was dead.

I heard a loud snap from behind me. I turned quickly to see a figure walking toward me through the dust and burning rubble. I winced as I began to push myself from the ground. My first thought was that it was Andy, and a burst of relief shot through me as I watched him come closer to me. He was okay! He was alive and moving. I was about to call to him when I realised the body of this person was by far larger than Andy, and he was moving too freely to have been involved in the explosion. Some sense within me knew danger. I threw myself behind a nearby car, praying he hadn't seen me. I pushed myself hard against the car, tucking my legs to my chest, breathing with shallow breaths.

His footsteps continued toward me. As I sat pressed against the car, I noticed bodies lying on the footpath just across the road. I could see an arm move—someone was alive! As I looked more carefully, I was able to make out the distinctive shape of my crossbow lying next to the arm that had just moved. It was the arm of a man—Andy! It must be Andy lying there!

I slowly rolled over so that I could peer under the car to the other side. Through the air gap beneath the dust, I could see black combat boots moving closer to the car—The Aztec! I pressed my eyes and lips closed. How could he possibly find us here, now?

I sat back against the car and looked again to Andy, who remained motionless on the footpath. I stared at my crossbow lying only centimetres from his outstretched hand. If I had hold of the bow, I would at least be able to defend myself and Andy. Damn, damn, damn! The bow was so close—but so far. If I did try to dash for it, The Aztec would see me.

Andy's foot began to move as he was coming out of his unconscious state. I was torn between my feeling of relief that he was alive and my feeling of terror that The Aztec would see him too—and kill him.

A gentle breeze blew past me, bringing with it the smell of trees of all the ancient forests of the world; the smell of Derrek. No, the smell of The Aztec. I had to force his memory from my mind; the memory of him holding me closely in the bookstore, of him pushing me from harm's way in the street. They weren't real. That wasn't him. He was only pretending to be Derrek. Derrek didn't exist. It was only The Aztec. I unwillingly breathed in the intoxicating smell of him, and as soon as I did so, I could feel my soul being drawn to him. I wanted to give myself over to him. I tried to draw back memories of what he had done to me at my house, but as soon as I remembered them, they were replaced by my greater need to be with him. I tried holding my breath, forcing myself not to inhale his scent. But it made no difference. It wasn't just his smell; I was drawn to him for another reason, one that I could not explain.

Andy bent his knees up as he started to return to the conscious world, letting out a long moan as he came around. The Aztec heard him as loudly as I did, and instantly stopped edging around the car near me and turned to the direction of Andy. The overwhelming desire to give myself freely to The Aztec subsided with the intense fear of what he would do to Andy if he managed to capture him. I needed my crossbow—I needed to protect Andy, just as he had done for me. Abde's words resonated in the front of my mind: 'You will love him until you draw your last breathe.' That may have been so, but love or no love, I would not let him kill Andy.

I stared at my bow, trying to figure a way of retrieving it without him seeing me. "Alexandra? Oh, Alexandra ... I know you are here, my darling." Her voice sleeked through the dust-filled air. "Come out and play."

This couldn't be happening! Andy was unconscious with The Aztec only metres from him, and now Veronika was here! I frantically sought some means to escape. I could hear the heels of her shoes click along the road, coming closer.

"Why do you hide, Alexandra? I am with you, always."

The eyes appeared in my mind, the searing pain rippled through my head like never before. The pain was too much to bear. I let out a piercing scream.

I felt someone slide their arms under my legs and shoulders and lift me from the ground. I couldn't open my eyes to see who it was—the pain was unbearable. It had to be Andy. He had regained consciousness and was carrying me to safety.

A moment later the eyes were gone, and I was dropped to the ground.

"Get up! Run!" Andy screamed at me as he hauled me from the ground.

I remained unresponsive for a moment as I realised what had happened. It wasn't Andy who scooped me from the ground at all; it was The Aztec, who was now lying face down on the road with a piece of metal debris through his back. A pool of blood was growing around him. It made me think of the bookstore— he had saved me that night, but then treated me savagely. How could he be wonderful, *and* be a monster as well?

"Alexandra! Run! She's here!"

I couldn't move. I just stared at The Aztec. Was he dead?

"For Christ's sake Alexandra! Snap out of it!" He slapped my face. "Run!"

I blinked several times as he drew me back to reality. He grabbed my arm and dragged me through the debris, further and further away from the wreckage.

"Alexandra!" Veronika's voice echoed through the desolate city. She wasn't following us.

"Andy. Stop," I said as I turned back to face the explosion site. "Why isn't she chasing us? She had such a strong hold on me, and then it was just gone. What happened?"

"I don't know. Keep moving," he said. "Maybe it was because I killed him. Abde said death was the only separator."

I thought of The Aztec, and I wanted to hate him, I wanted to despise him. I wanted to feel nothing but joy that his life had been stripped from him. But I couldn't. In spite of everything that had happened, and all that he had done, I felt only pain at his loss. I wanted to fall to my knees and weep for his passing. I wanted to pray for him to be given back to me.

"So he's definitely dead?" I asked.

"I bloody well hope so! I have to say, that was one of the best feelings ... killing that bastard. He's never going to hurt you again."

"Yeah, I'm glad he's dead," I said with little conviction.

~ 16 ~

CHAPTER SIXTEEN

For several hours, we walked along the desolate streets of Melbourne. We dared not speak to each other as our voices would float over the eerily still air. Each noise that sounded in the distance made us jump and caused adrenaline to race through our veins, so we were both exhausted.

We eventually came across a small real estate office, seemingly unaffected by the chaos. It wasn't anything special, and I doubted it ever was a vibrant place, but it was now our oasis in the rubble of the city.

"Do you think we can take five here?" I asked. "I really need to rest."

"I was thinking the same thing. There's probably a back office so we're not seen from the street. Might be a computer we can use to see if we can find something on the net; a news report or something," he said as he stepped through a door of broken glass. "We've walked for hours and still haven't crossed a single person. The power is out across the city."

"Well, we're in luck. There's an office behind the reception area. Yes, yes, yes! Look ... a laptop!" he exclaimed and quickly moved toward it. "It's a laptop and not a desktop," he said as he sat behind a small desk.

I looked at him with one eyebrow raised. I was too exhausted to ask why it would make any difference.

"A desktop needs power. A laptop can run on batteries." His hands flew across the keyboard, as the laptop came to life and responded to his commands.

"Ah," I said as I took Andy's blood-soaked jacket off and slowly lowered myself down to the floor, resting my body against the wall. I was too tired to feel the true extent of the pain.

"Maybe there's been a news report uploaded, or something ..." He sounded more hopeful than convincing.

I looked up to the night sky through the one window on the back wall of the office. The stars twinkled and glimmered as they shone brightly. A deep longing for home crept into me. I closed my eyes as I tried to remember the smell of the rain as it hit the hot, dusty roads.

Andy moved to sit next to me and looked up to the sky as well. "Don't normally see the stars in Melbourne. There's usually too many lights; we can only see them now because of the city's black out." I knew he missed Warrangatta as much as I did.

"How could you live anywhere where you couldn't see the stars?" To me the stars are, and always will be, freedom. When you can see the stars and feel the night sky hug the Earth, that's when you're home.

As I stared up at them, my eyes drew heavier and heavier. I only meant to close them for a moment, but hours passed before I reopened them.

*****

The stars had gone and the sun shone fiercely through the window. A couple of jackets had been rolled up and placed carefully under my head, and a large brown coat lay across me as a blanket.

"Andy?" I called, as I lifted my hands to wipe my eyes into focus. I stopped quickly as pain from my shoulders shot down my arms. "Jesus Christ!" I cursed at the pain. I rolled to my knees and used only my legs to push myself to my feet. "Andy, where are you?" I called again.

Something caught my eye. My necklace was snaking over a yellow note that had been left sitting on the lap top. The note read:

'Press play.

Had to go check on my family, you were out cold.

Hopefully I'll be back before you wake up.

If not, wait there! I am coming back.

And here's your necklace. You were right,

It is just a piece of jewellery!

Andy.

P.S. Eat the food!'

I tried to put my necklace on, but I couldn't lift my arms high enough—my shoulders hurt too much. I wrapped it around my wrist instead. A sense of calm washed over me as soon as I clipped it together. How was it that something so small and simple could have such an impact on my mood?

A large croissant and an unopened bottle of water sat next to the laptop. I pulled the seat out and lowered myself into it. I took a bite from the croissant; it was crunchy and stale, but I forced it down with some water. As I finished the last piece, I clicked Play on the laptop.

The screen filled with the image of a female news reporter. "In recent times, Melbourne has been subject to inexplicable, extreme weather conditions," she began. "Many are blaming separate religious groups for the cataclysmic weather, claiming it's due to displeased Gods. Others are blaming global warming. Just yesterday, a cyclone wiped out almost all of Adelaide and now is headed directly for Melbourne. Parts of Melbourne have been evacuated due to the explosions, which only hours ago ripped through the city. Many of the bombers have since been captured. This would ordinarily be welcome news. In this instance however, it is anything but. The bombers have informed police they have hidden countless more bombs throughout Melbourne and are set to explode at certain times. They say the bombs' locations will only be disclosed once their demands are met. These demands have not been released to the public. Thus far, no bombs have been discovered. Police suspect the possibility of it being little more than fear mongering. Even so, we have been told to inform all viewers to please go to the nearest Safe Station until the true extent of the situation is known."

The laptop screen went black. I pressed the power button quickly, and a red battery flashed across the centre of the screen.

"Damn it!" I hit the laptop with my hand.

I felt my pocket vibrate. I pulled out my phone and saw it was a call from Sam.

"Sam?" I asked, as I answered the phone.

"Alexandra! My God, it's good to hear your voice. You know how to give an old man a heart attack, don't you? I've been worried sick about you. Where are you? Are you with Andy?" I could tell he was angry that I hadn't contacted him to tell him of my absence, but his relief at knowing I was okay outweighed his anger.

"Yeah, Sam. I'm with Andy. Sorry I didn't tell you."

"Is that Alexandra?" I heard Emilee call out over him.

"Yes, Emilee, I've finally gotten a hold of her," Sam answered.

"Give it here." I could hear her snatch the phone from him. "Alexandra! What the hell is going on?" She sounded furious. "Where are you?"

"In a small deserted office in Melbourne."

The phone went silent for a moment. "Melbourne?" she shrieked.

"Melbourne? What's she doing all the way down there?" Sam called out.

"Yes, Melbourne. It's no big deal ..."

"No big deal! The entire city's in lock down!" She drew several heavy breaths. "It says on the news that most of the city has been flattened. Why are you still in the city? Why aren't you at a Safe Station?" She spoke so frantically I could barely understand her.

"What do you mean in lock down? We were in an explosion, but I didn't think it was city wide."

"You were in an explosion!" she cried.

"Explosion? Who was? What are you talking about Safe Stations?" Sam yelled at Emilee.

"We're okay. It was the rioters ..." I stopped short. I really didn't know if *we* were okay. I had no idea how long ago Andy had left or where he might be.

"Alexandra? Alexandra? Are you there? What is going on?" Emilee panicked.

I didn't answer.

Broken glass crunched loudly as my heavy feet stepped through the front door into the broken and crumbling city. The dust had finally settled, and the aftermath of the devastation was clear. The city was deathly silent as I stared out to it.

"You said the city is in lock down?"

"Yes, the News says that everybody *must* report to a Safe Station ... it's also saying this all started because the rioters are now blaming the insane weather on people's defiance to God or something. Morons! Just before it was the Government's fault, now it's Gods! Ugh, people do my head in! Basically it got out of control. Tell me that you and Andy are in a Safe Station now. They're saying anyone outside of a Safe Station tomorrow will be shot! They're declaring Martial law." She breathed down the phone as though she had been running for hours.

"Is it just Melbourne?" My mind raced furiously as I tried to plan an escape route. There was no way I could go to a Safe Station. The very first thing they would do would be to search me, not to mention I would be a sitting duck.

"I'm not sure, I think so. They've half fixed Barri-Barri tower but we are still only getting TV reception at irregular times; it's only luck if the News is reporting at the time we get it. As for phones, I've been trying to get a hold of you for over a day. We've been worried sick about you. Where's Andy? Put him on the ..." The phone went silent.

"Emilee? Hello? Emilee?" I pulled the phone from my ear and looked at the screen. The call had been disconnected. I hit the redial immediately, but instead of it ringing a 'call failed' message flashed across my screen. "Damn it!" I cursed and pushed my phone back into my pocket. As I did, I noticed something else in my pocket. I pulled it out. It was a small piece of paper.

"Abde," I said as I unfolded it.

'Rose and Jonah Persival.

65 Alpine Way, Falls Creek.'

I squeezed the piece of paper tightly in my hand as I paced the small office. Andy's note specifically told me to stay put— he was coming back for me. Phones were working, so I'd just call him and tell him I was awake and we would both go to the Persival's. I pulled my phone from my pocket and called Andy's number.

"Hi, you've reached Andy Munroe. I can't take your call right now so please leave a message. Unless you're a hot chick, in that case forget the message and get naked and lie in my bed." I smiled at his message.

But my smile quickly faded as I realised that I had an opportunity to save him. He didn't have to come with me any further. If I did tell him about the Persivals, he would follow me blindly. Death had been only inches away from both of us, and I was the cause of it. His life literally balanced in my hands. I pulled the phone from my ear and pressed the 'end call' button. A familiar feeling came gushing back to me; it was the same as when I had opened my eyes for the first time in the hospital after our house exploded—I was alone. But this time I didn't have Tess to help me, to support me and to guide me through my own obstacles. I realised at that moment how much I had relied on other people to push me through difficult times. I hadn't been capable of dealing with the harsh world by myself.

I looked down at my arm. The marking of the symbol was more vibrant than ever. I had no clue as to what was in store for me next, or who would be hunting me tomorrow. But I was certain that the time had come for me to face my own life, my own reality, without relying on anybody else to pick up the pieces. I walked across to the desk and took the note from the screen. I turned it over and wrote on the back:

'No, I won't wait.

Be safe, Andy.

I love you.'

I was well aware that these words would quite possibly be the last words I would ever say to him. I never had the chance to say a proper goodbye to Michael and Sasha. I had re-lived the moments before their deaths a hundred times, and I rehearsed what I would have said to both of them. But I now realise that no words, no matter how eloquently spoken or written, could ever suffice. There is no way to say goodbye to someone you love.

~ 17 ~

CHAPTER SEVENTEEN

I wasted no time in preparing to leave for the Persivals. A large bag filled with paperwork sat under the desk. I pulled it out and upended it. I carefully placed The Book of Narveere in the bottom of the bag. Andy had taken his backpack but had left my bow leaning against the desk; I put that in the bag next, along with the jacket, which he had draped over me, and a pair of gloves I found in the drawer. I was already wearing a pair of jeans, so I didn't bother to search for any more clothing.

I placed my mobile phone by the laptop. If I truly didn't want Andy to follow me, I had to make certain he couldn't trace me. I knew it would only take him a matter of seconds to trace me by my phone. A piece of me wished he would just appear and make all the hard decisions for me; to tell me what to do next. He had put himself in harm's way countless times in order to help and protect me. It was now my turn to do the same for him.

Veronika and Boris were still hunting me. I knew it would be only a matter of time until they found me. I just hoped I was able to find the Persivals before that. I took comfort in knowing that while they were hunting me, they were not hunting Andy.

There was a small staffroom next to the office. I looked through the cupboards and found some bottled water along with a couple of boxes of dry biscuits; probably stale, hardly nutritious, but better than nothing. I put them in the bag. I knew my shoulders would scream in agony as soon as I swung the backpack on my back. Yep. I positioned it as evenly as possible and walked out the door.

*****

I had to steal a car to get to where the Persivals lived. There were several vehicles abandoned along the roadways, so it wasn't difficult to get hold of one, and there wasn't anyone around to stop me. I hadn't seen any police since the square; I didn't dare think of what they'd be pre-occupied with.

I had driven for the good part of a day until I reached the Alpine region. I could have arrived more quickly, but I was certain the key roads would have roadblocks, so I had to resort to taking back roads. Driving through an abandoned city was surreal and disconcerting.

It was a relief to finally get to Falls Creek. Although it was summer, snow had lightly covered the ground; even the mountains weren't immune to the weather anomaly.

I had pulled the brown coat on almost as soon as I had left Melbourne and hadn't dared to take it off again. I could feel my shoulders burning and figured an infection had started, but for the time being, out of sight was out of mind, so the coat remained on.

The car had a built-in GPS, but I had disabled it. I had no idea if I could be tracked by GPS or not, but I wasn't taking that chance. Once I was at Falls Creek, I had to rely on an old red map I had found in the door trim to navigate my way to the Percival's. I found this infuriating because hardly any of the roads were sign-posted and there were no milestones to gauge my location.

Eventually, I found myself driving up their driveway. A neat stack of firewood stood out the front of the property. I appreciated the intense need for the abundance of firewood when I opened the car door—the icy wind felt like a million needles piercing my exposed skin.

I reached my arm across to the back seat, which sent pain shooting through my shoulder. I pulled my arm back and gently pushed my coat and shirt away from my shoulder. I hadn't inspected my wound since it had been stitched. I flipped the visor down and aimed the mirror to my shoulder; the stitches bulged angrily around the red skin. I winced as I applied a small amount of pressure to the side of my wound; a greenish-yellow substance was secreted from between the stitches.

"*Damn* it!" I let my shirt fall back to my shoulder. Even the lightness of my shirt made me cringe. The infection would soon spread, and when it did, I would need to be within reach of a hospital. If I wasn't and the infection leaked into my blood stream, I would not be able to recover. I grimaced at the irony of being hunted by century-old beings with super-human abilities, and my biggest threat now was microscopic.

As I went to flip the visor back, I caught my reflection in the mirror. I looked like hell. I was filthy, bags hung low under my eyes, and my hair was knotted and awry. I tried to wipe my face with my hands, but they were no cleaner, so all I achieved was to smear even more dirt across my face. I opened the car door and bent down to scoop up a handful of snow with my hands; the heat from my palms melted it almost instantly. I used it to wash my hands of dirt and blood and then repeated the process to splash water over my face. I wiped myself dry with my shirt. Every action caused searing pain, but it wasn't likely these people would talk to me if I looked like I had just woken up in a gutter. I tried flattening my hair into some sort of order, but it wouldn't cooperate, so I bunched it up and tucked it under my back of my coat. I kind of wished I hadn't left Andy's cap back in the office. Oh, bloody hell—the pain! I pulled on the gloves I had packed—they would hide the bruises and scratches on my hands, as well as serve another purpose should I need to show the Persivals the Book.

I carefully laid my crossbow under the back seat and tucked the Book into my belt again. I began to walk to the house along the small, concrete footpath, which had recently been cleared of snow.

The house was an inviting cedar-clad building with a verandah that ran the perimeter of the property. A chimney off the side of the house was producing thick, rolling grey smoke. I knocked on the heavy timber door. The door opened just enough for the owner to see me; I couldn't see anyone.

"Can I help you?" a woman's voice called from behind the door.

"Yes, please. I would like to speak with Jonah Persival, please." I squinted and craned my neck, trying to see the woman behind the door.

"He's busy," the woman snapped and slammed the door.

"No, please, this is important ... I have to speak to him about his research." I could hear the desperation in my voice. "Please, it will only take a minute of his time." There was no answer. "Please! I've driven for days," I pleaded.

It couldn't be happening. After all the effort to find them, to be standing on the Persival's doorstep only for them to deny me access; I felt like crying. Through the door, I could hear a man and a woman speaking quickly and quietly in another language;

a language I didn't recognise. A moment later, the door slowly opened a little more than it did before.

"What is it that you want?" a man asked. I still wasn't able to make out his face.

"Jonah Persival?" I asked as I took a step closer to the door in hopes of getting a glimpse of his face.

"Yes. Now, what is it that you want?" he demanded.

"I need to speak with you about something important." I paused for a moment. "It's about a book ..." The door slammed shut before I could finish speaking, and the two people began speaking quickly in raised voices. I couldn't understand what they were saying, but it was obvious they were arguing. There was a pause in their exchange before the door finally swung fully open. A slender, middle-aged woman with long greying blonde hair stood in the doorway, her arms folded. She had a small pointy nose and wide blue eyes, which were study-ing me intensely. The man stood behind her. He was a short, plump middle-aged man with a receding hairline and a thick, wiry moustache. He had a wide nose and small beady eyes that scowled at me.

They were both looking me up and down, no doubt assessing my haggard appearance, perhaps trying to gauge the extent of any threat I might pose.

"Please." My voice was thick with emotion. They couldn't turn me away, not after all that I'd been through. "I don't want you to do anything. I just need to speak with you. Please!" I begged.

"You have five minutes." The woman pointed a finger at me. "Then you leave."

"Yes, five minutes. Thank you. Thank you."

She nodded once and walked back into her home. I followed her before she could change her mind. Once I was through the front door, she closed it quickly and snipped five deadbolts that ran down the edge of the door. I knew something was amiss. People don't often lock their doors when they live in the middle of nowhere much less have five deadbolts. I settled my breathing; I needed to remain calm. I had only one chance to find the answers I was seeking.

Their lounge room had a large open wood heater in the centre of one wall. Around it curved a dark red couch which looked extremely comfortable. I had barely slept since I left the real estate office, and the comfortable couch was tantalising. But I wasn't asked to sit or offered any sort of refreshment. Instead, we stood at a stalemate in the centre of the lounge room.

"I am Jonah, and this is my wife, Rose," Jonah said as he waved his hand towards her. She held her lips pursed, glaring at me through squinted eyes. "You said you had questions for us?" Jonah asked sternly. He had a strong accent, but I still couldn't identify his country of origin, possibly Swedish.

"Yes. Um, for the sake of time saving, I'll skip the pleasantries," I began.

"Suits us," Rose said, clearly angry.

"Okay. You led a research team many years ago?" I asked him.

His eyes narrowed as he studied me. "I have led many research teams—ranging from the depths of the Congo all the way to icy plains of the Arctic. You will have to be more specific if you wish to gain any information from your five minutes." He folded his arms across his broad chest and looked at his watch. "Four minutes."

I swallowed hard. I knew I had only once chance to speak with them about The Book of Narveere and I could not afford to jeopardise it. I looked around the room; every shelf, every table, every bench was littered with books. As my eyes focused on them, I noticed he had written all of them. Surely he would have written a book about his studies of The Book of Narveere? It was only a hunch, but it was all I had. I bit my bottom lip and prayed my hunch was right.

"Yes, well it is in regards to a book that you wrote." I tried to speak calmly and plainly.

He unfolded his arms, and his eyes lit up. "Ahh yes, I can see why you would venture this distance to speak with me. My distinguished work is renowned throughout the world. People from many cultures have travelled vast distances just to speak with me for a matter of minutes. Tell me dear, which of my illustrious memoirs would you like me to elaborate on for you?" He sat down on his wide Chesterfield couch, rested his intertwined fingers on his lap, and pushed his head back, puffing his chest out even further.

I exhaled quickly. There was still no mention of Narveere, but at least I wasn't going to be thrown out immediately.

"Sit. Sit." He splayed his hand across the air towards the couch.

"Jonah!" Rose hissed, as she pulled her cardigan tighter around her waist. "Five minutes has expired." She spoke from the corner of her mouth as to whisper, but she made no effort to lower the volume of her voice.

"Nonsense, Rose." He waved his hand, dismissing her complaint. "No harm in having a little chit chat, now is there? We could do with some tea, though," he beamed. His smile almost vanished behind his thick moustache.

She dropped her hands furiously, spoke several words in her language and stormed from the room. "Sit dear. Let us reminisce of my many courageous expeditions." He adjusted his shoulders back further into the chair as he prepared to tell me of his countless 'courageous expeditions.'

I studied him intently, looking for anything that may prove to be Aztec-related, as he began to ramble about his many adventures. He wore a long sleeved jumper, so it was impossible to see if he wore any markings like the one I did on my left arm.

"... invaluable artefacts that I do believe one of the largest museums in England has a permanent display, dedicated solely to my research team and me." He puffed his chest victoriously.

Although I was not welcome in their home, Jonah would take any opportunity to gloat about his accomplishments, so I was being tolerated. I hoped that I would be able to coax information about the Book from him without raising suspicion as to the true reason I had visited. I couldn't afford to anger or scare them, or they would shut down completely.

He stood to his feet and waddled to a pile of books that sat near the fireplace. He carefully selected a book halfway down the pile and moved back towards me.

"This book—before you ask, yes you may keep a *signed* copy —illustrates in perfect detail the differences between two- and three-toed sloths." He pulled a pair of spectacles from his chest pocket and slipped them on as he prepared to begin reading from his book.

"Sloths?" I asked, taken aback.

"Yes, sloths." He narrowed his eyes at me.

I held my breath. How could I have been so stupid? I hadn't researched any of this other expeditions. My heart beat hastened, and I could feel my face burn red, any chance of learning more of the Book fading.

"Ahh, I see you are an adventurous girl, aren't you?" He chortled. "No need to be embarrassed. Many young girls have enjoyed a story or two of my telling." He held his hand to the side of his mouth as he spoke quietly.

"Oh yes. Oh, you got me." I said awkwardly.

"Here, this one is particularly interesting ..." He walked heavily to the corner of the room, where at least twenty books were piled in a perfectly straight tower. He carefully selected one and opened it slowly. "*My* team of researchers and I made some incredible discoveries ..."

"Wow. You have had such an adventurous life. I could only imagine." I tucked my hair behind my ear. From the outset, Rose appeared to be hostile and unlikely to be cooperative, so I had to play into his ego in order to have him reveal the information I needed. I wasn't the slightest bit interested in his 'incredible discoveries' or his so-called adventurous life.

"It must be incredible, having so many people admire your work." I gushed with apparent enthusiasm.

"It can be draining." He gave a sincere nod. "But it is a duty someone has to fulfil." He exhaled as though his *duty* was utterly exhausting.

"There is one expedition that most intrigues me. You see, I actually work at a bookstore and I came across a vague description of this particular expedition." I smiled as sweetly as I could, and it had the desired effect because the smile broadened across his face. "I was just so utterly fascinated by your work that I needed to know more. I hope you don't find it *inappropriate* that I sought you out." I threw a girlish smile and tilted my head down.

He slipped the book back to the pile. "If I had known you were visiting, I may have made other arrangements ... for a more private conversation?" He lowered his voice and lifted his eyebrows, sliding his eyes toward the kitchen where Rose still busied herself.

What a creep! His wife was only a room away, and he would carry on like this. If only he knew how revolting I found his self-serving manner and deceitful behaviour. The thought of him anywhere near me was repulsive, and it took all my strength not to show it. I had absolutely no intentions of letting him anywhere near me, but he needed to believe I did and, more importantly, he needed to want it so much that he would tell me everything he knew about The Book of Narveere.

"Perhaps I could make another trip out here." I stood and stepped closer to him. There were few people I felt comfortable being in my personal space, and he was not one of them. "We should get the *business* side of our meeting out of the way today. That way, when I come back, there will be little need for conversation." I lifted one eyebrow. I felt utterly ridiculous and somewhat grotesque, but it worked.

"Oh, yes! I do like the way you think," he said, eyeing me up and down suggestively "Okay then. Now the document I was reading was referring to ancient scrolls that *you* uncovered." My skin was electric. I was so close to getting the answers I had been searching for, but I had to remain calm. "They referred to a book in particular—The Book of Narveere."

All the air seemed to leave the room—the fire flickered unnaturally as soon as the name was spoken.

"Who are you? What business do you have being here?" Any pleasantness in his voice and demeanour vanished.

"I told you why I'm here. I'm interested in ..." I moved my hand to touch his arm, but he pulled away and walked back to the couch.

"You are not here because you *stumbled* upon information regarding that book. No one just happens upon any information about *that* book." His eyes weren't beady anymore. They were wide and dark, filled with fear.

"What do you mean?" I stepped closer to him, but he took a large step back to create distance between us.

"You need to leave." He pointed towards the door with a shaking hand.

Rose reappeared at that moment, holding a lightly coloured tray with a tea setting balancing delicately upon it.

"No need for tea—our friend was just leaving," Jonah said decisively, as he stood next to his wife, as to side with her. It sickened me.

"Look, I'm not here to cause trouble or upset anyone. I don't want you to *do* anything. All I need is information; then I'll leave. I swear."

"Information about what?" Rose asked slowly, as she carefully placed the tray on the coffee table in the centre of the room.

"Nothing," Jonah answered before I could.

"The Book of Narveere," I said firmly.

"What of it?" Rose said quickly, as she wrapped her cardigan around herself tightly and looked around the room as though someone may be listening.

"I just want to know all that you know about it. That, and if you happen to know anything of The Aztec. That's it."

Rose clapped one of her hands over her heart and the other over her mouth. "Who are you?" she hissed.

"It doesn't matter. Please, I absolutely beg of you. People are dying." For the first time since I arrived, I felt that I was being honest.

"Of course they are." She threw her hands in the air and sat on the couch.

"Rose, there is no need to entertain her anymore. I can send her away ..." Jonah spoke loudly, proclaiming his authority.

"Really? You want her to leave? Five minutes ago you were planning on her returning for a 'private conversation'." Rose shot a foul look at Jonah and held his gaze, till his eyes dropped.

He took a step back as though in retreat, unable to deny our conversation.

I looked at her again, and I recognised her look immediately. It was Tess all over again. I should never have wasted my time with Jonah. Rose was just like Tess. And right now, she was angry, so I decided to tackle her as I had always approached Tess—with direct and no-nonsense honesty.

"You've seen the Book, haven't you Rose," I asserted as a statement, not a question.

I looked at her, and she looked back at me, and we had some connection in that moment. She did not refute my statement, but continued to look at me and asked, "You've seen it?"

I pulled my coat aside and took the Book from my belt. The gloves I was wearing prevented it from glowing.

"Where did you find that?" Rose jumped to her feet and stood behind the couch. She behaved as though the Book was going to leap from my hands and attack her.

"I was given it," I answered quietly.

"Put it away," she hissed at me as she looked around as though someone was still watching.

"I just want to know what it is. Why does it burn some people ..." I spoke before I could stop myself.

"Some people?" she asked, taken aback. "It burns all people. The Book is made of dragon skin. The words are etched of light and fire." She cringed as she told me, as though her words also burned as she spoke.

My face fell. "Dragon skin? I asked for your help. If you don't want to help me, fine, but don't treat me like I'm an idiot."

"The Book is made of dragon skin! Dragons existed. Not in the same way you see them in story books, but they were certainly real." She pointed her finger at me, angry that I dared call her a liar.

"What do you mean?" I frowned.

"What do you know of dragons?" she asked.

"That they're mythical creatures. People dreamed them up years ago."

"You, like most people, are wrong. I don't care if you believe me. I don't care if you leave here thinking of me as insane. I don't care." She spoke with her lip turned up and waved her hands dismissively. "Dragons existed. You did not come here to learn of dragons. You came here to learn about the Book, and that is all that I will tell you. You want to learn of dragons; you find somebody else. Now get that thing from my sight." She threw her hands in the air.

I lifted my jumper again and tucked it into my belt, then slid my coat back across so it was completely covered.

"Listen and listen well. Whoever gave you that Book is no friend of yours. And be extremely careful of who sees you with it," she said in almost a whisper.

"Why? What is it?" I asked.

"Damn it, Rose! We swore we'd never speak of it again!" Jonah stomped his foot in protest, much like a child would.

"No, Jonah. You swore, not me. Now, you're the one that rambles on about *your* adventures. How about for once in your miserable life you be the hero instead of the coward. Tell the girl." Rose said coolly, as she reached for her tea and sipped it loudly.

Jonah's ego had been hit hard, and he didn't like it. A moment of self-deliberation passed until he finally spoke.

"We did some research ..." He paused. There was a slight noise outside, like a stick snapping. He quietly walked to the window to ensure it was securely locked and made certain there were no peeping holes in the curtains. "That Book, it awakens something. Something dark, and once it's awoken ..." He shook his head. "It doesn't stop."

I sat on the edge of the seat. "The Aztec? It awakens The Aztec?"

Jonah sat next to his wife on the double couch and placed his hand on her arm as though to comfort her.

"Open the Book to the first page," he instructed.

I sat opposite them and pulled the Book from my belt, again, being careful not to touch the cover with my bare skin. I laid it on the table and opened it to the first page. The page was blank apart from four symbols, which were imprinted across the centre of the page. It looked like there was once five symbols, but the fifth was too faded to make out.

"The third symbol across. What is it?" he asked.

I looked down at the symbol. "Um, it's a sort of squiggle with several zigzag lines through it."

He rolled his wife's sleeve up to her elbow and held her forearm up. There, replicated on her arm was the third symbol in the Book.

Rose said quietly, as she looked at it, "It doesn't fade, it doesn't change, and it cannot be removed or covered. I tried to get a tattoo over the top, but the following day the tattoo had disappeared, and the scar was as strong as the day I got it."

I could do nothing but stare at her; I could feel my eyes shaking as tears threatened to burst from them.

"Do you know of The Aztec?" she continued in a voice so low, it was barely audible.

"Yes."

"The Book releases him." She leant forward on the edge of the couch so as to speak more softly.

"Look, our research offers insight into how people, humans, have developed over the many centuries. A major part of the research is based on mythology. This is so important because we need to know why people believed such stories, to understand how our brains have advanced. For example, the Ancient Egyptian believed Ra, the Sun God, would travel on a 'boat' for twelve hours a day across the skies giving the world light. On days of storms or eclipses, Egyptians would blame serpents, or perhaps Ra would have to fight other Gods. After the twelve hours had passed Ra would travel through the underworld, hence giving night. The cause for this type of mythology is blindingly obvious; the Earth orbits the sun giving us day and night, but they had no way of knowing this, so they invented these stories. These myths were created to fill the void of unlearned science; myths only exist to explain what humans, what science could not. Myths were never created for entertainment; they're not stories. Each myth serves a purpose to explain the unexplainable—except the myths which surround that Book. Those myths only explain themselves."

"I don't understand, 'myths only explain themselves'?" I shook my head.

"That's right," Rose added. "Myths explained things such as photosynthesis, or the planet's orbit, or death. But the Book's myths only explained the Book, which led us to believe the Book was a tangible object. That is why we were so interested in it. We were desperate to know if the Book was real. We had several hypotheses, of course. Most of us agreed the Book was complete nonsense and never existed in the first place, but we needed to know for certain. Centuries ago, a tablet was uncovered in a language no one had ever seen. No one could translate or even guess as to what the writings could have been. This tablet had passed down from kings to princes for generations and all of a sudden it stopped. Instantly, all mention of the tablet ceased, until a team of prospectors accidently came across the tablet. It had been badly damaged over time, but more than half of it was still legible. So naturally it got shipped off to a museum."

"And that's where *I* come in," Jonah interjected. "The historian at the museum photographed the tablet and sent it to me. One of my team members happened across the image. She was the most incredible linguist in the world, second to none..." He clasped his hands together. "After weeks of working tirelessly through the translation, she discovered that it was not a message, but rather, co-ordinates; co-ordinates to lead us to the location of The Book of Narveere. Naturally, when the tablet had been written, actual co-ordinates hadn't been invented. Instead, it told of a place by the stars. Once we had discovered the location, I and my team of seven lost no time in heading straight for it. It led us into the deepest parts of Africa, through caves and tunnels, through crocodile-infested rivers ..." He stopped short, as though the next sentence would burn his throat to speak them.

"What else? What else did your team find?" I asked, my eyes not moving from him.

"Hangmen." His eyes shot back to mine. "Through the mist were so many trees filled with hangmen—rotting, decaying hangmen. There was only one path through the death, but by river—a river, black and still, made its way through the hanging corpses. But, someone had been there before us. We don't know if it was those who hung the men or perhaps they too had been in search of the elusive Book. Tied to an outstretched branch was a raft made from fallen branches and was just sitting there on the water. We knew at that moment, we had a choice, and there would be no going back whatever choice we made. It was either go into the forest of hangmen, which we knew would reveal more horrors the deeper we went, or abandon our mission and return empty handed.

We set out with eight researchers, but only three of us stepped onto the raft—myself, Rose and Tirra, the linguist who translated the tablet. At the time I thought how foolish the five who walked away were, how they would miss one of the greatest discoveries of our time. But now," he squeezed Rose's hand and pressed his lips together, "but now, I wish we had followed them."

Rose rubbed his hand soothingly, and she looked at him lovingly. "You weren't to know. None of us could have known."

I paced the floor, trying to take calming breaths. They had described with perfect accuracy the dream I had had on the bus the night I arrived in Warrangatta—the night I was given the Book, even though I didn't know the Book was within the parcel.

"You found it? You found The Book of Narveere. Where was it? What happened once you found it?" I said too abruptly. It was a matter of time until Veronika and Boris found me. I had to know how to kill them too.

Rose continued. "The very instant we stepped onto the raft it began to float along the river as though it was being pulled, but there was no one there. Ugh, I can still smell the rotting decay of the hanging people." She covered her nose and mouth with her hand. "We dared not speak or move," she whispered. "The dead eyes of the hangmen seemed to follow us as we passed. I could feel their eyes burning into my soul." Her eyes were still and distant as she recalled her memories. Although she sat in the room alongside Jonah and me, her mind was in the forest. "The raft stopped at a cove of yellow sand. It was so strange because the river did not lap the sand and the mist did not venture past the water's edge. Jonah was the first to step off the raft, followed by Tirra, then me. And there it was." She pulled a half smile.

"What? What was there?" I asked the question, but I didn't need to; I knew exactly what was there.

She turned her head to face me. "The Book of Narveere. Oh, when we saw it, do you remember Jonah? The elation we felt. Oh ..." She put both her hands over her heart and closed her eyes as she remembered the victory. "We did it. We were the ones to find the Book. It would be our names to go down in history. Our discovery would re-write human history. And that was our undoing. We were so bound up in our victory we did not see what was directly in front of us. How could a Book possibly survive in the deepest African jungle? Putting aside all the spectacle of hangmen and self-rowing rafts, how could a *book* survive without human interference?"

Johan waved his fist in the air. "I wanted it, Rose. I wanted it more than life itself. I wanted to be the first person to lay their hands on that Book. Years of searching, day and night, and criticism from sceptics ... and it was within my grasp. I took it without a moment's hesitation, and it felt good." He lowered his hand and stared back to the fire.

Rose quivered as her eyes began to fill with tears. I knew something was wrong. My stomach turned over itself. "What happened once you took it?"

"He came." Rose's voice was thick and her eyes were wide.

"Who? Who came, Rose?"

"The Aztec. His skin was as dark as night, and his scars shone in the moonlight. He was terrifyingly beautiful."

I felt my heart sink. She described him with perfect accuracy —he *had* been terrifyingly beautiful, but Andy had killed him.

Jonah walked to the pile of books, which were stacked behind me, as she continued to speak.

"Another woman appeared as though her body materialized from hundreds of black birds. That's when it happened." Her eyes widened as she recalled the memory.

Veronika. "What happened, Rose?" I pleaded.

She slowly lifted her eyes to meet mine. "The Aztec grabbed me." She held her forearm and rubbed it slowly. "His hand was like fire as it burned into my skin. *'We will never be apart,'* he said as he tried to pull me away from Jonah and Tirra. He tried to pull me into the jungle. I turned as I screamed for Jonah and Tirra to help me and that's when I saw her, the woman of crows. She was holding a knife and..." Rose choked on her words. "And she killed Tirra. She ran that blade across her throat without so much as blinking, and she just let her body fall to the ground." Rose wailed as she recalled the horrific memory. "I could hear Jonah. He was looking for me through the jungle. The woman of crows started to walk towards him with her knife poised. I was about to scream for Jonah to run, but before I could, The Aztec clapped his hand over my mouth so hard I could barely breathe. Jonah's voice was screaming for me. Rose slumped into the couch. "Everything goes black. I don't remember anymore. I don't know how we escaped. I can just remember running through the blackness and praying Jonah was close. I could hear him—The Aztec. I could feel him. I still can. He is always hunting me."

"That's why we live here. The cold—it dulls the senses." He gave a merciful look to Rose.

I inhaled deeply. "Well, you don't have to worry about him anymore."

"And why is that?" Rose asked.

"He's dead." I should have felt victorious, liberated. But I didn't.

"Ha!" Rose's laugh was dismissive. "And what weapon did you use?"

I frowned as I looked at her. I couldn't understand how the weapon I chose had any impact on his death. "A piece of metal debris—through his back ..."

"Metal?" she scoffed.

She leant her elbows on her knees and moved in close to me. "He is still alive." She stood to her feet and began to pace the floor. "You have the same connection—I can just tell. Can't you feel him? He's in your veins. You can feel him flowing through you."

She was right; I could feel him. I had thought it was a form of mourning, my longing for him. But it wasn't, he was still drawing me to him. As I looked at her I couldn't decipher my emotions; either I was rife with jealousy that she could feel him as I did, or I was relieved I wasn't the only one to be experiencing it.

"This is what you need if you want to kill him." Jonah passed me a sheet of thin tracing paper. I leant across so the fire would illuminate the drawing. I recognised it immediately. It was one of the many swords Andy had hanging on his wall.

"There is little known of this sword, except that it is the only weapon capable of killing The Aztec. As for the woman of crows, we know nothing of her."

A fierce gust of wind thrashed at their front door and blew one of the front windows open. Icy air forced its way into the warm room, sending chills through me. Jonah and Rose ran to the door and window, slamming the window shut and peering through the slither of glass.

"We have helped you more than enough. Please leave." He ordered me.

"No, there's still so much more I need to know." I began to protest. A hundred more questions flew through my head.

"Here! Take this! This is *everything*! There is no need for you to visit here again." He threw an old brown folder to me and pushed me through the front door, slamming it behind me.

As I turned to walk towards my car, I could hear them sliding the slide bolts on the door. As I clasped the folder in my hands,

I knew two things for certain: I had to go to Warrangatta to retrieve the sword that hung on Andy's wall, and I could never live my life in complete hiding like Rose.

~ 18 ~

CHAPTER EIGHTEEN

I left the Persival's house and drove for a few hours, feeling more and more unwell as I went. I decided to stop at a small clearing behind a stand of birch trees. Although their trunks were slender, they offered a fair amount of camouflage for my silver-coloured car.

I tried to reach across to the front passenger's seat to pick up the brown folder, but my shoulders burned furiously and sent pain running through my body to my stomach. I pushed myself back into my seat as I waited for the pain to subside, but it didn't. Everything started to spin around me, and I felt nauseous. I was going to be sick.

I pulled the door handle, and the door fell open. I leant out the side as vomit spewed out my mouth. I was in trouble. I had absolutely no medicine that could begin to help me, and the way my vision blurred in and out of focus, it was unlikely I would be able to resume driving.

A set of headlights caught my eye—a car was coming up the road. My heart beat heavily, as I tried to think of what I should do. I had nowhere to hide, and I was unarmed, apart from my crossbow; but it was useless to me if I wasn't able to wield it.

As the headlights grew closer, my breath quickened as panic began to rise from my stomach and spread through my body. The headlights were right on me, the car only metres from the turn-off to my hideaway. My immediate thought was that they had found me, and this time there would be no escape. But instead of pulling in, the car drove straight past.

I allowed myself to relax into the seat. It wasn't them; it was only another car—strange because I hadn't seen any other vehicles on the roads. I looked up to my rear view mirror to watch the car continue along the snaking road. But it wasn't continuing; it had turned around and was driving back down the road toward my hideaway.

I didn't have time to react before the car was idling by my side. My mouth was parched, and my breath was lost. I was going to die. I closed my eyes as I waited for a bullet to pass through the window or a sword to slide through the door. As I sat there, I wondered how it would feel to die. I thought of Suravi and the way the light disappeared from her eyes and her body stilled as I held her hand. There would be no one to hold my hand as I passed from this world. I wondered if Michael and Sasha would be waiting for me? I had once spoken to a man who had a heart attack. He had died and been resuscitated. He told me dying wasn't the scary part; dying was easy. It was the resuscitating part that was terrifying. I took comfort in his words, as I knew there would be no resuscitation for me.

I pinched my eyes closed, as I listened to a set of feet crunch loudly as they walked from their car to mine. *It will all be over in a second. Just a moment of pain and then nothing—it's okay.*

The car door swung open. I cringed down as I waited for the fatal blow.

"Alexandra? What the hell are you doing?"

I sprung my eyes open.

"Andy!" I cried as I threw myself at him, wrapping my arms around him. My shoulders burned and ached, but the pain was nothing compared to the elation I was feeling with him in my arms. Not only had I just come to terms with the fact I was going to die, but I had also been certain I would never see him again.

"What are you doing here? How did you find me?" I asked as tears streamed from my eyes. "I thought I was never going to see you again."

"Nah, you can't get rid of me that easily," he said softly, as he stroked the back of my hair. "Oh, and I have someone for you." He eased me away from his body and tapped his leg. Spud jumped from the back of the car.

"Oh my God, Spud!" I tickled his belly, as he licked my arm.

"How did you find me? Did you follow me in my car or something?" I asked as I rubbed Spud behind the ear.

"Your car?" Andy lifted one eyebrow. "Well, it really belongs to a Mr. and Mrs. McTullick." He smiled his big, warm smile. "As for how I found you, well that's easy." He pointed to the GPS mounted in the centre of the dash.

"No, you can't have; I disabled it," I frowned.

He laughed loudly. "Alex, hitting 'don't navigate' doesn't disable it."

Suddenly I felt incredibly stupid. I would never have taken a car with a built-in GPS if I knew I wouldn't be able to disable it.

"And it was very easy to find you. You're about the only car left driving around. Everyone else is in a Safe Station. I only just managed to get out without being noticed."

I sat up straight. "What? Were the Safe Stations a trick? Is everyone trapped? Are people hurt?" I blurted in a panic.

"No, no, calm down. The Safe Stations are exactly that—they're safe. They're scattered all around. Some are halls, others are sporting grounds, pretty much any venue that can cater for

a large number of people is being used—there's police everywhere now. Everybody has been given food, water and bedding.
It's certainly not luxury, but it is safe. And before you ask,
Leroy, Mum and Dad are fine. But no one knows what's going
on. I mean sure, I can handle crazy weather as much as the next
person, but I'm not joking when I say we had a forty degree day
followed by a day of snow. Needless to say, the rioters went nuts
again. They've blown up even more of the city, and they are still
saying they've got more bombs hidden everywhere. They won't
tell anyone where they've hidden them until the government
fixes it. The only problem is that no one knows what 'it' is to fix
—friggin' morons! So no one is allowed out of the Safe Stations
until each of the bombs have been accounted for. Anyway, right
after I knew my family was safe, I came back for you, but you
had already gone." He shook his head as he frowned. "It really
is impossible for you to do as you're told, isn't it? Anyway, I
only just made it here—the Army's everywhere. They're searching everything. Anyone outside the Stations is considered to be
a threat."

"Is it just Melbourne?"

He shook his head. "All the towns between here and there are
crawling with soldiers. The rioters have taken to social media,
accusing different races and religious groups for causing the extreme weather. Some are saying it's due to people extracting all
the crude oil from the Earth, and others are saying it's because
the world is overpopulated. Their solution is to wipe out third
world countries—even cows have been blamed by some for cre-
ating too much methane and depleting the ozone layer."

I couldn't help but spit a laugh at his last suggestion. Cows?

He bit his lip and looked at the ground. "Alex, it's practically a war out there. In the last few days, several groups have
banded together with one common goal. They believe that their

God is punishing the world, and the only way to salvation is for everyone to join them... and guess what happens to those who refuse?" He made a gun with his fingers and pointed it at his head.

"You've gotta be joking?! God damn religion! Why can't people just be happy believing in whatever they want? Let me guess which religion it is." I was furious. How can one group of people dictate what the rest of the world believes?

Andy was shaking his head as I ranted about how much I detested religion.

"What? You think they're right?" I yelled.

"No, I don't, but listen to this; until about three days ago, this religion didn't exist. They call themselves The Kunghi; they have founded a religion which honours no God. They are only using the religion part as a guise."

"What? Are you sure?"

"Yep. They're everywhere, worldwide. They claim they're new and that they've only just formed, but I don't buy it. It's like they've been hiding underground for the perfect opportunity. And the supporters they're getting ..." He raised his eyebrows and shook his head. "It's like all these people who are joining them are only joining because they have to follow someone. They can't think for themselves. They don't care who they're fighting or why just so long as they're fighting. And it's not isolated to one race. People from all different backgrounds are joining them."

I sat back in my seat as I patted Spud on the head. "How can all of this happen in a matter of days? Sam ... what about Sam, and Emilee? What about everyone from home? I spoke to them a while ago, but how are they now?"

Andy sat back in the passenger seat and inhaled deeply. "I dunno. All phones, all forms of communication devices have been shut down by the government in hopes of slowing the Kunghi. I can't reach anyone from home. I found you just before the government ban went into effect. I just prayed I could get here before you moved on again. What are you doing out here, anyway?"

I pulled a sideways smile. "I found them."

"Who? The Persivals?" His eyes widened.

"Yep. Well, Abde did. She slipped a note into my jeans' pocket as we were leaving her place. I had completely forgotten about it until Sam and Emilee rang and I pulled my phone out of the same pocket."

"Well, what are we waiting for? Let's go!"

"No, I've already been there, and trust me; they do *not* want to see me again." I widened my eyes and lifted my eyebrows as I spoke.

"Why what happened?"

I spent the best part of the next hour explaining everything to Andy, including Rose's belief that The Aztec had not been killed, I told him everything as objectively as I could. I needed him to listen with a clear mind, not one that had been swayed by my opinion. I needed to know if the facts lined up with their story; was there any point in charging back to Warrangatta to retrieve the sword, or would that be as useful as catching the wind?

"He's not dead?" He ran his hand over his face.

"No..." I answered quietly. The news had shaken him equally as much as it had shaken me.

"I know." I said slowly. It was a waste of time visiting the Persivals again—their story couldn't be true.

"It's so insane it has to be true." He looked at me. My face was disapproving. "This situation we're in is madness. So it's fair to say we need to turn to madness to solve it. And dragons being real is just freaking awesome!"

I rolled my eyes. "We don't know that for sure. Dragons are extremely far-fetched."

He bit his bottom lip. "You're right, they are aren't they? Glowing books, ancient supernatural people hunting you and women turning into crows are completely plausible."

I inhaled deeply. I was beyond trying to make sense of any of it.

"There's one more thing. They told me how to kill The Aztec, how to actually kill him, and hopefully, Veronika and Boris too. Remember when I told you that you were wasting your time hoarding all your swords?"

"Yes?" he answered slowly.

"Turns out, perhaps I was wrong," I said quickly and quietly. "One of your swords—it's the murder weapon of choice."

"My swords?" He asked, surprised.

"Take a look at this." I reached around to pick up drawing of the sword. But as soon as I moved, my shoulders screamed with pain, and I couldn't help but lurch forward and cry out.

"Alex! What is it? Is it the eyes again?"

I shook my head.

"Your shoulders?"

Before I could deny any problem with my shoulders, he had pulled my shirt aside.

"Bloody Hell! Alexandra!" he yelled as he looked at my heavily infected shoulders. "You need a hospital. Forget the Book, bow and everything else. We're getting you to a Safe Station before you die." He wrapped his arms around me as he started to lift me from my car into the passenger seat of his car.

"No!" I pushed him away from me.

"What do you mean, 'no'? Alex, do you understand you are going to die if you don't get to a doctor? Once that infection gets into your bloodstream ..."

"And do you understand that I *am* going to die if I don't kill them first? Jesus, just a few minutes ago I was preparing for my own death ... I don't know what they want. I don't know why Veronika wants me dead or what purpose the Book serves. I don't know why or how I love The Aztec or if it's really even love or what the hell it is. All I know is it has to *stop*. Andy, I can't keep going like this. Every time I go to sleep I see him, I feel him. I'm still taking my meds, but they aren't strong enough to stop Veronika from seeing me. If I don't do something they will find me—and they will kill me. That is a certainty." I looked down at my fingers. "I saw Rose, Andy. I can't be like her. I live in the middle of a vast country. I can leave my home and drive for hours—days even—and never see anyone, and yet I still feel trapped. I could never live like Rose; in hiding. It may not kill me, but it would destroy me. I have to take the risk."

He looked at me through solemn eyes.

"I am not asking you to come with me, Andy. I left that office because I didn't want you to risk your life for me anymore. On the tram, you told me that I had to live so you wouldn't have to fight this alone. Well, you shouldn't have to fight it at all. You need to stop risking your life for mine. You need to go back to your family—you need to go home." I didn't want to say a word of what I just did. I wanted to beg him to come with me, but I couldn't risk his life any more than I already had.

He looked directly into my eyes and held a firm face. "And what am I going to find there? A bunch of scared people. Alex, the entire world has turned to shit. I think it's pretty bloody obvious the Kunghi, The Aztec, and that crazy crow bitch have something to do with each other. And you're asking me to leave you to fight it alone, while I sit on the sidelines? Not happening. But, if you leave me behind or try to 'save me' once more, I'll hand you to that crow bitch myself! Now get in my car; we're going home."

~ 19 ~

CHAPTER NINETEEN

He drove on back roads the entire way to Warrangatta. Twice a day we would stop, and he bathed my shoulders in salted water. It didn't reverse the infection, but it slowed its spread considerably. It wasn't enough, though. By the fifth day of travelling, I could feel the infection had moved into dangerous ground. As I lay along the back seat, I could feel the fever spread throughout my body. My skin was an inferno, but my insides were frozen.

"Ally. Hold on. We've just passed the sign to Warrangatta. We're only twenty minutes away! We'll be at the bush nurse in no time, and even if there's no one there, we'll find some medicine," Andy called over his shoulder.

I heard his words, but I couldn't understand them. It was as though he was speaking through water.

"Oh shit!" he yelled as he slowed the car.

I rolled my head towards him. I tried to sit up, but my head spun too much.

"Wha..?" I tried to ask, but my voice wouldn't work.

"Shit! Shit!" He frantically looked through all the windows. "They're here! I can't see them properly in the dark, but they're here!" He ran hands over his head, as though trying to clear his thoughts.

"Run. Leave me here!" I yelled at him. "They want me! Just run!"

"No. Not a chance," he snapped.

He turned the steering wheel on full lock and started to turn the car around, trying to escape. There was no point because there was no escape. They had made it their mission to find me, to kill me. They would also kill anyone who was with me.

In that instant, I made my decision. I couldn't change my fate, but I could alter Andy's. I turned over onto my stomach and pushed myself closer to the door. I grabbed the handle and pushed the door open.

"Alexandra! No!" Andy screamed as he tried to reach for me to hold me in the car.

I didn't look at him as I fell to the coarse gravel road, the stones grabbing at my skin as my body skidded along to a stop. It should have hurt, but I didn't feel anything—my senses had become desensitized.

As I lay on the hard ground, I looked up to the sky. It was night. The stars twinkled as they smiled down at me. I rolled my head around. I wanted to see Andy's car driving into the distance, but he wasn't fleeing; he was running towards me. I tried to scream at him to run away, to just leave me, but my eyes grew too heavy; I was losing consciousness. Just before my eyes closed, two black hands wrapped themselves around my waist. Him! He promised to always find me, and he had. He was taking me. I belonged to him ...

*****

I sit with my head resting back, eyes closed, exhausted from my effort. I have done as they asked and filled the notebook with my memories.

The feeding door slides open again. A rusted tray scratches its way across the cold concrete floor. Another notebook has been delivered, to be filled with more of my memories. During the time spent filling this first notebook, no boxes have entered the room. But there could be another hundred boxes sitting on the other side of the wall, each to be filled with body parts if I deviate from my task; a cruel reminder that retribution awaits. So, I have no option but to continue to re-live my life and record my memories—for what reason I still do not know. I do know I am being watched, and I do know that they must still need some secret I hold locked within me; I have no clue as to what that secret may be.

Are my loved ones still alive? Are my allies searching for us? Perhaps it is foolish, but I still cling to something—I still cling to hope.

*****

Thank you for reading Hunted.

~ 20 ~

Tethered, book 2 is now available. Please head to my website to see where to grab your copy. Don't forget to sign up to my newsletter for all the latest info!

www.jsdavidson-books.com

~ 21 ~

Acknowledgement

The day I announced to everyone 'I've written a book, I want to be an author' was one of the most terrifying days of my life. Honestly, I had prepared myself to be laughed at, told I'd never succeed and another multitude negative statements to follow.

That didn't happen. I am still overwhelmed with the amount of support I received (and am still receiving) from friends, family and complete strangers alike. But I can't list everyone here, honestly I would need an entire novel just to thank everyone who has helped. So, if you notice your name isn't listed here, please don't be upset.

Firstly, my biggest thanks must go to Sandra Simmonds. When Helen Bosa referred my work to you, I thought you'd take quick look, maybe fix a few grammatical errors, send me work back to me and be on your way. You didn't. Over the last twelve months you've taken my under your wing, guided me, helped me grow, and now become a dear friend of mine. Sandra, without a doubt, you are the world's greatest editor – even though I know you'll shrug this compliment off, you shouldn't. You are a wonderful woman – thank you for everything.

My family shares a part in 'my biggest thanks'. John, my husband, Sam and Phoebe, my children. You endured the endless night I would sit up and write, you put up with two minute noodles far too often. But you supported me throughout this journey. Actually, funnily enough, it was all due to John that this book has even come about! I was far too nervous to speak to anyone about my work, I was certain I'd never have a chance of being an author. It was John who told Helen I'd written a book, he refused to allow my many years of work go unnoticed. If he hadn't mentioned it to her, I'd never have met Sandra – the butterfly effect at its greatest.

Rhiannan Haintz, you need a special thanks in here too! You are a tremendous nurse – now midwife (congratulations!) and you let me pick your brain numerous times in regards to Alexandra's hospital scene. Because of you the scene is far more realistic and believable – thank you.

Mum, well, you're my Mum! You put up with me when I was happily bubbling on about my book or the times when I was down and thought I'd never be able to do it. I don't often say it – but thank you for being there. Xx

Alana, what can I say? When I first wrote this book I came to you and cried, I was so overwhelmed with emotion. Each and every time I would go on about my book you'd just sit and listen – that means more than you'll ever know.

As I said earlier, there are so many more people who are deserving of being written into this acknowledgement – if you didn't notice your name above, please know that you support means the world to me and I couldn't have done it without you all.

J.S. Davidson xx

www.ingramcontent.com/pod-product-compliance
Lightning Source LLC
Chambersburg PA
CBHW070556120726
47909CB00007B/2361